Richard Malcolm Johnston

Two Gray Tourists

From Papers of Mr. Philemon Perch

Richard Malcolm Johnston

Two Gray Tourists
From Papers of Mr. Philemon Perch

ISBN/EAN: 9783337194130

Printed in Europe, USA, Canada, Australia, Japan

Cover: Foto ©Andreas Hilbeck / pixelio.de

More available books at **www.hansebooks.com**

TWO GRAY TOURISTS:

FROM PAPERS OF MR. PHILEMON PERCH.

— EDITED BY —

RICHARD MALCOLM JOHNSTON,

Author of "Old Mark Langston," "Dukesborough Tales," etc.

"His travel has not stopped him,
As you suppose, nor altered any freedom,
But made him far more clear and excellent."
—*Queen of Corinth.*

NEW YORK :
P. J. KENEDY,
EXCELSIOR CATHOLIC PUBLISHING HOUSE,
5 BARCLAY STREET,
1893.

PREFACE.

THIS work contains an account, written by Mr. Philemon Perch, of a brief tour, made by himself together with his friend, Major James Rawls, both natives of the State of Georgia (the latter yet resident therein), in England, Scotland, Belgium, the Rhine-region, Switzerland, and France. They are dear friends, and have been for more than forty years, though, in some respects, quite dissimilar. Mr. Perch, a student, tall and slender, is sentimental, often absent-minded, and perhaps too fond of anti-quarian research. Major Rawls, a planter, stout, rather below middle height, is practical, entirely modern, energetic, and, on occasion, somewhat pug-nacious. This is a record of the sights these tourists saw together, and the impressions made upon them. I found, on reading the manuscript, that their dis-cussions upon several subjects of former and present interest had brought forth many observations upon the classical, mediæval, and modern conditions of some of the scenes through which they passed.

To my proposal to publish, Mr. Perch assented more readily, because of a habit of printing his thoughts. Major Rawls, perhaps, would have preferred to keep out of print, but for his affection for his friend, and, partly, the urgent entreaties of his youngest son, Jake. Moreover, he argued (with himself), that among his numerous friends and acquaintances, he had been questioned about this journey some two thousand times, more or less, and he wondered whether it might not be about as well to let Phil (as he calls him) tell what there was in it, and so leave himself to have something else to talk about. He has not seen what is herein written ; but he was ready to conclude that if Mr. Perch could stand it he might also.

Acting on such consent, I submit these papers, hoping that whoever reads them may have some measure of the entertainment that I have had in editing.   R. M. J.

TABLE OF CONTENTS.

TWO GRAY TOURISTS.

CHAPTER I.

I T was a matter of some surprise to me one day to get a letter from my old friend, Jim Rawls, of Todd's Mill, Georgia, proposing that he and I should make a voyage to Europe together. When I was younger and more prosperous, I had often dreamed, and so had Jim sometimes, of a brief tour in the Old World, and we had been hindered first by one and then another obstacle: dread of the great waters, reluctance to put ourselves at so vast distance from home, business engagements, and so forth. Years passed, the war came, bringing what it brought, and leaving what it left. Not that it left Jim in as sad condition as that of most others in his section. He yet had a good plantation, with grist and saw mills, some State bonds and railroad stocks, with several of his neighbors as debtors. With the last he made generous compositions, and went to work with renewed vigor. One of his sons had died while serving in the army. This hurt him sorely; for the boy was very promising. But his two others had come through unscathed in health and character, and little Jake was born some years afterwards. There were two married daughters, and one single. Above them all was his wife, once Miss Emily Todd, whom he has always believed, and most probably always will believe to be, the finest woman in Georgia. His former slaves, or the most of them, have remained with him, and matters at his home look very much as in old times.

Yet his health of late had declined somewhat. He always would cry a little whenever the war was mentioned, and he thought of his boy. His family feared he had been yielding too frequently to that regret, and they persuaded him to take a sea voyage. Singularly enough, I had been entertaining a similar notion occasionally throughout the winter. His consent to go was conditioned upon my accompanying him; and certainly I could not have desired a more fit companion in travel than my old friend of forty-five years and upwards. For Jim Rawls is as true a man as I ever knew. Although he had never taken eagerly to books while at school, yet, after growing up, he has read extensively, especially on history, agriculture, and mechanics, and is right familiar with Shakspeare, the only poet he cares much about. He is brave, even inclining to pugnacity, but thoroughly generous and good humored. From the letter he wrote to me, I saw that, in spite of some loss of health and spirit, not nigh all the old fund of good humor had left him.

"The truth is, Phil, if you and I are ever to see the old country, it's got to be soon. It won't be long before it will be slow travelling for you and me. And then both of us are rusty; you not so much as I am, but you ain't bright like you used to be when you were young. I told Emily so the last time you were here; and then Emily laughed and said that Bob Dudley's wife told her that you had said exactly the same thing about me. Now a little travel, if we can make the trip, and get back all safe, will do us both good, freshen us up a little, make our folks think a little more of us, and, may be, even feel a little proud of us. Think on it, and think fast. If you'll go, I will. If you won't, I won't. But let us try and make the trip, and have a little bit of fun together one more time, and have something to talk about instead of hanging on to what we've talked out heretofore."

And yet, after we had agreed, the undertaking seemed to us both, especially to me, so vast and perilous, that I doubt if we should'nt have retreated but for the urgent persuasions of our friends and the fear of being considered as having too much levity for men of our age. Jim had the advantage over me of having been the first to take leave and break off from home. Besides, he was always a man of more resolute purpose than myself, and could do, thoroughly and without hesitation, whatever he had once made up his mind to. By the time he had reached my residence, he had the talk and the air of a man who had travelled considerably already. I caught as much of his infection as I could, and when the young people, in obedience to his request, brought out from the piles of old forgotten songs, "A Life on the Ocean Wave," and he pretended to keep time to the music, if I had been even more soft than I was already, I should have been forced to laugh heartily.

"Phil, my boy, we shall soon be laying our hands on old ocean's mane, and playing familiar with his hoary locks, as the ancient writers used to say."

"What do you suppose Byron meant by that sort of talk, Jim?"

" I never had the slightest idea; but it sounds plucky. Still, if old ocean will take us over and bring us back again safe and sound, I shan't meddle with his locks nor anything else that belongs to him."

We reached New York on the day before the *Gallia* was to sail. The interval we spent, for the most part, in our chamber, talking together with what spirit we could command, and writing repeated farewells to those at home. We boarded at the St. Nicholas. Once, while he was writing to Jake, I saw Jim brush a tear from his eye. How the sight touched me! He noticed it, and at once rose and rung the bell.

" Bring us up," he said to the servant, " two good, big, stiff juleps, with a plenty of mint, and everything else in 'em."

Upon my word. I doubt if I ever knew a circumstance, so inconsiderable in itself, to exert a more speedy, and sustaining, and even elevating influence upon persons at our time of life. Jim said it reminded him of home in a pleasant way; no sadness about *it*. He had had no idea that they could make such juleps so far north. We occupied the same chamber—for that was one of the items in our plans.

" The truth is, Phil, we are going a long way farther from home than we've ever been before, and we must stick together. I never was a man to be afraid much of robbers and pickpockets in *this* country. But when a fellow is about five or six thousand miles from home, and among outlandish people, its another sort of thing altogether."

"All right; but you somewhat exaggerate the distance, Jim."

" Oh, well, a few miles more or less don't make much difference when we are on as big figures as we are now."

He had always been a good provider. Although we had determined to take no trunks along with us, so as to avoid their incumbrance and the delays they might cause at railway stations, yet it was interesting to notice how many articles of necessity and convenience he had managed to get into his valise and bag. The most of these he brought with him from home. Yet here, he was frequently going out and returning with some new article he had purchased. At one time it was a couple of small phials of paregoric; for he always got two of every item: one for himself, and one for me. At another, it would be a couple of pipes and packages of tobacco or cigars. About ten minutes before we were to leave the hotel, he ran out suddenly, and, returning with two additional combs, handed one to me. I was leaning on the office counter, talking with one of the men.

"Why, what upon earth did you get them for, Jim? We had them already."

"Never do you mind. Do you put it in your valise. You're going among strange people, and you don't know what all you'll need.

And while he was unlocking his valise and wedging in the comb, he looked up at the man, and asked:

"Ain't that so, mister?"

"No doubt about that," he answered, with a smile. "That's a very useful article to take along. I wonder more people don't do it."

We shook hands with him the more cordially, because he had been very civil to us, and this was to be our last hand-shaking on the eve of a long voyage. Jim held his hand a moment or two, and, with tears in his eyes, said:

"Good-bye, mister. You've treated us civilly since
1*

we've been here, and I'm much obliged to you.   If you
hear of anything happening to us while we're gone, I
hope you'll write to my wife.   You'll see there, on your
book, where to direct your letter; and if I get back
safe, as please God I hope to do, and you ever come to
Georgia I want you to come right straight to my house."

The man thanked him, and promised to write, if necessary.   But he protested that it would be all right.
Never so safe, you know, as when on a Cunard steamer.

"Yes, yes.   Oh, yes.   Thank ye; good-bye; God
bless you."

And we got into the omnibus.

Arrived at the wharf in Jersey City, we went immediately on board and were led to our state-room.   It was
about amidships, on the lower tier, opening upon an
alcove of four or five feet, which, separating ours from
another state-room, led into the lower saloon.   Because
I suggested that, being the stouter man of the two, he
should take the lower berth, Jim at once insisted, as
being the stronger and more active, upon going up
stairs, as he styled taking the upper.   We compromised
by agreeing to alternate, according to circumstances.
He at once went to work arranging things.   Every article of mine he moved, evidently to advantage, from the
place where I had placed it, and I was delighted to see
how snugly we were fixed when he had finished.   Then
he took from his pocket several pieces of English silver
money, held them in one open hand, and laying his
finger on one after another, he asked of our steward :

" What's that?"

" Two shillins, sir."

"And that ?"

" 'Arf a crown, sir."

"A what?"

"'Arf a crown, sir."

Jim hesitated.

"You mean *half*, don't you?"

"Yes, sir; 'arf, 'arf a crown."

"And this big fellow?"

"A crown, sir."

"Then, by good rights, its worth, or ought to be twice as much as the little one."

"H'oh yes, sir; two 'arves make a 'ole one, you know, sir."

"I suppose they do among you English. Well, now, which is the most, the two shillings or the 'arf a crown?"

"H'oh, the arf a crown, sir. Sixpens' the most."

"Well, now, here's two of these 'arf a crowns to begin with ——."

But I put my hand on Jim's shoulder, and insisted that such as that must not go on, and gave the steward my own money. He put one of his pieces into his pocket, protesting that I was mighty particular. Besides, being one of the most liberal men, and with pecuniary means much greater than my own, I had suspected that somehow he had considered himself partially responsible for my undertaking an expense which he knew I could not very well afford, and that he ought to lessen it as far as he could with my allowance. But he respected my feelings, and generally let me have my own way.

Having arranged our state-room satisfactorily, we went ashore in order to purchase our deck-chairs. Jim listened politely to what each vender had to say, and then from the stock of the one who seemed the most needy, made his selection.

"Let me have the key to your valise," he said, when we were on board again.

"What for?"

"I've a few useful little things in my pocket that I'm afraid I have'nt room for in mine."

He took my key, and returning shortly afterwards from the state-room, said:

"If you ain't a traveller, I don't know one. Your things are upside down already. I see I'll have to look after you, young man."

I found afterwards that he had put into the valise needles, thread, and at least a gross of buttons of assorted sizes.

"I hope we have'nt forgotten anything, Phil."

"I have no fears on that score."

"You? No, I suppose not."

We were much interested in the scenes that were around us, the busy stirring of our fellow-passengers, the merry chattings of some, the sad words of others. There were smiles and tears. At last the anchor was lifted, the bell rang, those who had come to witness the departure descended from the deck, the gangway was taken off, Captain Moodie, with hand uplifted, gave the signal, the bell rang, and we were tugged slowly away. "Good-bye, good-bye," was sounded many times from hundreds of tongues. "Good-bye!" joined in Jim, with trembling, but hearty voice. And so he joined in the waving of hats and handkerchiefs when the voices were no longer audible; and though he did not know a single soul, I noticed that he was the last to make these mute farewells.

"Phil," said he, putting his handkerchief into his pocket, "these northern people are friendlier than I thought."

CHAPTER II.

GOOD, brave ship is the *Gallia*, and Captain Moodie as good looking and gallant a commander as any reasonable voyager might desire. Jim said that it made him feel stiffer in the back while, looking into his ruddy face, he heard him say that he had crossed the Atlantic more than one hundred times. The drawback, however, Jim argued, was in the reflection that if such luck was ever to change it was now about the time   Yet we both felt our greatest sense of security in reliance upon the protection of the Almighty, who, whatever He did, would do what was best and mercifullest.

To those whose minds were not preoccupied, it was a fair sight, that New York Bay, as we glided smoothly over its surface. But our thoughts were of our homes; and already these seemed becoming more and more immeasureably distant.

"We are in for it now, Phil, sure enough," said Jim, in a tone of half humorous, half sad resignation, as the pilot left us and we steamed off again. "Now let's sit down and take a good, civil smoke."

"No, let's wait," said I. "It's now half-past eleven, and lunch is at twelve."

"You don't mean dinner?"

"Of course not; dinner is at four. They have five meals a day here."

(9)

" The mischief you say."

" Certainly; breakfast at eight, lunch at twelve, dinner at four, tea at seven, and supper at nine."

" Well now, that's what I call good, fair, liberal board. Five meals a day *sounds* well."

He was fond of good eating, was Jim, and he always had it at home, although, as was and is the old Georgia country custom, he had dinner at a little past noon and only three meals a day.

" You see, Phil, if we ain't always hungry at meal times it is a good way to pass off the time, especially when a fellow is away from home. For no matter how he feels, there is something cheerful in all sitting down to table and hearing the rattle of knives and forks and plates. Even when I don't feel like eating myself—and that's mighty seldom—I love to see other people eat, and hear 'em talk while they are eating. Yes, sir, that's good; I'm glad to hear *that*."

His brightness served to relieve much of my own gloom, and when the eight bells sounded we were quite ready for lunch. Our seats were near the stern. Jim said he liked that because it gave us a better view of the saloon.

" I don't know so well about that, Jim," said I, " for in rough weather the pitch will be greater here."

" Why you don't expect to get sea-sick? *I* don't. I ain't quite what I used to be in some things, but my stomach is as sound as a dollar."

I said nothing more.

" I tell you they don't spare expense on these ships. Why here's a regular dinner, Phil, except hot meats. We must'nt eat too much lunch or we may get into the same case for dinner as Bob Minton got in for his pie."

" What was that?"

"Bob said that one day when he was a little boy and his mother had company for dinner, she said to the children, as they were stting down to table, that the one who ate the most meat and greens should have the most pie. In his eagerness to beat his brother Sam, Bob ate so much meat and greens that he had no room for any pie. He always said, Bob did, that of all the calculalations he ever did make, that was the foolishest. What made it worse was, that Sam laughed at him until he cried, and hit Sam with a potato, when his mother gave him a whipping. Bob says he had always had a disgust for meat and greens just by themselves since that day. He said also, that though he always had been and always expected to be a poor man, he intended to have some sort of désërt, as he called it, every day, even when he can't have anything but corn bread and molasses."

By this time, though the weather was fine, yet the roll of the sea was much more considerable than we had expected.

"My gracious!" said Jim, "don't she put up?"

But he ate his prunes with a relish; and smiting his breast proudly with his open hands, said that all was right there. As we went out of the saloon and through the passage between the upper berths, several ladies, looking quite pale, entered them in considerable haste, and we heard some suspicious sounds.

"Poor things!" said Jim; "got it already. You see, Phil, women's stomachs ain't strong like men's anyhow. Then they take so little exercise that, in fact, they ain't fit to travel on water. Well, I'm sorry for 'em. Do you know, Phil, that there's two couples here?"

"Two couples? Couples of what?"

"Two couples just married,"

"How did you find out?"

"I knew it from their actions; for one couple behaved as if they were especially anxious that nobody should find out that they were just married, and the other that they should. Well, it does seem to me that this is about the last place I should choose for my honeymoon, if I had that time to go over again. But people ain't all alike, I suppose. These northern people have a plenty of money, and they have to find various ways of spending it. Will you have a light?"

He drew a cigar, and puffed away delightedly.

We had placed our chairs near the mizzenmast, and not far from the captain's room. The latter came out where we were, when Jim rose and offered him his chair and a cigar. The chair was declined, and the cigar accepted politely.

"If you like that cigar, captain, we have a plenty, and will be glad if you will help us smoke them on the way, as they tell us we can't carry 'em into your country."

"Ay, ay. I guess they won't be very particular about a few cigars, especially with such gentlemen as you are."

"You think that?"

"Oh, ay."

"And, captain, I have some first-rate brandy in my valise. If you feel a little—unwell any time or—any wise—or disposed—"

"Oh, thanks! but I never take anything to drink when on the passage."

"The mischief you don't."

"Never; yet I'm much obliged by your kindness. This *is* a fine cigar."

"Glad you like it; have another?"

"Thanks; not just now."

"Everything looks very pleasant here, captain."

"Oh, ay. The June passage, you know, is always considered delightful. Will you be sea-sick?"

"Not the slightest idea of it. The June passage, you say, is a favorite one, is it captain? I'm glad we took it then, Phil. A clever fellow that captain is," he continued, as the latter walked away, "and a friendly fellow. From his jolly red face, I thought sure he must take at least one good drink a day. I knew he would like that cigar. I can't quite afford such as these at home; but I mean to enjoy myself as well as I can while I'm in for it. Emily said she wanted me to enjoy myself just as much as I could, and I'm going to do it."

His native heartiness and his facility to adapt himself to different circumstances led him soon to find perfect ease in the strange condition, and impart it to me. We walked about the deck, watched the in-coming and out-going vessels we met and passed, or sat in our chairs and chatted and smoked. The seven bells struck half-past three.

"I don't feel as much like eating, Phil, as I thought I would. I left off hungry at the lunch, so as not to get into Bob Minton's fix, and thought I should feel keen for dinner. That last cigar is the only poor one I've got out of the box."

At dinner we were getting along with reasonable relish. With a stiff westerly breeze, we were making about thirteen knots an hour, and the *Gallia* was bounding along in her-old-fashioned way. Once or twice, even while we were taking our soup, I noticed that Jim, as we would descend with the sweep of the stern, turned a little pale, and, laying down his spoon, pressed his knees firmly against the legs of the table, and uttered a

2

smothered ejaculation of "Good gracious," but looked at me very sympathizingly. When I said I thought I would go up stairs for a moment, he smiled dismally, but said nothing, and looked doubtfully at the meats as they were being brought in. I ascended the stairs, made for my chair, and put myself in as horizontal relation with it as possible. Five minutes afterwards, hearing behind me melancholy sounds, I turned, and Jim was holding to a rope, leaning over the side of the vessel and apparently complaining to somebody beneath. A sense of duty prompted me to rise and go to his assistance; but I could get no further than the rope next the one he had.

"Jim," I asked. "Are you——" But my own attention was also drawn to the objects beneath.

"Yesh. Oh, yesh. Oh, my goodness gracious! Oh, hello! What mat— Pill. You shick, too? Oh, yesh. Never spect—oh goodness gra— Never felt—so—life before. What—do—Pill?"

Disjointed as were his words, they were better than I could have employed. So I kept silent, at least of all articulate expression. Jim stood as long as he could; but he sank at last, and was in the attitude of a man at his prayers, except that his jaw was laid upon the rail in the few intervals of its rest.

Whoever has suffered from sea-sickness remembers it without description, and whoever has not so suffered would find no description adequate. There is no foul odor, real or conceivable, that does not enter or seem to enter the nostrils of a sea-sick man; no species of bitter, poisonous herb, of filthy, venomous reptile, that he does not feel to have eaten, and now to be destined to die therefrom. Added to these are the mental anguish, the sense of profoundest degradation for having deserted one's home, and family, and country, and being pursued as a deserter, and caught, and punished in the most humiliating and disgusting of all ways, the gradual exhaustion of life by body-and-soul sickness, and afterwards thrown out, worthless even for such a purpose, to the monsters of the deep. In sleep—for it is wonderful how much a man can sleep in such a time, his thoughts and feelings get no relief. Perhaps they are then more horrible, for then the imagination is wholly unrestrained by reason, and these horrible things seem real.

My friend suffered longer than I did, and, I think, more grievously. By morning I could creep upon the deck, while he could not be brought up until near sunset, and then had to be laid flat upon his back. He had been so ill that he was not aware how much I had suffered, and he afterwards made me promise not to tell all he had said to me in the messages which he sent to his wife. Not that his breast was not as clean of wrong-doing as that of any husband and father in this or any other country. But he had so magnified his little infirmities, and especially the great crime of going off, and, as it were, running away from his family, that were I to repeat, except to them, the terms which he repeatedly employed, he might, and justly, be hurt. Besides, such had been my own feelings, that, had he been in condition to listen and sympathize, I doubtless would not have varied far in the language I had employed with him.

But the getting well again. That was simply glorious. I desire to see, not often, a more serene and pleasant sight than when I would look at Jim Rawls two days afterwards. as he leaned far back in his chair, his appetite promising more and more assuringly to come back, and himself, while with sweet resignation, calmly saying he had no stomach at all—none whatever, yet slowly chewing delicate little morsels, and helping them down with sips of iced champagne. While he would divide most fairly, yet in the very last pouring he would linger in holding the bottle's mouth down over his goblet, and, imperceptibly to himself, give it a shake, and even a little squeeze, for the last and a possibly one drop more. That man will tell you to-day, if you were at his house in Georgia, that the most speedy, effectual and pleasant remedy for sea-sickness is champagne wine. It was, indeed, more delightful to notice in him than to feel within myself the relish of the tranquil happiness of convalescence. How kindly he inquired of others as to their sufferings! How fond he was to answer them at length. The sympathy he felt was rendered to him abundantly, as he would prolong the accounts he gave of his sufferings, innocently exaggerate them, and be reluctant to admit how fast he was getting well again. He had already made many acquaintances, and was on familiar terms with them. At lunch hour, on the third day out, when he had finished with his champagne and crackers, while half a dozen gentlemen were around him, he thus let himself out:

"Yes, gentlemen, I've been through what I never expected for this world, and even now I wonder that I ever got through and came out a live man and in my senses. My opinion on the subject of sea-sickness is, that it ain't a question of stomach. My stomach is as sound as anybody's. It's a—well, you may call it a sort of a—epidemic on some people—or, like mumps or measles, which everybody *has* to have one time, provided if he goes where the cussed things are. Oh, you northern people, you may laugh, but it's so. You all are used to such things. You live close to the water anyhow, and you get used to the smelling of it and traveling and meandering about over it. The case is very different with us down in Georgia, where the water, what there is of it, is fresh, and everybody has a plenty of fresh air. It ain't a question of stomach. My stomach's as sound as a roach."

"But we thought you had been very sick at the stomach."

"Of course I have; but I tell you it came on like mumps or the measels, and, just like them, the older a fellow gets the worse *they* get *him*. Sick at the stomach? Yes, indeed! Gentlemen, my opinion is, that since the creation of the world no *man*-person ever had such a sick stomach. I don't say women, for I know that's the nature of some women; but if any poor woman ever had such a stomach as I had for twenty-four hours, I pity her. Look here; would you like to know some, just only a few things, I conceited that I had in my stomach?"

Of course they would, and I never heard more hearty responses as, in the intervals of their laughter, he recounted:

"Toad frogs!"

"Tadpoles!"

"Peavines!"

"Old rotten fodder-blades!"

"Brass knobs! The reason I knew they were brass was, I smelt 'em!"

"Watermelon rinds!"

"Grub-worms!"

"Dish-water!"

"Scaly-bark lizards!"

2*

"Vinegar a thousand years old!"

"Stumps of mean cigars!"

"Old roosters, that died of the cholera!"

"And, what you northern people know mighty little about, little niggers, all greased up with pot liquor!"

How they did roar! A crowd of twenty or thirty gentlemen by this time had gathered around him, and several ladies, who were standing a little way off, actually cried with laughter.

"These," he wound up, "and many more besides, too tedious to mention, seemed to be in me and tangled and squirming among one another, not only in my stomach, but in my very brains. Why, gentlemen, it seemed to me that an old brass hoop was around my head, fastened on with a glue of some sort made out of every old, mean liquor in the world, that was everlastingly a melting and running down on my face, and the more it melted the tighter the hoop held on. The fact is, my mind was worse off than my stomach. If I ever stole anything from anybody I don't remember it, except it might be a few apples or a watermelon or two when I was a boy just for fun and mischief; but I tell you—no, I can't talk about my mind. But I hope as long as I live (and I don't think I *shall*) that I'll ever feel in my mind like I did then. My old friend here says he was about as bad off as I was, but I've no idea of any such thing. If he had been, *he* would'nt be a live man now, certain sure. Yes, gentlemen, I've been very bad off, and I'm far from being a well man yet."

He drew a long breath that was meant to be mournful, but it deceived nobody.

Having recovered entirely from sea-sickness, we came to thoroughly enjoy our new experience. The sight of the good which the travel and even the sea-sickness were imparting, made us glad that we had made the voyage. Jim, especially, with his old heart fresh as ever, relished fully the life peculiar to a sea voyage— watching the seamen at their work, and especially at their leisure, studying the ropes and machinery, playing at shuffle-board, sitting at those five meals in which he kept his vow to make up for lost time, talking with the passengers, and listening to them talking about the various sections in which they resided and their avocations.

One night, however, he became considerably disturbed. He was a sound sleeper always, and by this time was able to rest as well as if he had been home. Late in this particular night, while I happened to be awake and he was snoring well, the whistle suddenly sounded. It awakened him, and I heard him start up. In another minute the sound was repeated, when he immediately sprang from the berth, and going to the lounge put his eyes to the glass over the port-hole.

"Phil," said he.

"Hello."

"Sleep?"

"No."

"Did you hear that?"

"Yes."

"What do suppose is the matter?"

"We are in the fog."

"The fog?"

' Certainly, the fog."

"Are you awake, Phil?"

"I am."

"Well, what do you mean by being in the fog?"

"I mean what I say. We are on the Banks."

"What banks?"

"The Banks of Newfoundland. I heard the Captain say to-day that we would get on them to-night, and he thought the fog might be thicker than common."

"But what are they blowing the whistle for?"

"In order to avoid collision with other ships."

"Why don't they hold up till morning?"

"They could'nt see any further then than they can now."

"What?"

"Fact."

"Well, why don't they go slower, then?"

"Because self-preservation is the first law of nature."

"Phil, I do believe you are asleep. Wake up."

"I am awake."

"What's that you said just now?"

"That self-preservation was the first law of nature. If we go slowly, and another ship pitches into us, we are split in two. If she comes slowly, and we pitch into her, she goes up—or rather down."

"I do believe that fellow *is* asleep."

The whistle kept sounding at regular intervals.

"Phil."

"Hello, Jim."

"Is that so? In point of fact?"

"Certainly; and the whistle blows in order to warn any vessel that may be in hearing to get off the track."

"But suppose *it* was to whistle, too, and so go to warning *us?*"

"Why, then, we would turn one way and she another, and so we would pass."

"But suppose it was a sailing vessel, and had no whistle."

"It would blow its fog-horn."

"Its what?"

"Its fog-horn."

"Good gracious me! The idea of a fellow going about in the middle of the Atlantic Ocean such a night as this blowing a horn. Do you think there's much danger?"

"Oh, no. Collisions very seldom occur. The chances are thousands to one against."

"Do you suppose the captain is up?"

"No doubt of that; he is on the bridge."

"How do you know?"

"Because that's a rule of the service."

"A good rule."

He returned to his berth. Shortly afterwards, he called:

"Phil."

"Hello?"

"How big *is* a fog-horn? How far do you suppose a fellow could hear one of 'em?"

"I don't know; but, I suppose, about a mile."

"A fog-horn!" he muttered, as he turned with his face to the wall, "I've heard of many kind of a horn, but never before now have I heard of a fog-horn."

Shortly afterwards he called again:

"Phil."

"Yes, Jim."

"Why don't you go to sleep?"

"That whistle and you together won't let me. If one of you would stop, I think I could."

He said not another word, and was soon asleep.

We were both surprised that so few ships were visible during the passage, as well as the inhabitants of the sea Jim was particularly disappointed in the matter of the last. He had been, he said, always desirous of seeing a whale, and he suggested that owing to the quantities that had been taken heretofore the breed probably was thinning out. Many of the passengers left us at Queenstown, among them the two young married couples.

"A poor time they've had of it, I think, Phil."

"How so?"

"Why one of the fellows' wife has been sick nearly half the way, and the other woman's husband has been in the same fix, and when *they* got up, the other two got down. It was like the fox, and the goose, and the corn, all trying to cross over the river. One of the couples don't seem to be well matched anyhow. That's a beautiful girl with the yellow hair. That big-jawed fellow is her husband. He is a rich pork merchant from Ohio. Those jaws look as if they got to be so big from calling hogs."

He had invited at least half the passengers to come to see him in Georgia. Just before the arrival at Liverpool, he said to Captain Moodie:

"Well, captain, God bless you. You've done your duty certain this trip. If you ever come to Georgia, captain, and come to my house, if I don't treat you like a gentleman, you may tie me, bring me back to the old *Gallia*, and drop me in the biggest hole in the Atlantic Ocean."

"Any cigars or tobacco, sir?" asked the officer of customs.

"No, sir," said Jim, "I never use tobacco except for smoking, and I gave my last cigar five minutes ago to the second mate. I should not wish, sir ——"

"Pass on gentlemen, please."

CHAPTER III.

IN Liverpool: at the Adelphi Hotel. Looking out, and seeing, and hearing men, women, horses and wagons. Such odd-looking wagons, too, and those funny-looking, round-bellied, snug, little Welsh ponies, that seemed to know no other gait than a trot. Not to be rocking about as we had been for ten days. To see, for the first time, women keeping a hotel, and good-looking, smart, educated women at that. Those great big beds, so curiously canopied, with as much covering on them as if instead of June it had been November. The various windings we had to take in order to get to our chambers. To be waited on by servants in livery. When a pretty boy with violet colored livery and brass buttons brought to me the first things I ordered, I had feelings approaching the aristocratic. The service was trifling, and I hesitated whether I would offer him a sixpence; but he received it with such cordiality that I was glad I did it.

It was three o'clock, and, feeling like eating, we made known our wants, and were invited to the coffee-room.

"The coffee-room?" said Jim.

"Yes, sir."

"Why, my dear friend, we want our *dinner*. We don't want any *coffee* this time of day."

The boy smiled, and led us across the hall, and we entered the large room which, to his delight, Jim found to contain or to have the means of getting whatever the hungriest and the daintiest might desire. A very portly and elegantly-dressed man with steel-pen coat and white vest and cravat met us at the door, and directed a waiter to conduct us to a table.

"That's the proprietor," whispered Jim. "Don't he look well fed? And so they call a dining-room a coffee-room over here. Likewise, they call a horse-car a tramway. We've got a heap to learn in the language, I see, my friend. They've changed it a good deal since our folks left this country."

Our sojourn in Liverpool was brief. My own pursuits and studies had always been of such kind that I felt comparatively little interest in so new a city as Liverpool, and I am almost ashamed to say that I saw little more of the celebrated docks than what I could notice from the ship as they lay for miles and miles on the Mersey. But Jim had said that he would rather see those docks than anything in England. He always had had a turn for mechanics. His own mill-dam, of which he was very proud, had been constructed under his immediate supervision. While he was examining the docks, I remained at the hotel, and with the map I had purchased studied our routes. Before this, I had become convinced that the pleasure and the benefits of each in the other's companionship, instead of being impaired by the diversity of our tastes and dispositions, were enhanced. While Jim derived pleasure from studying the achievements of modern enterprise, and I was much more fond than he in looking upon the relics of olden times, yet this very difference served as a foil to divert the course of each sometimes, when it might have led to observation of things specially interesting to himself only, and at other times it gave occasion to pleasant raillery.

On the second day after our arrival, when Jim had returned from his visit to the docks, full of admiration for them and for the prodigious commerce of the city, I listened to his ardent accounts of them with an interest which I certainly had not felt in reading, and should have not felt in personally inspecting them. I made a mistake, however, when I began to admit that I did not at first understand his eager and minute descriptions, for the admission led him to make them yet more so, and I had at last to assume an intelligence which I certainly did not have, and, according as he was most enthusiastic in his descriptions, I exhibited satisfactory attention. I frankly admit now that I know little about the great Liverpool docks; yet what I do no know of them I owe to Jim Rawls

"Why, sir," said he, among many other things, "I got an idea to-day for letting the water into my mill-race and stopping it out that I would'nt grudge the whole cost of this trip for. It's so perfectly simple that I wonder it never occurred to me before."

And then he took my umbrella, both of our hats, and some books that lay on the table in the smoking-room, and he went on at such a rate that I had to say that it was very simple and—indeed—decidedly first-rate.

"You see how it is, Phil, don't you?"

"I think—I think I do. Let me see. The umbrella is—the—oh—the—"

"The mill-race, of course."

"I thought so, because—it's the longest. Yes, yes, that's the race. And now, let me see again. On reflection, I don't exactly remember whether it was your hat or my hat that was the, ah—the—"

"The gate, man, the gate."

3

"Oh! Gate! Certainly; what was I thinking about? I understand now; the gate."

"The two gates."

"Certainly; two gates. Of course, they've *got* to be two gates, I should suppose."

"Of course; else what in the dickence would come of all the water?"

Thus we went on for some time.

"Well, upon my word, Jim, I'm glad you went to these docks. They are more interesting than I had any notion of their being. And then, the valuable hints you got from them."

I looked intently at the umbrella and the other articles, and tried to understand the hydraulic principles they were meant to represent.

"Yes, yes, sir," I said, as soon as I could; "this thing will be of service to you, Jim. I have no doubt. I'm glad you went."

"Why, sir, I would'nt take five hundred dollars for it."

Late in the afternoon we took a long walk out on Prince's Road, intending to visit the public park, and were pleased to find that a city so mainly devoted to commerce exhibited so many evidences of taste. Having reached what we supposed was the park, we were surprised to find the gates leading into it locked. Standing at one of these, we were looking over upon the exquisite landscape, when an elderly gentleman, who had been sitting upon a rustic seat beneath a shade tree overhanging the walk, rose, approached us, took out of his pocket a key, and politely asked if we would enter. We accepted promptly, remarking that, supposing the park was open to the public, we had not provided ourselves with permits.

"Oh! the public park," he answered, smiling, "is

open to the public. That is further on. This park is private, belonging to those of us who reside for some distance along on this side of the street. I shall be pleased to show you this, however, if you wish. I see you are Americans."

"Ah?" we exclaimed, both well pleased.

"Oh, yes. We recognize Americans at once."

Jim evidently straightened himself yet more, but said nothing. We wandered for half an hour amid one of the loveliest landscapes I had ever beheld. Some young persons of both sexes were rowing on a lake. Jim lingered several moments looking silently at them, while our guide and myself were slowly walking and discussing the various species of vegetation. We had, at length, to call him away. I knew where his thoughts had been. He sighed gently but not painfully, as he came up briskly.

It began to grow late, and having gone considerably from the entrance, we proposed returning. The gentleman said he would lead us to a place of exit nearer home. Winding about through other and continually varying scenery, we came suddenly to the rear of a fine mansion. We looked at him in astonishment.

"This is my residence, gentlemen. If you will do me the honor to walk in, I will let you out this way."

We entered, through a veranda, a large dining-hall.

"But here," said our host, "you must rest for a few moments. You've had something of a walk."

While we were admiring the pictures on the walls, and the stuffed birds of game in a large glass case on a table in one corner, a servant brought in a bottle each of sherry and port. Pledging in a glass apiece, we parted from him at his front door, expressing his satisfaction for having met us.

"Upon my word," said Jim, "a politer or a friendlier old fellow I should seldom wish to see. Sensible, too. That man knows whom to ask into his house, no matter if they are strangers. Rich folks up along here, Phil, to be able to have private parks in a town of five or six hundred thousand inhabitants. You may be sure of that; and if you had seen those docks and that Exchange you would'nt be surprised. Well, I don't mind a fellow getting rich and enjoying his money if it don't make a fool of him, and keep him from being civil."

The next morning, as we were preparing to depart for Chester, Jim, who, it was arranged between us, should keep the accounts, went to the office and called for our bill. One of the ladies answered, that she would make it out and send it to the smoking-room. He looked at her somewhat surprised, but politely retired.

"What *can* she mean by *making out* our bill? I never paid a tavern bill in that way. Can't they just say what it is at once? We've been here exactly two days."

"They don't charge by the day over here, Jim."

"How do they charge?"

Just then a porter brought in the bill. Jim put on his spectacles, looked at it awhile intently, frowned, turned it upside down, looked at it that way, turned it back, took off his spectacles, and handed the paper to me.

"I can't read half of it, and don't understand one word of what I can make out. As nigh as I can come at it, it's a regular old-fashioned sum in Daboll's Arithmetic. What in the world these things are that you've been getting, I can't tell. This English handwriting and these figures are too much for me."

This he said in very low tones, so as not to be overheard by the porter, who had retired as far as the door and was waiting to be called. I took the paper and showed how the items had been set down separately for each day, added, carried from the first to the second, and footed.

"I see, I see. It is a regular old sum in compound addition. What does it foot up? Oh, that's reasonable. But what's that word?"

"Apartments."

"Apartments? What—does she mean; *rooms?*"

"Certainly."

"Why, we did'nt have but one."

"Yes, but you see the charge is right."

"I see, I see. I suppose it's just a general way of calling them rooms. But what word is that?"

"Attendance."

"Does that mean the waiters?"

"I suppose so."

"Certainly, that's it; but I wonder if they suppose anybody who considers himself a gentleman would be willing to go off without giving the waiters something? I never got that poor and that mean yet. I expect they've had a heap of mean people to stop here, and it has made 'em put this item in their bills. I mean to give these fellows something extra, for they've been very attentive."

He took the bill to the office himself, apologized for having kept it so long, said it was very reasonable, paid it, and bowed himself away. He then said that he was going to the dining-room to hand James a couple of shillings and take leave of the proprietor. The latter he met at the door.

"I beg pardon, sir; but I was looking for the waiter. I wanted to hand him a couple—"

3*

"Hi am the waiter, sir."

"You! Ain't you the proprietor?"

"H'oh no, sir. Hi am Daniel, the 'ead waiter."

"Gracious fathers! I thought—"

He had a half crown piece in his hand. He looked at it for a moment in confusion, thrust it back into his pocket, and taking out several pieces of various sizes put them into Daniel's hand and rushed away. It was not until we had gotten into the cars at Lime Street Station that he said:

"Phil, did you know that old fellow in the coffee-room was a waiter?"

"No. You said he was the proprietor. I thought you knew. You are so ready to find out everything."

"I never asked a soul about him. I took it for granted that he was the proprietor; but he's the head-waiter. Well, sir, this is an aristocratic country, to have such as him for waiters. When he told me he was the waiter, I *could'nt* get so far down from my opinion of him as to give him half a crown, so I gave him about all the change I had in my pocket and broke off as soon as I could."

As it was my province to select the places to be visited and Jim's to arrange the routes and the hours of departure, he soon made himself familiar with Bradshaw's Railway Guide, a feat I think I never could have accomplished. The shortest route to Chester was by ferryboat to Birkenhead, and thence by rail. But the hours that way not suiting, we went by the longer route of the Great North Western and the Grand Junction, crossing the Mersey about twenty miles from Liverpool.

"I should like, if we had time," said Jim, looking out of the window as we sped along by the margin of the

Bridgewater canal, "to travel on that awhile and see how they manage those locks."

"I don't see where the water comes from to fill that canal," I said.

"Why, man, from the air and the ground. This is the wettest country in the world, you know. I've read about this country through here often. Look what crops and what cows. You've ate, my friend, many a piece of cheese that came from here."

In less than an hour we were at Chester and quartered at the Grosvenor House.

"Another pretty girl, Phil," he whispered, as we approached the office. "Great country this for women."

As we stood upon the vestibule of the hotel and looked out, Jim said:

"Now what could you ever suppose put it into the head of people to build such a town as this? This is what they call the Rows. Why look, will you? The street belongs to the wagons and the horses, and are away down below; and the people have to walk on that piazza above."

It was indeed a strange sight as we wandered along the piazzas, far above the street, the dwellings below us and the stores to our left, with an occasional booth to our right boarded in and jutting over the vehicles below.

"I call this doing business up-stairs. And then look down that cross street yonder. See how the houses lap over on both sides as they go up. Upon my word, it don't seem to be more than six feet from some of the windows in the upper stories on one side of the street to those on the other. The town is about three times as big at the top as at the bottom. I wonder it don't fall in. A little more and that street would be a tunnel.

If the houses did'nt look so old, I should guess that
that's what they intended to make of it after a while.
But *ain't* they old?"

After dinner we made the full circuit of the walls
within which the town is enclosed.

"And the old king stood here in this window, did
he?" said Jim, when we had mounted into Charles the
First's Tower. "And over yonder is Rowton Moor.
Oh, these kings, these kings! They have to have their
times of trouble like the rest of us. How he must have
felt when he stood in this window and saw his army
defeated. Let's go on."

We went on by the race-turf, lingering to look upon
the lovely view towards the north and west. Further
on was the bridge over the Dee with that magnificent
arch of two hundred feet, the largest in the kingdom.

"Now that looks sensible," said Jim, "about the first
thing of the kind I've seen in this old burg. Why they
don't pull down this old wall, and let the town grow
some, if it can, is what I don't understand. They might
give it a chance, anyway. No wonder the Dee is drying
up. I should think such a town as this would dry up
any river after awhile. And that's the field where they
caught the other king, eh?" (pointing to a hill-side
across the Dee), "and along here old Edward was rowed
by the seven princes up the river to that old St. John's
Church on the hill yonder? This place seems to have
been quite considerable with those old kings, and some
of them had hard times like other folks. Yes, sir.

> " Princes, this clay must be your bed,
>   In spite of all your towers."

"They are not *buried* here, Jim."

"I suppose not. Still—somehow, I thought of that

old song ever since we were in King Charles' Tower, but it did'nt seem exactly to fit in there because it's no great shakes of a town, and old Charles was'nt in much of a bragging mood, I take it. From the way you look, it don't seem to you to come in much better here. Well, you know, Phil, poetry ain't my strong point."

"When will this circuit end?" said I, nearly broken down after more than an hour's walk. "Have you any idea how far we are from our hotel?"

"Oh, an immense distance," he answered, with mock seriousness. "This is a big place, Phil, you know, counting every way, up and down, especially up."

"Why it has only about thirty thousand people in it, inside and out."

"And they inside living all in one district another, too, eh? Yes, but you see it *winds*, you may well say, inside and out. I take it that this town of Chester has about as many insides and outsides, and as many insides that ought to be outsides, as any that can be found. I'm glad I've seen Chester *one time*."

We had not gone ten steps further when Jim stopped at one of the numerous flights of steps that led down from the walls.

"Are you really tired, Phil?"

"I am, indeed."

"Oh, you old fellows; you can't stand anything."

"I'm just three weeks older than you are."

"Yes, but three weeks make a difference. Well, do you know where you are? Do you know what house that's the top of?"

"I certainly do not."

"I suppose not. T'was'nt for me you'd never get down from these walls, but keep meandering round and round 'em. Well, that's the Grosvenor, and these are the very steps we came up when we started."

"You don't tell me so."

"I do. Can't *you* think now of a bit of poetry, or a piece of a hymn that would suit your lost condition? What is that about

"Weary sinner, lost and wounded?"

"Let's get down and rest a while first."

The next morning, we considered whether or not we would go out to Eaton Hall, the seat of the Marquis of Westminster. Our time was so limited, we rather chose to visit the Cathedral. We entered this most imposing old structure just as morning prayers were over. One of the vergers very kindly led us around, pointing out and explaining many things; which, however much we may read of them, we must see in order to fully comprehend and appreciate; the varying architecture of the ages, and the relations of the various parts of such a structure to one another. Jim was especially impressed by the cloisters of the monks of former times, and the great hall in which they used to dine in common.

"What upon earth is that thing up there?" he asked of the verger, pointing upward to where, high on the wall, a very small sort of pulpit of stone was fastened, to which several steps of the same material led from the floor.

"That," answered the verger, smiling, "is the pulpit from which, when the monks were at dinner, one of their number was accustomed to read aloud sermons and homilies."

"Sermons and what?"

"Homilies."

"You mean preaching?'

"Not exactly that, but—the next thing to it, I suppose."

Jim laughed aloud, but instantly checking himself, said:

"I beg your pardon, sir, for laughing in your church; but it struck me all of a sudden the idea of a set of preachers sitting down to their dinner and having to listen to another one a preaching to 'em. Do you suppose that fel—, that gentleman I mean, had *his* dinner first?"

"Ah, I can't say that, sir, but probably not."

"Well, well, this town of yours has seen times, in its—time, if I might use such an expression. I see you are all mending up the old church?"

"Oh, yes; the Dean is very much interested in renewing the Cathedral"

"Well, I wish him good luck; but I should say he had a job on his hands."

"And now, gentlemen," said the verger, "I shall be glad, if you are to remain in Chester, to show you, at another time, other interesting things about the Cathedral and the Priory. But, with your leave, I will bid you good morning for the present, as I have not yet breakfasted."

"Why, bless me!" answered Jim, "have'nt you been to breakfast?"

"No, indeed; we never breakfast until after morning prayers."

"I beg your pardon a thousand times, sir, for keeping you away from your breakfast. We leave the town in a couple of hours. We are very much obliged to you, and we would'nt have thought of trespassing on your time ——"

"Don't mention such a thing, gentlemen."

"Good gracious!" said Jim, after we had left the grounds, "did'nt you suppose he had had his breakfast? Why, it's half past eight o'clock, and the sun has been up nigh on to five hours."

"They don't rise here as you do in Georgia."

"I see they don't. Well, I suppose their business here goes on about as well, what there is of it, as if they did get up in decent time. This is a slow-going, but an economical town, Phil."

"How economical?"

"Why, don't you see the object of putting that pulpit on the wall in the dining-room of that church? And have preaching going on while they were at dinner?"

"I think I do. It was to remind the religious who were eating of the source from which all blessings come, and lift their thoughts to contemplate the feasts of the soul as superior to those of the flesh."

"No, sir; not a bit of it. It was to spoil their appetites, and make 'em eat as little as possible, and save expenses, and maybe to keep 'em from complaining of their victuals. That's the only effect that such a thing would have on me, or any other reasonable and healthy man. About two weeks' preaching to me at dinner would make me as thin as a down stream shad. But, do you know, Phil, I've been thinking how this head preacher here, what did he call him? Dean? might economize in fixing up that immense old establishment? If I was in his place, I should get my material from this old wall. It's of no manner of use for anything else in this world than for building material. The idea of keeping it here just because it has been here always, is nonsense. It ought to be put to some earthly use besides for strangers to get the rheumatism in walking over it. For the people here don't seem to use it in that way themselves. We've walked the whole round, and I should say it was pushing on to two miles, and we didn't meet the first native man, woman, or child. Maybe they keep it just to toll people here; for I don't see much business here of any kind. If this is so, I should say that it was about as curious and unsatisfactory kind of merchandizing as I would seldom wish to see. But then it can't wear out, not even like wax figures, which it certainly makes me think of. Well, I'm glad I've seen old Chester one time; and now I'm ready to leave, and go where a body can get some fresh air."

4

CHAPTER IV.

N the carriage, sir; in the carriage," urged the railway porter to Jim at the station, as he was lingering on the platform taking a last look at the old town.

"It's well they call it a carriage," said Jim, when we were seated, and the train moved off, "for it's no railroad car. I'm astonished, Phil, that these English people should be so far behind the times as to have *carriages* instead of cars on their railroads. No chance to walk, nor not even to stretch your legs, without putting them between other people's. No water to drink, whether you are on a slow train or a fast one."

"I don't see what the speed of the train can have to do with the question of water."

"That's just what I say; it has'nt got anything to do with it; and the reason is, the people over here don't keep any water to drink, and don't drink it themselves; otherwise, a fellow might get a drink at a station. No, sir; no water on the cars, and none on the route. But, Phil, there's an advantage in taking a smoking-car: for they don't use the weed much over here, and the smoking car is seldom full."

The morning was fine, and it was pleasing that prospect of well cultivated fields bounded on our right by the Rhuabon and other hills in Wales. Further on, the meadow-lands of Shropshire, on the Severn. in their unbroken green, seemed well worth a journey through them. even if they had not been full of historic interest. The low, dense hawthorn hedges, the clumps of shade trees in every field for the laborers and the cattle to rest beneath in the noontide heat, the winding rivulets with shaded banks along which led narrow paths for the country folk, the fat kine and the full dairies,—looking upon all these, we had continual delight. As we ran into Shrewsbury, I expressed regret that our brief time would not allow us to linger here for at least a day.

"It looks a little livelier than Chester, and for that reason would certainly suit *me* better. It isn't as big, I should say, but it has'nt any wall, and can grow."

"It did have one for a part of the circuit, and would have had it all, but that the Severn, you see, nearly surrounds it. There was a wall across the neck of the peninsula, but it seems to have all gone."

"There's a part of an old something just above this station on that hill."

"That is the remains of the castle which was built by Roger de Montgomery, created Earl of Shrewsbury by William the Conqueror. This town and Chester, being on the frontier, had to be strongly fortified against the Welsh. Shrewsbury especially was so important that several of the early kings spent much of their time and held parliaments here. In that old castle up there were born two of the sons of Edward IV, the oldest of whom was one of those afterwards murdered by Richard III in the Tower. Shrewsbury was the great stronghold of the Yorks in the wars of the Roses. See yonder old abbey with the tower. You don't forget Falstaffe?"

"Who? Old Jack? Of course not. Is this my same old Shrewsbury?"

"The same; and in that tower was the clock which timed Sir John's fight in the field over yonder to the left."

In five minutes we were off again. Jim strained his eyes, as long as it was visible, to the old abbey, then turned them in the direction of Shrewsbury Field.

"Well, well, many's the time I've read that play of Shakspeare about old Jack, and Douglass, and Glendower, and Hotspur, without ever expecting to be this near Shrewsbury Field. That same clock, eh! Well, it ticked to a good, long, old fight. Ah! that was a grand old fellow. It was a mean thing in the prince to throw him off after all they had seen and done together. Of course, he must stop all such larks when his father died and he got to be king; but he might have made some provision for the poor old fellow. I always feel a little like crying when I read old Mrs. Quickly's account of how he died: because the king 'killed his heart.' Poor Jack! He put all his money on one card, and that's always a mistake. But, see here, Phil, if I remember right, it was somewhere along here that the young King Charles, while running from old Cromwell, hid in the oak. What's the name—Bos—something?"

"Boscobel Manor-House. Here it is on the map. It is only about five or six miles from the town of Sheffnall, the next station. We can't be further than three or four miles from the Royal Oak."

"They had him up a tree there, did'nt they?"

"They did, indeed; that was a narrow escape."

"I expect he felt about as easy as his father did in that old town at Chester. Oh, these kings! What won't they go through to gain and to hold on to their crowns! But that's not so wonderful. What *is* won-

derful to me is that the people will risk more and suffer
more for the same than the kings themselves. I don't
mean the big men; for they always expect something in
the way of reward; but the people, the poor people
that expect nothing, and get nothing, no matter how it
goes: how such as these can leave their wives and children, and little pieces of land, and follow these kings,
who care no more for them, as a general thing, than so
many mules or hogs, and travel over mud, and dust, and
snow, and rain, to get killed, or come home broken
down in health and poorer than ever, this is what I
don't understand."

"That's a matter, Jim, that used to perplex me,"
said I, "very much. I have thought over it many
times, and I think I am getting to understand it better.
There are several reasons why even the poorest are willing to undergo such dangers for kings. In the first
place, pity is a thing which, my reading and observations have led me to believe, tends upwards instead of
downwards. Misfortunes are the common lot of the
poor. Born in low conditions, they, for the most part,
remain in them throughout their lives. Calamities
among them are too small reductions from their habitual
states to excite very much commiseration either among
their superiors or their equals. But when a very great
man, and especially a prosperous king, comes to grief,
the descent seems so immense, that the lower and hum-
bler a man is, the greater his awe and his pity. They
have been used to look up to the great as the favorites
of heaven; and when these fall, they have a sort of
undefined dread as if such vast ruin, unless reversed,
must overwhelm all mankind. It is pleasing, besides,
to pity such unforeseen and such great suffering, because

4*

thus the lowly feel some exaltation of themselves in
thus sympathizing with, and, in some sort, rising into
the society of the powerful. Look at the tragedies that
have excited so many tears among the poor. To say
nothing of the older, take those of Shakspeare that you
like so much. They don't recite the misfortunes of common people, but of the mighty—King Lear, and Hamlet
and such men. If they were common men, even you,
Jim, would get tired of reading them, because, with all
your independence and self respect, you feel, while reading such exalted language, that the suffering it describes
can befall none but those who have fallen from the
loftiest estate. Were you less intelligent than you are,
that idea would be yet more decided in your mind·
The poets who wrote these tragedies understood well
the hearts of the masses, and that they extend more
pity towards the powerful than they receive from them,
or than they bestow upon one another. Besides, there
is the sense of greater personal security in the success
of the chieftain of their choice, their pride in his glory
and in the feeling of their identification with his fortunes, whether in prosperity or adversity. And so they
will go to his wars, suffer and fight for him, and die for
him, and their children will be proud of having had
such fathers. What do you say to that?"

"I expect you are about right. In fact, we see something of the same sort, though, on a small scale, in our
elections at home. Parties choose their leaders, and
when the campaign gets hot the more ignorant a fellow
is the more ready he is, if not an arrant coward, to fight
for his candidate. I suppose it's natural to us all to
have our leaders."

"Just so; and the more ignorant we are the more

necessary seem to us their triumph, and the more disas-
trous their fall. Then there is to be considered that even
the weakest and most incapable has his share, small as it
may be, of personal ambition, and looks forward to his
portion in the aggregate successes of his cause. These
are the secrets of loyalty and patriotism. A man must
look *up* to some one above him, even in this world. If
he does not, he will be unhappy. It is God's work.
The kings and the great rulers are necessary, but they
have not been generally happy, because, for the most,
they had no higher personages to look up towards in
whose glory they could feel pride and common interest,
or whose misfortunes they could pity. We are glad we
are not kings, Jim, are'nt we ? "

" Yes, indeed, or queens either; especially queens."

We were soon out of Shropshire and into Staffordshire,
and my friend was full of admiration at this the great
coal and iron region of England. The scores, the hundreds of factory chimneys near Wolverhampton, from
which the fires and smoke, rushing day and night continuously, made it seem as if the whole region around
was a forest on fire, were intensely interesting to a mind,
which, in spite of age and adversities, yet delighted in
the evidences of energy and prosperity. As we were
approaching Birmingham, he said :

' Now, sir, if I had had the picking out of the stopping places on this route, yonder's the town I should
have selected, instead of your Chester with its old walls—
not that I ain't glad I've seen old Chester *one time*, just
to find out what a curious kind of a town people can
make when they try."

" Why Jim, we might have given Birmingham a day.
Why did'nt you mention that you would like to see it ? "

"Oh it makes no difference; it's all right. Our time is too short for us both to see all we want to, and it's easier to leave the routes to one, and that one, you. In your programme I shall see enough sights to last the balance of my life. No doubt about that. I just said what I did to be talking. But I bet I can tell more about this town than you can."

"I've not a doubt of it. I have often regretted, Jim, that I could not take more interest than I do in the history and progress and varieties of manufacturing business."

"Yes, I see you think more of seeing and talking about old towns and old things than new. You always did, Phil. You were even a sort of an old boy."

"I admit that my conclusion to come out here with you was brought about mainly—besides the pleasure of having *you* for a companion—"

"Ahem! of course."

"Was to see old, historic places. To tell you the truth, I am ashamed of my ignorance of the march of mechanical industries, but more so of my unwillingness to make the effort to learn something about them."

"As to that, Phil, people are not alike. It's well they ain't. No one man can know everything, or like everything. Such things ain't in your line, and your old histories ain't in mine. You and I suit to travel together very well, and a heap better than if we had exactly the same ideas. We can have and do have some variety, and —if you was'nt so poky—we might have some little fun. I must see if I can't wake you up a little out of your dreaminess, my old man."

"I wish you would, my sweet youth."

"Hello, that's the liveliest thing you've said since we left home. I'm having hopes of you."

"But speaking of old things, Birmingham is a very old place."

"I thought it was modern."

"It was a town in the time of the Romans, called then Bremerium. The old *Strata Vitellianas*, now called Watling street, is not far from here. Even in those times this was a considerable place for the manufacture of arms. I doubt if there are many Roman relics now; but I should have liked myself to see old St. Martin's Church in the Bull-Ring. That is more than a thousand years old."

"Good gracious! I'm glad you did'nt bet. I find you know a sight more about the place than I do. Tell me some more."

"No, that's about all I know, except that in later times it was the capital of the Kingdom of Mercia."

"Upon my word, those items of information had escaped me. Well, your knowledge and mine will dovetail very well. Between us, we can make something of the town. In the first place, Birmingham is the healthiest of all the large towns of England. You know the reason why? No? Well, in the first place, it is built on the sides of three hills, and the drainage into this river Rea, as they call it, is perfect. Another reason, as they say, is the immense amount of vitriol which is made here and in the works at Soho and Smettick, close by. But a better reason still, is that the houses are not so crowded here as in Liverpool and the other towns."

By this time we were at the station, and although we had only five minutes, Jim declared he meant to run out of the enclosure and take one look.

"Get a couple of bottles of beer and something to eat," he said, as the train stopped and he rushed out.

"In the carriage, in the carriage."

"Certainly, certainly. In the carriage. Let her move on. Good-bye, my friend," he said to the porter who fastened our door, "I would have given you something to get me a drink of water, except I suppose it would have cost you twice as much to get as it would have been worth to me. Do you love beer?"

"Oh, yes, sir. It's better an' water."

"There, you take this and drink our health. It's for giving me the hint when your *carriage* was going to move."

Jim took the front seat, and looked back at the town as long as it was visible.

"Don't she look old and solid? This is a live town, Phil. The very walk of the people is different from that in that old *tarrapin* we've just left. They have some air here. I've read that Birmingham has twice as much room to the man as Manchester, and three times as much as Liverpool. But as for me, I could'nt live in a big town. Why don't they make the streets wider and have more shade trees? I suppose it's because they don't know, when the town first begins, that it is going to grow so big. I begin to like this beer. It *is* better than water—such as they have here. Oh! if I *could* get one drink of water out of my well. But that *if*. F, you know, my friend, is the longest letter in the book."

Thus rattling on, he took his lunch, and afterwards we lit our cigars and looked with delight upon the ever-changing and ever-pleasing views in this the so-called heart of England—the county of Warwick.

"There don't seem to be any poverty in this region, Phil; in the country I mean. I see from the map that we are in Warwickshire."

"Yes, of all, the country I have most desired to see."
"I bet it has a plenty of old worn-out things in it.
Well, I guess there's a few fresh things scattered about
here and there that a young fellow can pick up."

CHAPTER V.

LEAMINGTON is certainly the cleanest-looking town I have even seen. It was too early for the season, and not many strangers were there. These were invalids, for the most part, who had come for the benefit of the waters and the baths. But all, including invalids and inferior sorts of persons, seemed to be trying to keep in harmony with the general cleanliness and brightness of the town, the shining bath-chairs, which here we saw for the first time, pushed leisurely along the sidewalks, their occupants looking leisurely into the bright shops, and the shop-keepers seeming as if they had just come out of the baths, and preferred quiet to selling merchandise. After a good dinner at the Regent, on the Lower Parade, we strolled over Leicester, Regent, and Warwick streets, Holly Walk, The Lansdowne Crescent and Circus, and thence through the fine Jephson Gardens.

"She shoots well for a woman," remarked Jim, as we lingered where a party of young men and women were exercising themselves in the Archery. "She looks like she has some energy, and that's more than I can say for the men of this town as far as I've seem 'em. Did you ever see such an indifferent set? They must all be rich people. At least, everybody looks as if he had a clean suit of clothes for every day; and the very houses look like they were washed this morning with soap and water, and afterwards varnished. I thought you were after something old in these parts, Phil, but this is the newest-looking place that ever I saw."

"Yes, Leamington is a new place. It is only within the few last years that it has become a favorite resort for the wealthy. We are in advance of the season, you see, and the shop-keepers are waiting for the crowds to come in hereafter."

"I see they are waiting for something, and everybody is dressed up as if it was a wedding. But ain't these gardens pretty? What a delightful little stream that is in the bottom."

"That's the river Leam, you see."

"River! Well, it takes mighty little water to make a river in this country."

"Leaving our baggage at Leamington until the morrow, we took a carriage for Coventry, *via* Stoneleigh and Kenilworth. My companion remarked, in an undertone to me, as the coachman ascended to his box, that few men of our age would often desire to have a portlier, red-faceder, well-fedder, dignifieder, and comfortable-lookinger driver than the one we had. When the latter had taken his lofty seat in the open barouche, he slowly turned his head half way round for instructions, seeming as if he was in communication with some person under the front seat.

"He's like the rest of the Leamingtonians," said Jim, in a whisper, "and so, my gracious, are the very horses. Nobody and nothing else here seems ever to be in a hurry. But we've got the whole afternoon before us, and, upon my word, a man ought to want to travel slowly through such a country as this. My sakes, Phil! I had no idea that there was one-tenth of the timber in

5

this old country.   Can you tell me, my friend," addressing the driver, "whose land this is?"

In due time, the imaginary gentleman under the
front seat might have heard the solemn response:

"Lord Leigh's, sir."

"What?   He owns land this far from home?"

"H'oh, yes, indeed, sir."

On we drove through lanes, on both sides of which
alternated the greenest fields we had ever seen, and
forests from which one would have believed that never a
tree or even a shrub had been removed.   The approach
to Stoneleigh Abbey reminded of the old stories of
fairy-land, so enchanting were its shaded avenues and
irregular plantations amid undulating grounds.   The
Abbey, with its surroundings, from every point of view,
were most picturesque.   We would fain have lingered
and entered within the grounds, but after admiring for
a brief time the old gateway (of the time of Henry II),
we proceeded on.   A mile further, in the direction of
Kenilworth, we passed through another gate, and then
the great forests of oak and beech became more and
more dense and imposing.   The ivy, climbing high up
among the branches, and the thick underwood, made
these forests seem impenetrable.

"None but rich folks hunt in these woods, driver, eh?"

"H'oh no, indeed, sir."

"That's plain enough.   Common folks don't shoot
these rabbits.   Look at that fellow yonder, and that one,
and that one.   That's eight I've seen in the last half
mile.   They've come out, I suppose, just for a little
walk—or rather a little hop—in the fresh air.   They
can't get any in them bushes and briars.   It would do
the people here more good, I should say, to clear up

some of that land and sow it down in wheat. But that's none of my business, and so far as I can see, everybody about here seems to make a living with mighty little work. Ah, yonder's your Kenilworth! Now for a sensation! Now for a right smart plucking up in the old man."

We drove leisurely through the long straggling main street of the village, with its frequent displays on faded sign-boards, of the Bear and Ragged Staff, the ancient crest of the Leicesters. But our eyes, Jim's as well as mine, though he would have pretended otherwise, peered before us eagerly for what was left of the castle. Arrived there we were surprised and discontented not to find guides ready for employment; for, although we had freshened ourselves up by reading, while on the ship, Scott's novel, we desired to inspect minutely, and in the brief period allowed us, the famous old ruin. Finding by inquiry of the keeper, another portly man, with blue coat and brass buttons, that there were no guides, and nothing was to be had for our purposes but photographs of the separate parts, Jim merely remarked that he had 'arf a crown in his pocket for which he had no very particular use that he knew of just then. The keeper called from the lodge a woman who might have been his wife, and saying he was called away on business and would be gone for an hour or two, we passed, under his lead, through the Great Gateway into the outer court. To our right, Cæsar's Tower, the Leicester Buildings to the left; before us, and across the inner court, the Banqueting Hall and the Strong Tower, and adjoining, the famous Pleasaunce; on our left, Mortimer's Tower, and beyond it, the lake and the tilt yard.

I cannot say how I should have felt if I had visited

this scene, so replete with historic and romantic interest,
when I was younger, and my warmer blood bounded
with the recital of knightly deeds. Even as it was, I
seemed to feel as much emotion as the youngest and
most ardent could have felt. Jim partook fully of this
emotion, quite unexpectedly to himself, he contended;
and he minutely studied the ground. We walked to
the tilt-yard, plucked some of the eglantines which
grew in profusion on the banks of the little stream
where once was the bridge which the Earl, three hundred years before, had built in honor of the visit of the
great queen. Returning, we ascended the steps of the
Strong Tower to Amy Robsart's chamber, descended,
and strolled through the Pleasaunce and the garden.
An hour was sufficient for all. We spoke but little.
My thoughts had never gone so wholly and so inter-
estedly into the past. The Clintons, the Montforts, the
Lancasters, and the Leicesters, the Kings Henries, Edwards, and Elizabeth, and, lastly, Cromwell, the great
hater of kings and lords, and the fell destroyer of their
works. I was where, all my life-time, I had desired to
be for one time, where these great ones had had their
days of triumph and misfortune, their jousts and feasts
in times of peace, and their battles and sieges in times of
war. These had been here, where now all is desolation, and the very ivy, with its huge, brown, knotted
trunk, looks almost as old as the ruin on which it feeds.

"A tolerable old pile of buildings that, my friend,"
said Jim to the coachman, when we were off again.

" Very old, sir."

" Who does that piece of property belong to now?"

" Hurl Clarrun "

" Who?"

"Hurrell Clarrunen, sir."

Jim looked enquiringly to me.

"Earl Clarendon"

"If he would talk *at* me," whispered Jim, "I could understand him better."

"To what base uses we descend," I remarked, as we looked towards where the ancient abbey once stood and saw only the gateway and another small part now used for a cow-house.

"A cow is a very useful animal, sir," said Jim.

I looked at him reproachfully.

After a travel of five miles over the very finest road in England, we came in full view of the "three tall spires," and shortly afterwards were driving briskly up the street, making for "The King's Head" of Coventry.

"Where is the man carrying us?" I said to Jim, as, suddenly taking up his horses, he turned from the street into a narrow alley.

"Drive to the King's Head, man," I called out, excitedly.

Jim laughed silently, as the coachman, making no reply, drove on in a slow walk until the horses, of their own accord, stopped before a door in the alley, out of which a well-dressed, elderly woman, followed by two remarkably pretty, sweet-looking girls came forth with smiles and curtsies. I was much embarrassed, and looked at Jim.

"Oh, you must do the talking," said Jim, assuming an embarrassment that approximated alarm.

The coachman dismounted, opened the carriage door, and was proceeding to take down our bags and umbrellas.

"Madam," said I to the elderly lady, "I beg pardon. We are not the persons you seem to take us for; but really, ladies—"

My embarrassment painfully increased as I noticed them becoming suddenly grave and as suddenly arch (especially the girls), as they noticed my friend behind me whom, turning around, I saw making strenuous efforts to avoid laughing outright. Never having known him to be otherwise than gentle and most respectful towards women, I had not the slightest notion of what to make of his conduct.

"Ladies," said I again, "there is some unaccountable miscarriage in this matter. We are a couple of American gentlemen, merely traveling for entertainment, and are not those whom you have been evidently expecting. I directed the coachman to take us to the King's Head Inn, which I had been informed was the best known in Coventry, but by some misunderstanding he has brought us to a private house"

At this the young ladies laughed out, and so did Jim. The elderly woman again curtsied, and smiling, said:

"The coachman is right, sir; this is the King's Head, and we shall be happy to entertain you."

There was nothing that I could think of to say that would not have made matters worse. I only looked imploringly around for pardon. It seemed to be freely bestowed by all except the coachman. He rolled his great, red, moist eyes upon me for a moment, and as he led his horses into the court-yard, muttered:

"Thought I did'nt know the King's 'Ed! Private 'ouse!"

This being the first time I had seen an inn of the fashion which afterwards we found so common in England and Europe, I considered my mistake not unnatural. I was slow, however, in learning the relations of the different parts of this ancient but most respectable establishment—the coffee-room, the smoking-room, the bar, the office, and the route to and from our chamber. For my life, I could not definitely get the localities; and the smiles exchanged frequently between Jim and these girls made more vain my efforts in that direction. Not that I do not own to a natural absence of mind which has been wont to manifest itself, especially in the forgetfulness of places, excusable in some sort, I contend, in such as are as inconspicuous and comparatively capriciously arranged as those in an English inn.

We had but a part of the next morning in which to view Coventry, as our programme was to return by rail to Leamington and then by carriage again to Stratford. I determined, therefore, to rise betimes the next morning and see as much as possible before breakfast. At five o'clock I was up. I asked Jim if he would go with me.

"Not if I know myself," said he, "to see nothing but old things this time of day. I'll find you out somewhere in the course of a couple of hours and see whatever is alive in the old town; that ain't much, I take it, as far as I've seen, except some pretty, rosy-cheeked girls. At present—" he turned over and immediately fell back to sleep.

I began my descent, and it was soon evident that I had taken the wrong way at the first turning. A man unused to such buildings, constructed at numerous intervals through scores of years around a court yard, has little notions of the numbers of turnings the passages have and the irregularities of the plans of the various apartments. Discovering that I had lost my way, I thought to retrace my steps. The eagerness, strange at my time of life, that I felt not to be caught in so embarrassing condition as in the afternoon previous, made me the more confused, as I walked rapidly on. I saw very soon that I was utterly lost. I rushed on, however, as rapidly and as noiselessly as possible, now descending three or four steps and turning into a new passage, now ascending and diverging into another. I began at last to suspect that I must have gotten into the most private recesses of the house, possibly the apartments occupied by the females. In spite of the consciousness of the entire purity of my intentions, I reflected that I was a long way from home, entirely unknown here—well, the truth is, such feelings as I had cannot be well described. In my desperation, I determined henceforth to follow every descending suite of stairs that I should meet, until I should reach some point of egress on the ground floor. After having taken, as I really believe, more than two hundred steps, I found two large folding-doors, which, I could see by a side light, when opened, would admit me into the court-yard. To my amazement, I found the doors were locked from without. My feelings now partook of the indignant and even the angry. I seized the bolt and shook the doors with great violence several times. At last, the Boots, the only male person I had noticed about the establishment, was aroused where he had been sleeping, came to the door, and after scrutinizing me as closely as possible, with wide-open but not fully-awakened eyes, put in the key he carried, and let me out.

"In the name of thunder," said I, "what do you people mean by —"

But on a second's reflection, I knew that Boots ought not to be responsible for the building, or rather the numerous buildings of the house. Upon mild inquiry of where I was and how far from my chamber, on giving my number, he opened his great blue eyes to the very fullest, made with his fingers two sides of an imaginary parallelogram, running up the long and down the short side. I had travelled, it appeared, over the greater part of both these sides. If I had not descended when I did, I should have gotten among the stables in the loft of which Boots had been sleeping. I did not tell him in words, that I would rather he would not mention the circumstance; but the size of the piece I put into his hand made him appear grateful and intelligent.

I saw not a soul upon the street except a policeman, though the sun was now fully up. He accompanied me to the old priory, rather the few remains yet left of it; then knocking at a door at the corner of the same street, he roused a woman who, at his request, took a bunch of keys, and leading us to St. Michael's Church hard by, let us in. I felt amply compensated for the preceding anxieties of the morning by the sight, first of the lofty tower, prism and spire of this the largest and most tasteful of the parish churches of England, and afterwards, the interior, nave, aisles, and chancel with aisles and transepts, the latter most fitly divided from the body of arches rising from columns in clusters. From the wall of one of these transepts I copied an inscription which I afterwards submitted to Jim's criticism. While standing outside, and looking up at the tower, the bells, ten in number, sounded chimes, which, if I did not consider such music among the inferior sorts, would have impressed me much. They certainly were far the best that I have ever heard. Returning to Hertford street, on which was our hotel, at about seven o'clock, I met Jim, who said that he had just been into a watchmaking establishment.

"By the way, Phil, I heard a tremendous racket down stairs and about the house generally just after you left."

I took no notice of the remark, but stopped suddenly and pointed to a curious wooden figure in one of the open windows of an upper floor.

"What in the name of Davy Crockett is that?"

"That is Peeping Tom," I answered.

"What sort o' Tom?"

"Peeping Tom."

"I'm about as wise now as I was at first."

I then recounted the old legend of the Lady Godiva, and the signal punishment that befell the poor fellow, who, while the other citizens kept their eyes shut as, in obedience to the brutal conditions of her husband, she rode through the streets with no other covering than her long hair, looked upon·her, and was smitten with blindness.

"And how long ago was that?"

"Oh, several hundred years."

"You don't mean that that grinning old thing has been there so long?"

"It is well established that it has been there for at least three hundred years."

He looked at it intently for several moments.

"Well, old fellow, it was put on you right heavy for your curiosity. Why did'nt you just go *one* eye? Still, I think you were served about right."

After breakfast, we took leave of the women. We all shook hands, and, as pleasantly as I knew how, I apologized for my mistake of the evening before.

"Is that all?" began Jim; but one of the girls shook her finger at him.

"That Boots is a shabby fellow," said I, after we were

off, and I found that my morning's adventure was known.

"Boots? He had nothing whatever to do with it. You scared those women half to death while you were prowling about their rooms. If it had been a little sooner in the morning you would have finished 'em. As it was, they saw you, and rang the bell for the Boots to let you out. What were you doing in that part of the house, any how?"

"I had lost the thread of Ariadne," I answered, gravely. Jim looked at me seriously and interrogatingly for a moment, but said not another word on the subject.

"I wish," said I, "that we had had time to ride over yonder to Gosford Green."

"That's the ground of the duel between the Duke of Norfolk and Henry Bolingbroke. I remember that. There was'nt any blood spilt, however, and it's been a long time ago. Well, Phil, a man at your time of life old things suit. A man of my age likes new things. While you were going about those old churches, I was looking around to see what the people did for their living. That's a right live town, if it *is* old."

And then he gave me an account of the business done there in the watch, ribbon and silk trades: he had all the figures."

"By the way, Phil, what did they mean by putting 'in Coventry?'"

"There are various accounts of the origin of the phrase, but none satisfactory."

"I suppose when they put a fellow there, in the old times, they—as it were—located him—at the *King's Head*, and let him—get lost—as it were."

"Possibly. Look here, Jim, here is a curious epitaph

I copied in St Michael's Church. It purports to have been written by the deceased himself "In the agony and Dolorous Paines of the Gout and died soon after."

> " Here lyes an Old Tossed Tennis Ball,
> Was Racketted from Spring to Fall,
> With so much heat and so much hast,
> Time's arm for shame grew tyr'd at last.
> Four Kings in Camps he truly seru'd, '
> And from his royalty ne'er sweru'd.
> Father ruined, the Son slighted,
> And from the Crown ne'er requited,
> Loss of Estate, Relations, Blood,
> Was too well known, but did no good.
> With long Campaigns and paines o' the Gout,
> He cou'd no longer hold it out.
> Always a restless life he led,
> Never at quiet till quite dead.
> He marry'd, in his latter dayes,
> One who exceeds the common praise ;
> But wanting breath still to make Known
> Her true Affection and his Own,
> Death Kindly came, all wants supply'd
> By giving Rest which life deny'd."

"Well, sir, I should say a meaner piece of poetry I should seldom wish to hear read. No wonder the fellow that wrote that died soon after. None but a dying man ought to be expected to write such poetry as that. You ain't going to carry that home with you ? "

"Certainly. It's a very remarkable thing."

"Oh, it's remarkable. No doubt about that. It's remarkable that anybody, even on his death-bed, should make such stuff as that, and want it put on his tombstone ; and then it's remarkable that a well man in his senses should want to keep a copy of it."

I was surprised and pleased to notice how I had scotched Jim in his intentions to plague me about my blunders at the *King's Head*. He asked me very particularly about the Christian names of most of my female acquaintances whom he knew. I answered all his questions with prompt accuracy, never returning his intent looks. As we took the carriage again at Leamington for our afternoon's drive, he said:

"I thought I would buy a couple of handkerchiefs in this town, but they are too indifferent, these merchants. Well, good-bye Leamington. I'm glad to have seen you all, and to leave you all, looking so clean and contented in your minds."

Opening his bag to get out cigars, he said:

"Well, I see *my* thread is all safe yet."

I detected the mischief in his tone, but at the same time, the uncertainty.

6

CHAPTER VI.

HE afternoon was fine. The coachman, though partaking of the general steadiness of his fellow-citizens, was more communicative than the one of yesterday. Jim had given him a cup of beer before starting, and he was easily induced at our cordial invitation to join us in the weed. We had journeyed for some time over a beautiful, undulating road, when halting at the foot of a hill, and pointing to the left, he said:

"Guy's Cliffe! Yonder's the mill."

We alighted, and following the level pathway for a hundred or so paces, arrived at the old mill, and passing it a few steps stood upon a narrow bridge over the Avon and looked up at the mansion. A sweeter place for a man of culture, who sought compensation for absence from the city in the charms of nature, could no where be found on this earth. The clear river, widened by the embankment which backed its waters to the very foot of the mansion in its rear, the huge rock out of which the latter's foundation was hewed rising on either side, the dense, green shrubbery extending along the bank and up the cliff, mingling with the low-hanging branches of majestic shade trees above and beyond, all conspire, in perfect harmony, to make a home that "to one who desireth a retired life, either for his devotions or study, the like is hardly to be found." After gazing upon this scene for a few minutes, we retraced our steps to the road and walked up the hill to the front gate. It was open; but the portress, emerging from the lodge, politely informed us that Lady Percy was at home, and that strangers were not expected to enter the front grounds. We could only look down the fair avenue, through the lofty firs, and imagine to ourselves what manner of place it must be, the approaches to which were so exceeding beautiful.

A short drive brought us to Warwick Castle.

"This looks like worth coming to see," said Jim, as advancing through the deep, semi-circular road cut out of the rock we had full view of this magnificent structure. "Another Cæsar's Tower. They seemed in those times to have believed in old Cæsar in this country; and a Guy's Tower—our same old Guy of the Cliff, I suppose. Where's the part that was burnt some years ago?"

"There," I said, pointing to the Baronial Hall, and the suite of rooms following over a portion of that side of the court.

"Why the fire did'nt even kill the ivy on the wall."

It was surprising to see, in spite of the withered trunks, the green leaves which here and there dotted the walls. We entered along with about a dozen other tourists the great Banqueting Hall, and passed through the Red Drawing Room, the Cedar Drawing Room, the Gilt Drawing Room, the State Bed Room, and others. It was rather tiresome to listen to the poor woman whose business it was to point out to tourists the objects of interest, and the more so as the monotony of her occupation, it was plain to see, had become extremely wearisome to herself. She seemed surprised and even slightly

disgusted when any one exhibited special interest in anything, or enough to linger even for a moment in its con-
templation; and she showed evidently her displeasure
whenever she was called upon to repeat any of her remarks.
The ladies paid little attention to this, but the gentlemen were somewhat considerate, and would have been
more so except for her fretfulness   Jim, who had kept
very much in the rear, having become tired of the monotony, and not having noticed her infirmity, spoke up
just as we were emerging from the Banqueting Hall.

"Just one moment, madam, if you please   Will you
be kind enough to say again what it was you called this
—ah—sideboard?"

The woman turned and looked at him, and while
subdued smiles were on all other faces, she frowned
visibly.

"That, sir, is the Kenilworth Buffet, as I said as dis-
tinctly as I could, made of the Great H'oak of Kenilworth."

"Oh!" said Jim, "I took it for a sideboard."

"I will thank the gentlemen, *and* the ladies, to listen
as well as they can, for while they 'ave two ears apiece,
Hi 'ave but one voice."

Jim colored and said:

"I beg pardon, ma'am, I had no idea of being specially
troublesome, and will try not to be so again."

The woman noticed the perfect sincerity of his apology,
and evinced slight signs of regret by appearing sometimes to address her remarks, specially such as were
laudatory, to him mainly, and at such times taking unusual pains to make her utterances distinct and em-
phatic. He received these little demonstrations as a
gentleman should have done, with complete apparent

attentiveness. She called our attention, in one of the
rooms, to the view to be had from the windows. As
we were looking out upon that fair horizon, the
winding Avon, the alternations of fields and woodlands
extending far away into Worcestershire, we noticed that
the woman, with a pained expression in her face, was
leaning wearily against the door-facing. We were an
hour or more in this round As we descended at last,
Jim was the last to leave. Each of the rest having put
into the hands of the guide a small piece of money, he
handed her half a crown.

"H'oh! thanks, sir. But really, sir—Hi—am—sorry—"

"Not a word, ma'am. All my fault. I ought to have
known you must be tired. Thank _you_, ma'am. Good-
bye, ma'am."

"She ought to be paid well for that work," he said, as
we were walking off. "Now, if I could ever learn all those
everlasting names of old pictures and such things, it
would kill me dead to have to go over them as often as
she has. See yonder, she is there at the window above
where we went in waiting for that other party coming
up. But, by gracious, that's a right sizable bowl."

"My patience, Jim! call the celebrated WarwickVase
a _bowl_. _Here's_ the Warwick _bowl_," I said, as we lingered
at the old gate and inspected, among other relics of the
giant, his punch-bowl.

"Do you call this _pot_ a _bowl_, ma'am?" he asked of
the portress.

"H'oh, and it is a bowl, h'and many the time h'it was
filled and emptied when the Hurrul come to his h'age."

"_I_ should call it a pot, a regular old-fashioned wash-
pot However, when they call a sideboard a _booffay_,
there's no telling what they may'nt call bowls and pots."

6*

As we passed through Warwick, we had a good view
of Leicester's Hospital and the West Gate.

"With the exception of these old things, and a few
others, the town looks tolerably new, after all," said Jim.

"The old town," said I, "was mostly destroyed by
the great fire of 1694."

"They have gates yet, but I'm thankful, for the
people's sake here, that they have'nt got any old wall to
keep out the air. Driver, what old chap is that with
the blue gown, going up to that church, or whatever
that is up there, on top of the gate, and what's that he
has on his sleeve?"

"'Ee's one of the Brothers of the 'ospital, sir. They
'ave to worship in St. James' Chapel. That's the Bear
and Ragged Staff on 'is sleeve. The Hurrell of Leicester, 'ee founded the 'ospital."

"He did, did he? Well, I think he might have
picked out a prettier uniform for his people, and not
made 'em have to go up so high to say their prayers.
Do you suppose, driver, that any good beer could be got
in this town? It seems mighty long between drinks."

"H'oh yes, sir;" and although a Leamingtonian, he
laughed with reasonable appreciation of my friend's
jocularity. After a few moments' rest and refreshment,
we set out again. We can never forget the drive, the
sweetness of the fields and forests that June afternoon,
the rich green wheat, in its midst the red sparkling
poppies, the abundant cosy road-side shades! Yonder is
Shirburn, and yonder Fulbroke Park, and yonder Hampton Lucy. Here is the little church at the opening to
Charlecote. Halting for a brief space, we climbed the
railing, entered, and passing into the Lucy Chapel, saw
the tombs of Sir Thomas and his lady; then we drove

slowly along the circuitous road around the grounds, yet well stocked with fallow deer, getting ever changing views of the ancient hall. Again we halted at the further gate where the angry boy posted his first poetry, for which crime, more heinous than killing the deer, he must go into the exile so prolific of great results.

"Well," said Jim, "the family seem to hold on well to it, and a good piece of property it is."

"It looks, Jim, as if Slender's prophecy was a true one, that as the Lucies have written themselves *armigero*, any time these three hundred years ' as all his successors gone before him have done, and all his ancestors that come after him may, they may give the dozen white luces in his coat.' "

"Yes, indeed; and when a family gets hold of as solid a piece of property as this, and the law won't let it go out of it, a fellow even smarter than Shakspeare may write himself blind, in making fun of them, but he can't put 'em down."

Into Stratford, and down another alley. We had expected never to get to an inn where the women were nicer-looking, and things generally more snugly arranged than at the *King's Head*. And yet, it did seem to be so at the *Red Horse*. I was not slow to understand the cordial greetings that, before the carriage fairly stopped, we were receiving from three girls any fresher and prettier than whom (to use a favorite expression of Jim's) I should seldom wish to see. Having been conducted to our chamber, which, fortunately for me, was easily accessible, we descended the stairs, and were shown the coffee-room, smoking-room, and "Washington Irving's sitting-room." These were all so entirely satisfactory that we would have sat down and enjoyed the serenity

we felt. But the day was far spent, and the morrow
being Sunday, which we desired to spend in Oxford, we
sallied out to see the Shakspeare mansion. A poor house,
indeed, whose occupants of old time doubtless had little
foresight of the fame it was to have, and the pilgrims
of all tongues who were to resort to it. Yet, I thought,
who knows what joy might not have been in that low-
roofed upper chamber on that April day when another
man-child was born into the world. For joy, and even
pride and expectation belong not alone to mothers of
princes and lords, who bear them on costly beds, beneath
gilded canopies, but also to those who, in such poor
chambers as these, hear, for the first time, their beloved's
voices, and wrapping them in homely garments, lay
them on their breasts. Who can say what prophecies
may not have been in that village woman's heart when
she looked upon the face of that fair child who was so
much more worth to her than all the Lucies, and the
Beauchamps, and the Dudleys, theretofore and there-
after! Surely, such a being could not be born here
and there be no recognition in her who had travailed
with him, that he was not of the kind of the village
folk around them.

A sweet walk it is across the fields to Shottery. In
the narrow path along the hedges, we met several persons who had been to visit the cottage where the poet,
yet a boy, was so strangely wedded. The thatch was
sunken and patched on this house, yet more humble
than the one we had just left. We both sat, by invitation of the genteel woman claiming to be a descendant
of the Hathaways, upon the rude stone seat, where, she
confidently asserted, the lovers had often sat in their
trysting time, and then, ascending to the nuptial cham-

ber, we inscribed our names upon a book that lay upon
the table; then descending, and thanking Mrs. Taylor
for the flowers she pulled for us, took our leave On
the way home, I gave expression to some of the thoughts
that were in my mind while in the chamber where the
great man was born. Jim meditated awhile, and then
answered thus:

"I should'nt be surprised, Phil, if the woman did
have some such ideas as you say. But that is'nt an
uncommon thing. Women, the world over, are always
proud of their babies when they are first born, and even
up to the time when they find out that they are no
greater shakes than other people's. I suppose the good
Lord made 'em so, in the first place, to keep the poor
things in some sort of heart before their children come,
and then to keep 'em from neglecting 'em when they
do come, and make 'em take that everlasting care of 'em,
which, if they did'nt take, they would die, or get crip-
pled, or sickly, and come to nothing. I've noticed
often—no matter how little they think of themselves,
and how big fools and no account generally they know
their husbands or even their other and grown-up children
to be—why, sir, if they have nothing else to tell you
about their babies, they'll brag about how quick they
cut their first teeth, or of their falling out of the cradle
and not crying about it, or their reaching out their
hands and trying to take hold of the moon, as if they
were the only ones that ever did or could do such wonders. Why, there's my wife, as sensible a woman as anybody else's wife, she's had eight children, and I tell you,
Phil, what is the fact, not a single one of 'em, if he was
a boy, that she did'nt have some idea that he was to
grow to be a tremendous big man some day, presiden⌐

or governor, or judge, or something of the sort. Sometimes I've said to her, 'look here, Emily, that baby is
my baby, and I don't think my baby can be expected,
except as to what he has got from his mother' (his
mother, you know, Phil, I have to fling that in), 'that
my baby can be expected to be much, if anything, above
the run of just good, common men like me.' You think
that woman don't pinch me on the jaw, and tell me
that it's all because I ain't ambitious, and if I was ambitious I would have been equal to any of the rest of 'em
that go to Congress, and all such? And by gracious, I
do believe she thinks so. Yes, sir; yes, sir; I should'nt
be at all surprised if the old lady Shakspeare did
have some right high notions about William when he
was born at last, and she saw that he had a good big
round head. But that's no sign; they all have 'em
whether their babies' heads are big or little."

"Jim Rawls," said I, "if it was not for your wife, I
would knock you down right here."

"Thanky," he answered, in great glee, "she's got me
off from worse dangers than that many a time."

A pleasant evening we had in the cosy chairs in the
smoking-room hard by the little bar, waited on by the
bar-maid, so pretty, and snug, and neat, and friendly.
Jim ordered one extra mug of ale because, he said, it
seemed to do her good to have the opportunity of oblig-
ing us, old as we were. When we got to our chamber,
he suddenly exclaimed:

"There, now! If I have'nt left my spectacles at that
Anne Hathaway Cottage."

"I noticed," said I, "that you took a good deal of
pains when you were writing your name in that book;
but I supposed, of course, that you put your spectacles

back into your pocket. You observe that other people can *lose* things as well as I."

"Well, well, I don't know when such a thing happened to me before. Never mind, it's too late to get 'em back, and I won't need any before Monday, or if I should, I can borrow yours. I don't grudge 'em to the old lady Taylor if they suit her. She looked like a monstrous clever old lady. By the way, Phil, I thought I would ask you what thread that was you said you lost this morning."

"Why did'nt you?"

"Well, I did'nt exactly—I know I put some needles and thread in your valise; but—who—whose thread did you say you lost?"

"Ariadne's."

"Well, but how—what made you think *her* thread might have got away down there where the women stayed?"

"How could I know where it was?"

He thought awhile. Suddenly he broke out:

"Who in the dickence *is* Ariadne, anyhow?"

After teasing him awhile, I related the myth of Theseus and the Labyrinth.

"You got me that time, old fellow. I give it up. You answered so seriously this morning when I asked you about it, that I did'nt know what to make of it. I owe you one for that. Well, old Anne Hathaway's Cottage may go for me. But it was a polite old lady that showed it to us, and she's welcome to my spectacles if they suit her."

It was long before my eyes were closed in sleep. Even after we had ceased to talk, and my companion was taking the profound slumber that comes to a man of

sound body and spirit after a day's travel, I lay awake,
dreaming awake of him who had made this place so
famous. What mystery around him, what little known
of the interior life of this the greatest of mankind, though
born in the very heart of England and in the times of
Elizabeth. That such a man should have left no record
of his history, not even a letter to a friend. What a
marriage! What is the meaning of those unhappy sonnets which contain the saddest complainings that mortal
ears ever listened to; that pursuit of a business which,
although it brought him shame and grief, he persisted
in for the sake of providing a home for Anne Hathaway
and her children; that indifference not only to fame,
but to even a good name in refusing to notice even the
charges of plagiarism, one of the meanest vices; and
then that silent withdrawal from the great city and return
to his humble place of nativity, dying and leaving a
curse upon any who might come to molest the tomb
which was to hold his dust? What tragic loves had he
told of—the young love of Romeo, the married love of
Othello, the old man's love of Lear! What frightful
thoughts he had had of death! I suspect he did not
greatly love this Anne Hathaway, but that he had loved
another, younger and more fair, whom he failed to obtain
from accidents agonizingly painful and abjectly humiliating. Those sonnets, though so purporting, must surely
have been addressed to no man. That lamentation of
Venus for Adonis was written long after he had been a
married man. Who but one whose heart had been
blasted by disappointments and those that had been
attended by disgrace, could have put such words as the
following into the mouth of the goddess as she stood
over the corpse of her lover:

Since thou art dead, lo here I prophesy;
Sorrow on love hereafter shall attend:
It shall be waited on with jealousy,
Find sweet beginning, but unsavory end,
Ne'er settled equally, but high or low,
That all love's pleasure shall not match his woe.

It shall be fickle, false, and full of fraud,
Bud and be blasted in a breathing while;
The bottom poison, and the top o'erstraw'd
With sweets that shall the truest sight beguile:
The strongest body shall it make most weak,
Strike the wise dumb, and teach the fool to speak.

It shall be sparing and too full of riot,
Teaching decrepit age to tread the measures;
The stormy ruffian shall it keep in quiet,
Pluck down the rich, enrich the poor with treasures;
It shall be raging mad, and silly mild,
Make the young old, the old become a child.

It shall suspect where is no cause of fear;
It shall not fear where it should most mistrust;
It shall be merciful and too severe,
And most deceiving when it seems most just:
Perverse it shall be, where it shows most toward,
Put fear to valor, courage to the coward.

It shall be cause of war, and dire events,
And set dissension 'twixt the son and sire;
Subject and servile to all discontents
As dry combustious matter is to fire;
Sith in his prime, Death doth my love destroy,
They that love best their love shall not enjoy.

What words from a married man! No, indeed; this
Anne Hathaway, eight years older than himself, of yet
lowlier estate, was scarcely the first or chief, or only idol
of his heart. Yet, he was a man, and he would get such

7

things as she and her children would need most, and this seems to have been the only purpose for which he lived and wrought.

What had been the varying feelings with which he trod to and fro in that sweet walk across the fields to Shottery, and what when after his great career he returned, we can never know. The simple folk among whom he dwelt may have considered that a curious epitaph he was leaving. But such things were not uncommon in old England. So they let down the coffin beneath the chancel in the church, laid back the stones smooth as before, and, when night came, mingling gossip with sympathetic speeches, they at last grew sleepy and went to their beds. In time, sleep came to me also.

CHAPTER VII.

UST come here, Phil. Look at that."
Jim was in the smoking-room, and was noticing with a smile the bill which had been made out against us below the receipt of the payment of which were written the words "with thanks."

"Now did you ever see such as that at the bottom of a receipt? and would you ever wish to see a politer or a friendlier set of girls?"

They did look even more charming than the evening before, with their Sunday frocks, fresh roses in their hair, and perpetual ones on their cheeks. We shook hands with them reluctantly when bidding them good-bye.

I thought there never could have been a sweeter Sunday morning. The dew was long in drying on the grass and leaves, and, even in our car, we could smell the flowers in the hedges and fields. The green, so deep it was, darkened among the woods. The air was still and soft. We had a slow train, and we saw very many of the country folk, some going to church, walking or in their carts drawn briskly by their round-bellied, sleek, snug, little cobs, some leisurely strolling along the gentle hill sides gathering nosegays, or lying at ease beneath the shady clumps of trees, while others, a few, were angling on the banks of the Cherwell and the streamlets leading into it. Quite a number of third-class cars were in our train; these were emptied and filled again at every station.

"They seem the quietest and contentedest people I ever saw, I think," said Jim. "There don't seem to be much poverty among these country folks. The very smallest of their houses look clean and comfortable. What a people they are for flowers and vines. I tell you what is a fact, Phil, there's something about flowers and vines that makes poor people get along well and live contented on a little. I've noticed that often. They keep them from letting things go loose generally, and somehow it seems to me that the ones who have them about their homes don't complain and don't get sick as often as the others, and when sick they get well sooner. I tell you that there's something about flowers and vines that's healthy. Banbury Station, eh? I see we are in Oxfordshire.

> Ride a cock-horse to Banbury Cross,
> To see a fine lady get on a white horse,
> With rings on her fingers and bells on her toes,
> She shall have music wherever she goes.

Oh dear, oh dear! how often I've heard my little ones sing that, and how I wish I could hear 'em sing it this morning. But never mind, we'll all sing it together when we get back. Let's try another of the weed."

The old fellow had made up his mind in spite of his tenderness not to be homesick, and so he lit up, the bell rang, and we were off again. As we passed Enslow Station, he said:

"According to the map, those woods yonder to the right belong to Blenheim Park. Ah, that old Marlborough! He was one of 'em."

"Yes, indeed; but I should have thought more, if we could go there, of Alfred, and the Henries, and the other kings, Saxon and Norman, who made it their residence."

"I'll be bound for that. Well, men at different ages like different things. Maybe I'll like old things myself when the time comes But yonder's your Oxford. Let's stop at the *Randolph*. That sounds old Virginny like.

At the *Randolph* we stopped. Things were on a broader but not more comfortable scale than at Stratford and Coventry. We spent the hour before dinner in a visit to Worcester College in order specially to see its gardens. The walk was not long up Beaumont street. Having easily obtained admittance through St. Bernard's Gateway, after surveying the quadrangles, the chapel, hall, common-room, and library, we walked into the gardens. Surely, five acres of ground could not easily have been made more beautiful. The walls completely covered in green, the narrow, winding waters, the variegated beds, shaded by the horse-chestnut trees, and the walks with elms, make this the favorite resort of townspeople as well as students. It was vacation, and we saw only one student as he sat in the windows of his room.

"Poor fellow," said Jim, when the porter had told us that he was staying here in order to make up in the studies on which he had been cast.

After dinner we strolled out again, wending down Magdalen and Cornmarket, passing Magdalen Church and Jesus Colleges, thence into High street, to All Saints and St. Mary's Churches, lingering before the latter (built for the university by Alfred the Great shortly after its foundation), to recall the fate of some eminent persons whose history was associated with its own. There rest the remains of Amy Robsart, there

7*

the unhappy Rosamond, sometimes when she could in
safety leave St. Peter's in the East, might come timidly
to Vespers. That porch, with its elegant twisted columns, so Italian in style, made one of the items in the
impeachment of Archbishop Laud. Retracing our way
to High street, passing into Oriel, by St. Mary's Hall,
Oriel and Corpus Christi Colleges, we reached by Canter-
bury Gate Christ's Church. A citizen of the place whose
acquaintance Jim made immediately after meeting him
while coming out of the Cathedral—a lay-clerk—kindly
led us through the great *Tom-Gateway* into the quad-
rangle, the hall, common, and kitchen.

"A tolerable sizable gridiron, that," said Jim, as the
guide pointed out that relic of the times of the founder,
the great Wolsey.

" Yes, indeed, that was before ranges were invented,
and you know that in the old times the part of a college that was built first was the kitchen."

" The mischief you say! Stomachs first and brains
afterwards; not a bad idea. If you excuse me, sir, I'd
like to know why they call that gate the *Tom Gate?*"

" That is from *Tom*, the name of the great bell of
the college."

" Yes, yes, I've heard of the "*Mighty Tom.*" That's
him, is it?"

At that moment the bell sounded.

" He lumbers right well. I'm glad I've heard him one
time."

On to Pembroke College, and into the room occupied
by Samuel Johnson.

"Out of that window," said the guide, "he threw
into the court the new pair of shoes that had been left
for him at the door, when his own were worn out, and
he had not money to buy others."

"I'd have done it too," said Jim, with emphasis. "The old fellow was right."

"He was but a youth then, Jim," I said.

"It makes no difference; a man's a man, or ought to be, whatever his age is. And this is the desk he wrote his dictionary on, eh? It ought to have been a book by good rights after he spent seven years pegging away at it on such a piece of furniture as that."

Jim insisted upon our new acquaintance going with us to the hotel, taking tea, and smoking a cigar.

"My friend here," said he, after tea, "always prefers something ancient. What is about the oldest thing in or about this town that we can show him in the morning before we leave?"

"I should like," said I, "to visit Godstowe Priory."

"The very thing," answered the clerk. "You can do that before breakfast."

He accepted our invitation to accompany us, and betimes the next morning we were on our walk to the river. When we had reached Queen's Lane,

"There," said the clerk, "is something old for you, St. Peter's Church in the East, the oldest church in England. The fair Rosamond used to go there to worship, secretly wending her way through a crypt in order to avoid the observation of Queen Eleanour."

"Poor thing! I suppose she thought she must go to meeting *sometimes.*"

Arrived at the water, we hired a boat, Jim and the clerk took the oars, and we shot up the river, passing old Oxen Forde, and about a mile further on, landed and walked to the place we sought. Nothing of the priory was left except a part of the wall and a small stone turreted structure. To yet baser uses this celebrated spot had descended than that at Kenilworth, in being kept for breeding swine I was sorry Jim had gone with us.

"And this is it, is it? The great Godstowe Priory? You see, Phil, they are beginning to put these old things to some use at last. Kenilworth Abbey a cow-house, you tell me the Martyr's Tower is a horse-stable, and here's Godstowe Priory a hog-pen. Now, if they could put that old wall at Chester to some use, it would be about right. But let's go back. Make haste, Phil," he continued, after getting out of the enclosure, and looking back at me who was gathering a few ivy leaves from the old wall, "look out for fleas."

His loud laugh rang out in the morning air. Returning to the river, we untied our boat, and sped swiftly to the landing. I paid the boatman in haste, insisting that it was my treat. We had not proceeded a hundred yards when the man came running and calling after us. We halted.

"Beg your pardon, sir," said he, addressing me, "but the price was 'arf a crown."

"Certainly," said I, in some embarrassment, "I so understood it, and thought I paid you."

"H'oh yes, indeed, sir; but you gave us two 'arf-crowns. I did'nt know—but John said—"

"Did'nt you mean half crown a piece?"

"H'oh no, sir; for both."

"Certainly," said the clerk.

Jim took the money from his hands, and gave him a shilling of his own.

"Take that for your pains. Here, Phil, take your money. That comes from bothering yourself with other people's business. You never saw such an absent-minded man," addressing the Englishman. "I have to watch him like a hawk, to keep him from losing everything he's got, and himself to boot."

Jim pressed the clerk to breakfast with us; on his declining, he asked him cordially if he ever should come to Georgia, and so forth.

Another fair day. The country along the Isis, now become the Thames, was delightfully diversified with field and woodland, level and undulating surface. The prospect was most fair when culminating in the Chiltern Hills. As we passed through Berkshire, we remarked that the farms were smaller, and there seemed to be fewer landed proprietors than in those in which we had travelled.

"My goodness!" exclaimed Jim, "what a country for farming! They say that the sheep on those hills are uncommonly large and fine. Was there ever such a country for water as this? Not a field without it. And don't these smaller trees on them and the paths along them look nice? Here we are at Reading. This is a live town. Look at the foundries and mills, and there's a big business here also in velvets and silks. A priory, too? You don't say so. I wonder what animal owns *it*."

On to Maidenhead, into Bucks. The Chilterns continue, but here their sheep, at least in the fleece, yield to those of the Aylesbury Vale. Now the farming gives way to the dairy and chicken-walk, and junking, as some there name it, begins in milk, and butter, and poultry for the London market. What perfect economy! Not an inch unoccupied. We look over yonder to the right, a couple of miles distant, and see from the battlements of Windsor Castle the huge flag which indicates that the queen is there. We strain our eyes towards it, but the dashing train in a moment carries us out of sight, away across the Coln, into Middlesex, and the gardens grow smaller and more prolific, save where the elegant villas and pleasure-grounds vary the smooth landscape in the valley of the Brent. For several miles already the atmosphere has become clouded, yet not with clouds. Soon the great city rises on the horizon, near, but seeming distant. The farms, and villas, and pleasure-grounds have disappeared. For miles and miles, dark brick houses are thick on either side. At last we slacken our speed, the train slowly comes to a halt, and while we are looking out upon the crowds of cabs and other vehicles, the guard opens the door and announces "Paddington."

CHAPTER VIII.

ARRIVED at the Langham on Portland Place, a police officer met us before the vestibule, who, after taking down in a small book the number of our cab, asked if we had engaged rooms. We answered in the negative.

"Better see if the 'ouse is full before you trouble to take down the loogage."

I felt much embarrassed.

"Oh, nonsense," said Jim, and walked in with the air of a proprietor. It was several minutes before he returned.

"It's been a touch-and-go thing, Phil. The house, big as it is, runs over with Americans." We went in, and, after proper attentions at the lavatory and coffee-room, walked from the office through the long hall, surmounted at the extreme end with a statue of Shakspeare. From this place, styled "the Poet's Corner," a door leads into the superb smoking-room. At the entrance of the latter was a small office about five feet square, in which were two young women, for all the world like those at Stratford, except that they were dressed in city fashion, and did not give any recognition of the fact of our arrival. Jim paused a moment in passing by the open window, prepared to receive in a becoming manner the cordial greeting he had evidently expected. But

they looked at us only for a moment to see if we desired
any service, and immediately turned away.

"A fine house, Phil," said he, after we had taken our
seats, "and a tremendous big one. I was afraid for
awhile that we could not get in. The fellow at the
office said so in that many words, and said that we ought
to have telegraphed him from Liverpool. I urged him,
for goodness gracious sake, not to turn off a couple of
old fellows, one of whom (meaning you, of course,)
was a sort of invalid and very rich, who, neither of
us knew a single man, woman, or child in the town, big
as it was. I said we were a couple of Americans
just traveling for amusement, and that they told us at
home that when we got to London we must be sure to
stop at the Langham Hotel, because it was the best in
the town and had the very cleverest and most accommo-
dating set of men. I did'nt say *fellows*, fearing he
might think I was a little too free at the start. The
fellow, that red-headed one, looked at me a moment, and
smiled, glanced over his book, and then said, that if we
could put up with the Race-Way to-night, he could fix
us up conveniently by to-morrow night. 'The Race-Way,'
said I; 'you don't mean the stable?' That got him.
He laughed right out, and said that that was only a
name given to a long sort of attic story that they made
into rooms, with curtains between, when they were
crowded as they are now. I told him all right, and
so here we are. But this is a nice place," he continued,
looking around at the luxurious chairs, and sofas, and
snug little tables, and the huge windows opening out
above the street. "And those girls! more style than the
Stratford's, but not nigh so friendly; they see so many
more people, I suppose."

About twenty gentlemen were in the room—some quietly smoking, others sipping coffee or other drinks on the tables, and others writing. These reminded us to write letters home. At bed time we took the "lift," as they call the elevator, and after a tardy and apparently vast extent, and long perambulations afterwards, reached our quarters.

"I don't know why they call this a Race-Way," Jim said, when we found ourselves behind a curtain and our heads touching the roof. "Let alone running, we can't even stand. We shall have to get on the floor to dress and undress. But they are nice, clean beds. All right."

The next morning after breakfast, while I was looking over a map of the town, Jim, who had been to the office to arrange for a change of quarters, came into the smoking-room.

"Phil, what's an 'ontraysole?' That fellow said he could give us a room on the ontraysole or the first floor, and gave me this paper to look over the prices, etc. I told him, that being old fellows we would prefer to be as low down as possible, and would probably take the first floor if it was'nt too expensive. He smiled, he did, and I come to see you about it; but I can't find any such outlandish word here."

I took the paper and pointed to the word *entresol*.

"The mischief! Ah, I suppose that's a French word they have brought over here. I know it is, because I never saw one of them that was pronounced like it was spelt. But look, will you? I thought this was the first story. Instead of that, the first story don't begin until you get up above the—what ever you call it. You say so? Very well, we'll take the *hic*—the onthraysole. But I never expected to stay in a place of that name."

8

Whoever has only about fourteen days in which to see London must distribute and economize his time with great care. By so doing, it will surprise him to find how much more can be accomplished than by desultory visitations, as we found afterwards in comparing notes with other tourists. Jim and I studied the map thoroughly in the first instance, and then we arranged, every night, our places for the next day's operations. Not that we were at all unanimous in our preferences; but we had agreed to disagree whenever we pleased, each to visit such places as he should choose, when our tastes and dispositions did not coincide, and discuss, when we should meet again, what we had seen. We were to keep together, however, for the first day, partly because we knew we should find quite enough objects for our joint inspection, and because Jim said he wanted me to get a little used to the place before he could consent to my starting off by myself.

"I don't want to lose you over here, Phil, and have to advertise for you, you know."

On the first morning we started out for a stroll, having Westminster Abbey for our last objective point. Turning the corner at "All Souls'" we took our way down Regent street.

"This is'nt the street for *us* to trade in, Phil," said he, as we noticed the handsome shops on either side, into which, so early in the day, very few buyers were entering. "These stores are for folks with big money-bags; they hav'nt come out yet, you see."

Arrived at the foot of Piccadilly, I spoke of my long entertained wish to see the National Gallery of Paintings.

"Yes," answered Jim, with a lazy sigh, "I knew it, although I should have thought you saw enough pic-

tures at Warwick Castle. If it was'nt that I should'nt
care about having to give a long list of reasons when I
got back home why I did'nt take in such a place when
I had the chance, I should'nt go in with you, but wait
out here in this square until you got through. But lead
on; I'll try it for awhile."

"Of course, you should see the National Gallery, Jim.
There were some fine pictures at Warwick Castle; but
that was comparatively a very small collection."

"Whee—oo!"

"Whereas here, notwithstanding they have none from
the Spanish, there are more than seven hundred works
of the old masters."

"Well, let's go in and pay the old fellows a call.
Make it short, Phil. We are not much acquainted with
'em, you know, and good manners would require a short
visit."

We entered the building, and passed hurriedly through
the rooms. Jim regarded with considerable interest a
few pictures which were specially striking in the exhi-
bitions, either of great beauty in women, or great physical power in men. After emerging, we sat down for a
short rest in Trafalgar Square.

"Bigger lions than them," said Jim, pointing to the
immense bronzes at the foot of the Nelson Monument,
"I should'nt *ever* desire to see, that is alive. It would
take a sizable eagle to fly off with one of those fellows,
as our Fourth of July orators used to norate about
before the war. But speaking of pictures, Phil, ain't
there some humbug in this everlasting talk about
the old masters, as they call 'em? I've been hearing
of them all my life, and often from people who, I am
certain, knew about as little about 'em as I do. Such

people have a sort of idea that these old masters, as you call 'em, were a set of old fellows that painted, and painted together a long time ago, in a sort of partnership, and left some things which nobody could understand, but which they thought was powerful smart, just because they could'nt understand it, and then these old fellows died pretty much all together, and carried their secret with 'em. Now, all such as this strikes me as a piece of foolery. · But, were they so tremendous old?"

He frowned in the intensity of his doubts.

I answered his question; he was astonished to hear that Raphael was only twenty-seven at his death.

"My goodness!" said he, "I thought he was about a thousand."

In answer to what I had to say about the preference of men of taste for the older pictures, on account of the prevalence of the ideal amongst them, and how this ideal in art had been made in great part to give way to the practical of trade and commerce, he asked:

"And ain't the world better off for the change?"

"In some respects," I answered, "not in all. There is room enough in the world for other things besides trade. If a man is always at his work, or thinking about it, he will get to be a sort of machine himself, and, like all machines, will soon wear out. The ablest and most thoughtful of the men of trade understand this fact very well. They know into what a state the world would grow if there were nothing but trade and physical labor, and physical pleasures; and so they build houses like this, and put in them these great pictures of olden times, and encourage modern artists to strive to produce others like them. The effect of such things is something like that of flowers, which you said were so helpful to the poor. What do you say to that?"

"You are about right, I suppose. My wife says that what few pictures we own have done the children much more good than the worth of the money they cost, and I'm sure that the music my boys and girls make at home make me feel younger, and perhaps be better than I should without it. You are right, Phil. They are all right. Let's go ahead."

We walked along, and soon were in Charing Cross.

"What do they call it that for? You were to do the history part, you know."

"*Charing* is the pronunciation the English common people gave to *Chère Reine—dear queen.* This was the place where the last halt was made while they were bearing the body of Queen Eleanour, wife of Edward the First, to Westminster Abbey; and here was the last of the nine crosses which her husband caused to be erected in her memory. It was taken down by the republicans under Cromwell, and the stones used in paving the street at Whitehall. But they paid for that desecration; for at the very place where the cross stood, the regicides were beheaded. And here we are at old Whitehall, the royal residence of the monarchs from Henry VIII to William of Orange. In the latter's reign, all was burnt down except the Banqueting Hall, which is now used as a chapel. Just up yonder, where, you notice, the window has been bricked over, Charles I was beheaded."

"Do you suppose he had any idea of such as that when from that old tower at Chester he saw his army defeated?"

"Hardly. He probably had no apprehension, whatever else might happen, that they would take his life."

"Well, what do you think of my poetry now? It would'nt sound so bad here, eh?"

8*

"Not quite; but one would be more apt to think of it presently."

We were walking slowly up Parliament street.

"That's a fine statue," said Jim, just as we reached the head.

"A statue of the same king. It was sold by Parliament to a brazier with orders to break it in pieces and apply it to other uses. But the buyer concealed it, and at the Restoration of Charles II, made a great profit by bringing it forth unhurt. But yonder is the place, Jim, for your poetry about princes and their beds of clay." Then we entered Westminster Abbey.

Two hours we spent in the sacred edifice we had both so long desired to see. Silently and reverently we passed along its transepts, and aisles, and chapels, reading and musing upon the epitaphs of the great and the gifted who were buried there, or to whom, though buried elsewhere, cenotaphs were there erected. We paused not long in the chapels where was the dust of the long lines of kings and their offspring, but long enough to think how small places hold the relics of the generations of princes, Saxon, Norman, Plantagenet, Tudor, Stuart, and Brunswick, and yet have room for uncounted generations to be brought there hereafter. The accidents of life had made them great. These other tombs and cenotaphs outside the railings around the royal graves, these were they on which we looked the longest, and with solemnest emotions: statesmen and philanthropists, poets and orators, warriors, on land and sea, all of them heroes—some of gentle, but most of common blood. Never was my mind so impressed with ideas of the power of death, as, while standing amongst those multitudes of the tombs of the great. First and last, and longest we were in the Poet's Corner. In life, these almost, without exception, had not been great nor happy. Shakspeare, the lessee of Blackfriars and The Globe, who had patiently borne

"The whips and scorns of time,"

and Chaucer in his old age, impoverished and humbly repentant; and Spenser, first an exile on the Mulla, and afterwards a fugitive thence and finding death in a poor inn in his native city; Dryden, bartering intellect for bread in Soho, leaving, when dead, not enough wherewithal to pay the cost of being carried to the grave; Marlowe, struggling in vain with the ruffian for the love of the poor wench of Deptford; Goldsmith, the sizar of Trinity, and the many, many others; some more fortunate, some less. How sweetly had they sung in their days, in spite of poverty, and neglect, and improvidence and

"The spurns
That patient merit of the unworthy takes."

For, like the birds of song, they must sing, whether in prison or in fields and orchards. Their times of honor came latest, but they shall last longest. Shakespeare and Leicester, Spenser and Raleigh, Dryden and Buckingham, Goldsmith and Newcastle. What, if both the premier and the poet could have foreseen the future? It might have been well for one, but not for the other. Such singings could have been rendered only by the inspiration which comes from the seriousness of sorrow. Yet there is compensation in nature, and most benign it is that each prefers his own to another's lot. Achilles

would have been Achilles over again, and Tithonus
would have been Tithonus, though quick death snatched
the hero in his bloom, and old age, when it could not
destroy, changed the beau into a grasshopper.

CHAPTER IX.

ELL," said Jim, after we had dined at a restaurant, and strolling out again, passed the Bird-Cage walk and taken our seats beneath a tree overshadowing the smooth lake in St. James' Park. "It's a grand, solemn, old place, that abbey, but cold! Ain't it cold? I tell you that way of burying don't suit me, Phil."

"Why not?" I asked, just to hear what he had to say, for I knew his sentiments, and in part shared them.

"You remember, how they used to laugh at me when I was a child for being afraid of graveyards and dead people?"

"Very well. You were the scape-goat, Jim; for I was myself as weak in that respect as you were."

"Well, sir," he continued, very gravely, "nobody in this world, not even my mother, who was as careful and tender of me as she could be, knew for some time what I suffered. In a country neighborhood, like the one we were raised in, deaths happen so seldom, that every one makes a stronger impression than in towns. I remember that the first time I was ever in Augusta, and I was then sixteen years old, I saw a hearse going along the street, and I asked of a bystander, in a whisper, who it was that was dead, and was astonished and shocked to find that he not only did'nt know, but did'nt seem to care, while the rest of the people went along and acted as if nothing uncommon had happened. In the country it's different. When anyone dies, everybody goes to the burying, and they talk about it for a long time after, and about other deaths they knew about, and tell of many things that happened, or were said to have happened, some about people having been buried alive. The negroes in old times had tales to tell of ghosts, or *"sperrits,"* as they called 'em. Such as these used to scare me nearly out of my life. I was tormented with the idea that they would think I was dead when I was'nt. I got so that if anybody held me down on the ground I was badly frightened, and had a feeling of suffocation, and thought of how it was going to be with me in the grave. You see, Phil, I could'nt ever *realize* that I should be dead. Well, my mother found out some of this, not all; and she took a wonderful amount of pains with me, and always talked cheerfully about death. Then she was careful with our graveyard, had more trees and flowers planted in and around it, and used to talk about how these would die in the winter and come to life in the spring. Ever since then, I have had in my mind spring flowers joined with the resurrection of the dead; and it always pains me to see a grave with no flowers around it, and especially where flowers could'nt grow if they were put there. The idea of death is not so sad to me when I think about my grave being in the open air, where my people, when I'm gone, can come sometimes and tend the flowers and listen to the birds singing over me. I've long ago quit being afraid simply of the grave, especially since I've put away some of my children —"

He paused—for his words would have failed him.

"I agree with you fully, Jim," said I. "Time and reflection have subdued most of my early fears. When a boy, I used to be tormented with the very certainty of *having* to die at last, even if I should resist the perils of foregoing ages and survive to old age, horrified at the ideas of the mattock, and the spade, and the darkness, but—would you be young again, Jim?"

He considered a moment.

"No; not, by gracious, without Emily and the children could, too. No, sir, not a day. A man that has been blest as I have, would be a rascal, if not a fool, to want any such thing."

We rose, and wended our way into the Mall, passing Marlborough House, St. James', and Buckingham Palaces into Green Park.

"They don't seem to use old St. James' much these days. It looks dingy."

"It has not been used much," said I, "except on special occasions, since George the Fourth, who gave it up for Buckingham Palace. But its rooms are so spacious that they hold great State occasions there. Many a gay season have those walls witnessed, beginning with Henry the Eighth."

"Yes; now was'nt he a lively old cuss, with his seven wives?"

On we went, into Green Park, turning to view Stafford, Spenser and Bridgewater Houses.

"As our guide book says, Jim, that pretty mansion with the bay windows belonged to the poet Rogers. Greater numbers of illustrious men and fine women have been entertained there than in any other private house in the world, it is probable."

"I thought poets were always poor."

"Generally they have been; but he was a wealthy banker."

"That surprises me. Banking and poetry are two things that I should seldom suppose would go along together. Why not? Because one of 'em requires a man to have common sense, and the other, so far as I've seen, requires him to be without it. I don't know much about poetry, that's a fact. But poets seem to me to do exactly opposite to what bankers do. While bankers go right straight ahead, *they* go all around and about, and have an immense amount of talk about nothing, or next to nothing. And then they have a way of running down money as if it was a thing too dirty for a man with clean hands to touch. Was he a married man?"

"No; bachelor."

"Ah ha! there it is now."

"What is it?"

"If he'd been a married man, he'd have stuck to one thing, banked, and let poetry go, or poeted, and let his wife make a living for both. I expect the old fellow met with an accident, as Joe Wiggins called it when Bettie Rhodes kicked him. I bet his sweetheart married a rich man, and he went to work to get money and make her sorry that she did'nt take him; and then he went into poetry, just to keep up the idea that he was a badly treated man."

"But for what purpose?"

"For what purpose? Why, sir, to make people sorry for him; or, if not that, to keep on being sorry for himself. Have'nt you noticed, Phil, that most people want it to be believed that they've been badly treated? It's so; and it's specially so with these poets, it seems to me; and that's what makes 'em be so everlastingly talking

about broken hearts, and blighted prospects, and comparing themselves to withered leaves, and broken links,
and dried-up springs, and pretending to want to die
right away, and—all such. Yes, I thought he must be
a bachelor."

"But his was one of the healthiest minds that ever
was."

"Oh, he might have been healthy enough. I'm not
talking about the old fellow's health. They are all of
'em *healthy* enough, Phil, as to that, and can eat their
allowance when they can get it; but, I tell you, he met
with an accident, or he never would have mixed up
poetry with banking. Well, I'm thankful that he was
liberal with his money. Many a poor fellow, I suppose,
praised the old man's poetry and got a good dinner
which he could'nt have had at home."

"Shade of Rogers—"

"Come, come now, Phil, don't *you* begin. You've
got something of a hankering that way I know," and he
punched me playfully.

We turned up Constitution Hill, the Palace Gardens
on our left. To our right, men, women and children,
and even numbers of sheep were walking, or lying
on the green grass. It seemed the outskirts of a
country town. The gardens on our left and the growth
on the east, skirting Piccadilly, excluded the sight and
almost the sound of the city. What a blessing such an
open green space to the poor; for we noticed that most
of those whom we then saw were of this class.

"Have you any pennies about you, Phil? I'm out,
and I hate to pass that poor woman without buying
something from her."

His pockets were then full of boxes of matches and

9

such other trifling things as the poorest vend along the
public walks. As we passed the woman, being without
small change, he emptied his purchases into her basket
and passed on.

It is a sudden transition from Green to Hyde Park on
a summer afternoon. Emerging through the west gate
of the former, the multitudes in carriages, on horseback,
and on foot that one sees pouring up Piccadilly, warn
him that he is at the favorite resort of the middle and
upper classes of London, and he knows that other multitudes are gathering along Park Lane and Oxford
street. As we passed in view of Apsley House and the
statue in honor of Wellington, Jim, looking at the latter,
asked why they had put upon it such a costume, and
being told, answered:

"Well, they may compare him with Achilles, or any
others of the Greeks and Romans; but if it had'nt been
for Blucher, Napoleon would have whipped him. However, I like to see a people stand up to their own men.
Even if I believed that there ever were two greater men
than General Washington and General Lee, I should'nt
think it was right to say so."

We edged our way through the throngs, and passed
under the arch into the enclosure.

"You like live places, you say, Jim. Is this enough
for you?"

"Plenty."

Surely, no where on this earth is to be seen a fuller
display of life in its abandon of business for the enjoyment of leisure. Thickest about Rotten Row and the
Ring, yet there seemed no place in the great enclosure of
four hundred acres where there was not life in liveliest
relish. Jim looked alternately upon the endless lines

of equipages, equestrians, and pedestrians with unabated delight; for although as little envious as any man I know either of the rich or the young, he had exquisite pleasure in the sight of enterprise and activity. We took our seats on one of the benches on the edge of Rotten Row. He pulled out his watch, held it in his hands ten minutes, without saying a word. Suddenly he turned to me and said:

"It beats the world. I have counted, in ten minutes, over four hundred carriages, just like that passing now with that elegant pair of greys, all the drivers grey headed and with fat legs. But they handle the reins better than those fellows over there on horseback. I can beat any of them I see riding. They don't seem to know how to sit on trotters, but gallop themselves while the horses are trotting."

"And here's the Serpentine, as they call it. All this water is supplied by the Chelsea Company. Those houses are put up, they tell me, for taking care of people who happen to break through the ice here in winter time while skating."

We advanced into the Kensington Road, strolled past Albert Hall and Albert Memorial, and entered Kensington Gardens.

"No great shakes that old palace, Phil. I guess the queen don't stay here much."

"Not at all. The Count and Countess of Teck reside here. The queen was born here, you know. Little thought her father, the Duke of Kent, then that she would ever be queen."

"I suppose not. No danger of *her* line giving out. They say there are about thirty of 'em already. There has never been much talk of her marrying again."

"I have no idea that she ever had any notion that way herself."

"Sensible woman. At her time of life, with as many children as she has, nobody, woman or man, has any business marrying again. Too set in their ways. Well, she made a good wife and a happy one, and it was because she married to suit herself. I believe in that strong, for high and low, rich and poor. Four hundred acres in this park! and the map shows that Regent's, the biggest of 'em all, is not far off. No wonder London is the healthiest of all the big cities. See, here's a stretch of nearly three miles of open country from Westminster. Why don't our people in the United States learn something of the importance of open places in the big towns, where the people can get some fresh air? And that's the reason why I thought as I did about them confounded old Chester walls—"

"Jim," said I, "my notion is to ride home. I am tired of footing it. Here we are in the Uxbridge Road, the same as Oxford street."

"All right. Hello, Hansom. To the Langham. Eighteen pence? You know it is'nt over two miles; but go ahead. You look like a clever fellow. Quick; my old friend here is tired, and I think a cup of 'arf-and-'arf would suit you; so be quick, my lad."

At the hotel that night an incident occurred which I do not believe that one of the parties interested in it can have forgotten. Among the acquaintances which my friend, whose qualities in that regard were more facile than mine, had made was a young American who professed to be from the State of Missouri. He, together with a companion, a youth of about his own age, had been sight seeing in London for a couple of weeks, and

were purposing to leave the next day for the continent.
While I was looking over the map, arranging my own
plans for the morrow, Jim, who had announced his
intention of going around generally, as he styled it, sat
for some time and talked with the young man, to whom
he had taken, he said, a fancy, on account of his friendly
ways.

"It's so seldom you know, Phil, that one of these young
fellows cares about having much to do with old fellows
like us. He's been well raised."

After a while, the young men rose and left the smoking-room. Jim then came to the table by which I was
sitting, and, after inquiring, in his usual way, what old
piece of furniture I was after next, said:

"Phil, there's a place we must see together," pointing
to a large building some distance beyond the continuing
of Piccadilly into Coventry street.

"Why, what do you mean, Jim? That's the Argyle
Rooms."*

"I know that; but that young fellow—and he's
studied this town well, he says—he tells me that's the
only place here where strangers can see, without regular
introduction, the upper classes. Not that I care specially about the upper classes, but I did think I would
like to see some of 'em one time, just to notice how they
carried themselves."

I gave him a short account of this establishment. He
sat for some time silent, then spoke:

"I would'nt have believed it; it is'nt often that I'm
deceived in a man, but I suppose everybody is liable to
be sometimes."

We sat for an hour or so together, talking of what we

* Here resort leading characters in the *demi-monde*.

9*

had seen. I noticed that he frequently looked to the door whenever any one entered, and twice, after excusing himself, he had gone to the great hall and returned. At ten o'clock I proposed to retire. Jim said he would'nt keep me up, but he thought he would'nt go just yet. I turned to the table, took a sheet of paper, and began to write. He sat smoking his cigar, and slowly patted his foot with his cane. After a few minutes he rose, and I noticed that the young men had returned.

"Oh! how are you?" said the Missourian, addressing Jim. "Up yet? I supposed you had gone to bed. Glad to see you again. Been out?"

"No," said Jim, blandly "I've been waiting to see you once more, and tell you good-bye."

"Oh, you are very kind."

I folded my papers quickly.

"Yes," continued Jim, smiling more and more, "you've been so kind to me since I've been here, and made me so many valuable suggestions that I've been thinking about you for a couple of hours; and as I knew you were going to leave to-morrow morning, and might get off before I could see you, I made up my mind not to go to bed until you came back"

Then he shrugged his shoulders, and his face had the expression somewhat of a man who was about to sit down to a good dinner. The other seemed somewhat uncertain.

"Let me ask you a question or two, my young friend. You are from Missouri, I think you said. Yes. Well, have you ever found out, either from your own acquaintance or from other people's telling you, where the best society is there, and what sort of people they are that make it?"

"I don't understand you, sir."

"I see you don't; but I'm going to explain right away, for it's important to you."

He spoke in low tones, and with his back turned towards the bar, where two of the girls sat. Then, taking up the map, he said:

"You deceived me about the character of that place, sir."

The young man smiled derisively.

"What do you say, sir?" asked Jim, very mildly.

"I say that nobody but an old—"

"Say *that* or anything like that any further, if you dare."

Several gentlemen in the room, notwithstanding the low tones in which this conversation had been conducted, noticed that something unusual was going on, and they looked towards the disputants. One of the maids glanced out of her window for a moment, and then drew down the glass. Jim seemed as if he was just ready for his dinner. The other whispered with his companion, and patronizingly said:

"You are too old a man, sir, for me to have a difficulty with." Then he was turning away, when Jim seized him by the arm and drew him facing.

"No, sir, not quite yet; in a moment or so. Old man, indeed! I thought maybe you would apologize for your conduct; but that did'nt seem to suit your ideas of good society, and all you have to say is about your not wanting to have difficulties with old people. If I had been young, there would'nt have been any occasion for difficulties. You are not a man for difficulties with young or old, unless they are too old to take any care of themselves. Oh, you've got to stand here until

I get through with you. *I* want no further difficulty with *you*, more than to tell you what I am telling you; and if you change your mind, and think I'm not quite too old for you, and conclude to have a difficulty, look here; do you see that window? I'll take you up by the neck and breeches and drop you out there on the pavement. You took that liberty because I *was*, as you have no better manners than to call me, an old man, and you thought you would be safe in it. Young man, *no* man that thinks anything of himself or the people that bore him, would try to lead any other man, old or young, into places where the presumption is he would be sorry and ashamed to have been; and when one does such a thing with me, I'm bound to tell him that he is not only a scamp, but a coward. Now, you can go. But be quiet about it. It depends entirely on how quiet you are, whether you go out at the door or there." Loosing him, he pointed to the window. The young man was livid with rage; but his companion, with the air of one bent on preventing a very dangerous person from doing great damage, led him away. When they had reached the door, the Missourian turned suddenly round. Jim walked briskly towards him, shaking his left hand towards the bar in token of silence, and pointing with the thumb of his right backward ominously towards the window. They vanished without another word.

"Served him right," exclaimed, but not loudly, a young man from the same State who was standing near, and the rest, young and old, echoed the sentiment.

"Old man, indeed!" said Jim, with a tremulous laugh, "I could thrash out a cowpen full of such as him; yes, a quarterly meeting of 'em. Now, Phil, I'm ready for bed."

"I'm *not*," said I. "You've put me wide awake. My dear Jim, I'm afraid you have not considered how far the pavement is below that window, nor how hard it is."

"That was'nt a part of *my* business."

In five minutes after we got into bed, he was asleep.

CHAPTER X.

THE following morning we went out each in pursuit of the objects he preferred to visit. To me, it was continuously interesting to travel over places of historic renown, lingering as long as possible at each, and having my reluctance at leaving it consoled in quick succession by the sight of another. I dismissed my cab at Somerset House. Although this massive, solid structure was now filled, for the most part, with government offices, yet I was fond to recur to the old palace which formerly occupied the same ground, where the great Protector for whom it was named, dwelt, and later, where the queens of the First and Second Charles held their courts. Here, I mused, began, under the brilliant Henrietta Maria, the revolution in the literature of England, not less important than the political events which the introduction of foreign manners and tastes was destined to produce. As, in the days of the Conqueror, the proud Norman disdained the simple-minded Saxon, and sought for the native tongue of that people to substitute the polished language of the South, so now, that young gifted queen and her courtiers inaugurated, with Cowley and his like, that change which culminated in Dryden and Congreve, and Pope, and delayed for a hundred years the native English growth. Leaving this place and strolling into the

Strand, to the left was the old Globe Theatre, in front the Church of St. Clement Danes, in whose yard lay Otway and Lea; then into the Fleet—famous old Fleet, crowded from end to end with recollections of the work and the travail of men of letters. How heavy on them were the burthens of life, as, hungry, and thirsty, and ragged, they pleaded with book publishers and play managers for the purchase of those soiled and blotted manuscripts which were to delight the generations to follow! Then to Temple Bar, where many a king has waited for the bar and chains to be lowered before passing from Westminster upon the priviledged soil of the old city, and where many a dissevered head has hung on high to show to the world how terrible is the vengeance of princes. Turning to the right, I made my way to the Temple. Eight hundred years ago! How brave, how powerful those old knights! In this church, so faultless in its Norman architecture, they worshipped. How different they from these Benchers of the Middle and Inner! Yet other names besides those of knights and benchers are here. On that plain, marble slab in the churchyard, close to the choir, are these words: "Here lies the body of Oliver Goldsmith." Near that gate once resided Samuel Johnson. How often these two, the strong man and the weak, trod these places together; the one so helpless from the absence of all self-reliance, the other so imperious from the remembrance of the things over which, without help or sympathy, he had triumphed! The one fearing, yet relying upon the other, and that other contemning but protecting him, suspecting yet not fully knowing how great was he. How little either could foresee their posthumous relationship! I wonder what each thought of the comparative worth of

Rasselas and the *Vicar of Wakefield;* of *London* and the *Traveller;* of *Irene,* and *She Stoops to Conquer.* In this lovely garden, doubtless, many a time on summer evenings they sat down together and talked, scolding and pleading, yet never thinking of parting from each other for good:—not until the harmless quack should doctor himself to death, and be laid away in this churchyard.

In these gardens also, Shakspeare had often sat and meditated. Yonder, among that plantation of rose trees, York and Lancaster plucked the badges preparatory to the wars of thirty years. Along these walks the great of earth—princes, statesmen, warriors, poets, judges, philosophers—have strolled for longer time and in greater numbers than on any other grounds of equal limits and similar purposes in Christendom. Not that the poets in the olden times were often there before nightfall. For their apparel was ragged, and, in spite of these, the bailiffs were watchful. Yet Whitefriars was not far away with the protecting Alsatia, from which, but not too far from which, they and the thieves might steal in the darkness to the sweet arbors and smell the flowers and balmy evening air.

Back to the Fleet. There is St. Dunstan's, famous for the wooden giants long removed, and now striking the hours for the Marquis of Hertfordshire in Regent's Park; before me, to the right, the beautiful spire of St. Bride's, the masterpiece of Sir Christopher. In the churchyard lie Milton and Butler; how near each other now, how far apart when alive! Wynkin de Worde lies here also. In Shoe Lane, hard by, dwelt Ben Jonson; and in the workhouse graveyard was buried Chatterton. Not far off Dryden once dwelt, but afterwards in Soho, where he died. In the Blue Ball Court lived Richard-

son; in Bolt street died Johnson. I passed on to Ludgate Hill, where was the city-gate of King Lud long
before the days of Cæsar; thence to Newgate and the
Old Bailey. What a book it would be that should chron-
icle all the sufferings that have been endured here!
There were yet the notches in the stones on which the
gallows was erected; and yonder St. Sepulchre's, from
whose steps the nosegay was extended to the doomed,
and whose bell tolled the funeral knell.

Another flood of historic recollections met me as,
turning again, I found myself in St. Paul's churchyard. Roman, Briton, Pagan and Christian worshipped
and suffered within this semicircle of the "Bow and
String." The great Diana once had a temple here.
Here was one of the fires with which Diocletian the
slave ravaged the Christian world. A little later another sprang up on the ruins, which, in its turn, fell
before the Saxon in the reign of Constantine. And yet
another was built by the pious hands of Ethelbert of
Kent. Then, after other sequences of overthrows,
there rose this majestic structure, destined to immor-
talize its builder, and be one of the wonders of the
world. I entered, and as I cast my eyes up to the vast
concave, it seemed to be the most fitting of all places I
had yet seen for the worship of the King of Kings. I
ascended first to the Whispering Gallery and afterwards
stood upon the high parapet around the dome and
looked upon the pigmies in the street below. What
varying scenes have been enacted in the thorough-
fares along this lofty pile. The history of the British
drama is most intimately associated with St. Paul's.
Merry times had the ecclesiastics there, when returning from the Council of Constance they brought back

10

from the East the Mysteries and Miracle Plays. What a droll budget of religious fun was that Sacred Comedy, in which our arch enemy was whipped, and pinched, and knocked down, and trampled upon, amid the roars of laughter which this pious frolicking would evoke. Such scenes must in time be removed from the precincts of the House of God to the universities; but the merchandizing will go on around the churchyard until now, when even strangers can notice that the bargains offered are suspiciously cheap and the shopkeepers too eagerly solicitous.

Having to meet my friend for a joint visit to the Tower, I called a cab and drove rapidly on Cannon, East Cheap, and Lombard streets, stopping once on the way to look upon that other notable work of Wren—the Monument—a splendid Doric column of fluted Portland stone; a memento, not only of the fire of 1666, but of the folly and madness which attributed it to the Catholics. The great Protestant city, in the consciousness of its security against all assaults except those of the devil, and believing this calamity to be due to his machinations, in the absence of the power to avenge itself on him, could at least erect this lofty column, place upon it a burning urn, and record upon the plinth its angry protest against the Antichrist who had stimulated his followers to the perpetration of that horrible crime. Removed under James II, restored under William of Orange, it was made to disappear finally under the mild reign of William IV.

Punctually to the hour of appointment, Jim and I met at the Tower Gate.

"You look tired and serious, Phil, like a man that's been to a burying. Seen any old priories to-day?"

"Not exactly."

"Where they used to be, I suppose. Well, while you've been rummaging about among the dead, I've been mixing with the living; for this big town has a plenty of both. You do look tired. It is'nt quite dinner time yet; but had'nt we better fall in around here somewhere and get it before going into this old concern. I'll bet you have'nt had even any lunch."

"No, indeed. I have'nt had time to think about it; but it will be too late to see the Tower after dinner."

"All right. I've had my lunch punctually at twelve. I tell you this English beer grows on a fellow. I don't think a glass would hurt me now, and I know one would do *you* good. We've got ten minutes. That fancy-dressed old chap there, the keeper tells me, is waiting for the half hour to be out, to start with a new batch of visitors. I don't know how you feel," he continued, after we had taken the beer, "but you *look* better. You see, old gentleman, that a man has to take something in his stomach occasionally, even while he is working in old graveyards. Now for the beef-eater * as they call him."

Solemn as the place was in its recollections of the sufferings of ages, yet Jim, and so did I, thought they were needlessly magnified by the measured sepulchral tones of the guide.

"Did you ever," Jim whispered, "hear such a solemn old customer? That fellow's in debt, or lost his wife, or been henpecked, or had his house burnt up, or had no beef for his dinner to-day, or don't expect any. Upon my word, he makes me feel like I had been confined

---

* *Buffetiers* are so named those who conduct visitors through the Tower.

here myself twenty years or such a matter. Besides, I don't understand half that he says."

"He is a *buffetier*, you know, Jim, and your mind is apt to become a little confused when it gets upon the *buffet*. Can't you ask him to repeat, as you did the woman at Warwick?"

"Not if I know myself. Not an extra syllable would I wish to hear of that sort of talk. I suppose that being here so long, he's got to be like the place."

It required about an hour to make the regular circuit. When we emerged, Jim took off his hat, and looking back at the ancient fortress, announced that he had seen it one time. Then we took a hansom and rode to a restaurant on the Poultry.

"Things are even nicer here than we had yesterday, Phil. Let's just one time get a square dinner, and talk it all over. We've done a big day's work, and we want some rest, and then it will make us feel rich to be dining down here among the big merchants and imagine we own a big store apiece on Cheapside, or Leadenhall, or Threadneedle, or Bishopgate, or some other of these outlandish named streets. Now ain't it curious, into what a small bulk great riches may be pressed when you put 'em into jewels? Why a fellow could carry all those crown-jewels we saw just now in a tolerable sized basket. It gives me a sort of contempt for money when I see so much of it in such a small lump. What pleased me most of all I saw in that old Tower, was old Queen Elizabeth, standing there in the Spanish Armory with the same clothes she wore when she spoke to her army at Tilbury. The old lady was on her metal that day, sure. You don't suppose she meant what she said about going herself to fight the Spaniards?"

"I should'nt be surprised. She was a woman of a mighty spirit, and then she had a glorious precedent in one of her predecessors, Queen Boadicea. But what interested me most was the room in which Raleigh languished and wrote his history."

"I can't see how any man, no matter how good a writer he might be, could make a book in such a place as that."

"Ah! there lies the interest. I know of nothing in the history of literature so melancholy. The gayest, cheeriest, brightest, most gallant of all knights, the great discoverer, the sweet poet, the Shepherd of Ocean, as his friend Spenser called him, to languish in that prison, without guilt, from manhood to old age by order of the meanest of kings, while his wife, on the hill just outside the walls, mourned with her son their captive husband and father! What must such a man do in his captivity with that mind so active, so generous? He can only write. He *must* write—not poetry: for the pipe of the Shepherd has been broken and he must see ocean's billows, or even green fields and restful shades no more. Therefore, he will delude some of the loneliness of captivity by writing history. And a history of what? Not of England, or of France, or of Germany, or his own Orinoco; or of the Roman Empire, or of Europe. No. Such a history might be finished in his lifetime, and leave him unemployed. Therefore he will undertake a work that never can be completed, in the midst of which he will be able to look ever forward to a goal. So he takes the history of the world! His mind, untrammeled, began away back in the Golden Age, remote from the times of Tudor and Stuart, and wandered over the historic fields of Asia. He had barely crossed the Bosphorus and the Aegean, and was

narrating the deeds of the Macedonian Empire when
the doors of his prison were opened, and the historian
was carried, with the block and the axe, to the summit
of Tower Hill."

"That stopped that business. Oh, those old kings!
I suppose, when Anne Boleyn's time came, they thought
it would'nt do to cut off her head where other people's
had been, and they had it done there in the court.
How do you suppose old Queen Elizabeth felt when
she would go near that place?"

"She never went there. With her, the Tower ceased
altogether to be used as a royal residence."

"She showed 'em though that Anne Boleyn's daughter
could hold her own with the best of 'em in cutting off
heads. They say the poor old woman died a horrible
death. She had better died along with her mother."

"Indeed, she had. That death-bed was the most
tragic in the history of princes."

We rose from dinner and strolled leisurely amongst
the dense throngs in Lombard, Cornhill, and Bishops-
gate, along by old Crosby Place.

"The idea that Crosby Place," I said, "so connected
in renown with the Yorks and the Warwicks should
become a restaurant."

"Crosby Place? Crosby Place? I remember it now.
It was where Anne of Warwick was to meet King
Richard. I can quote some of his words:

> That it may please you leave these sad designs
> To him that hath most cause to be a mourner,
> And presently repair to Crosby Place,
> Where, after I have solemnly interred
> At Chertsey monastery this noble king,
> And wet his grave with my repentant tears,
> I will with all expedient duty see you.

He got her, but he did'nt keep her long, as he said he would'nt. A restaurant, eh? That's not so bad. Times have changed. The main business of those old times seems to have been to find out the most effectual ways of killing people in order to put up and put down kings. Now, it is how to let people live longer and more comfortably by giving them better houses, better clothes, and better victuals. So, I say, go it, Crosby. Set the best dinners you can; you are in much better business taking in people to feed 'em than having young widows moping about and being courted by the assassins of their husbands. Ain't it so, old man?"

"I give it up."

"Well, let's go on."

On to Lothebury, where Founder's Court suggests the great copper foundries that had to give way to banking houses; across Moorgate into Gresham; to Guildhall. Here we entered for a few moments. They were taking up the carpets from the great hall in which a State dinner was lately had. There were Gog and Magog, "two more unlikely old cusses," Jim said, "he should seldom, etc." We looked admiringly upon the statues of the two Pitts and Mayor Beckford.

"See what a brave man, Jim, can say to a king when the right of petition is denied: 'Permit me, sire, farther to observe, that whoever has already dared, or shall hereafter endeavor, by false insinuations and suggestions, to alienate your majesty's affections from your loyal subjects in general, and from the city of London in particular, and to withdraw your confidence in, and regard for your people, is an enemy to your majesty's person and family, a violator of the public peace, and a betrayer of our happy constitution, as it was established at the glorious and necessary revolution."

"That was the way to talk it," said Jim. "It was
that sort of pluck that brought these old kings down
after a time, and learned 'em to be reasonable. And
now, I'm for going back to the Langham. I'm tired.
Besides, I've got my head full of more things than I
shall ever remember the half of."

"Well, let's just go down King street into Cheapside
and look at Bow Church for a moment, and then we'll
take a cab."

"Are you going inside? No? I will go with you,·
then. This Cheapside is about the busiest street we've
seen."

"It is the most crowded street in London, perhaps in
the world. It was the northern boundary of the city in
the time of the Romans. Long afterwards were held
here the tournaments in the time of the Edwards.
Here also was another of the nine crosses which Edward
erected for the "dear queen." Like that of Charing Cross,
it was torn down by the regicides. Cheapside is now
the centre of the retail trade. And, now, we are in the
centre of cockneydom. There is Bow Church."

"A good-looking building, and a capital steeple. How
old is it?"

"About the age of St. Paul's. It has the best chime
of bells, they say, in London."

"I hope they won't sound 'em till I get away. That's
a music I don't fancy. Why do they call those cockneys
that live within the sound of the Bow bells?"

"Cockney was a name of reproach that outsiders
gave to city people, on account of their luxurious and
effeminate habits. It seems now to apply only to those
who know little except city matters, and believe none
others are worth knowing."

As we passed slowly along in the cab, I pointed out the Old Bailey and St. Sepulchre's.

"A curious name," said he, "for a church whose bell tolls while they are hanging folks. From the looks of both of 'em, the church and the gaol, I should say that both of those things had been going on some time. Do you know, Phil, I hate the very *looks* of a gaol?"

"That's not uncommon with some people."

"Oh, I don't mean that I'm much afraid of 'em for my own sake; although along towards the last of the war, when they were getting so fond of grabbing up people, I did'nt know what might become of me when those little enrolling and impressment officers might get a little more audacious. But I hate the looks of gaols for other people. My opinion is, that the keeping a man in a place like that a long time does him more harm than good. You see how it has been since imprisonment for debt has been stopped. In old times people could'nt pay their debts while they lay in gaols, and when they got out, they would'nt. They do so now more punctually and honestly than before. As for close confinement for crimes, that, nine times in ten, makes men worse. I've noticed that all my life."

"Why what else could society do with criminals who, not bad enough for hanging, should go without confinement?"

"Whip 'em, my gracious! whip 'em for small crimes, and drive 'em out of the country for great ones, with the understanding if they come back within a certain time and are caught, they shall be hung."

"Moving them, eh? What about other communities? Such people, according to your plan, would be coming in as well as going out."

"'That's so, and in that way every poor fellow would have a chance to improve himself by getting into a new community. I tell you, Phil, that the punishment that people dread more than anything else, except death, is to be driven away out of their native and regular beats, and—hello! I know where I am now. I've been all over this region to-day. This is the Holborn Viaduct. While you've been prowling around among the insides of those old temples and houses and things, I've been studying the modern improvements. When I get a chance at you, I'm going to make you understand, whether you will or not, something about the great works that are in this town. Now, here's this Holborn Viaduct," and he proceeded with the account, which I foresaw was to be an extended one. He was telling how, just below where we were then, the old Fleet Ditch, once a stream between Holborn and the Hill, used to run, and how the Fleet Ditch water was supplied, and what a nuisance both of them used to be. "Hold on, Jim," said I, "a minute. There's Lincoln's Inn Fields, where the Chancellor and Vice-Chancellor hold their courts. Over to the right is Gray's Inn, and just beyond Lincoln's Inn is the College of Surgeons."

"Drive up, coachman, let's get out of this neighborhood as soon as possible."

CHAPTER XI.

THE next couple of days were spent similarly to the last. While I visited places of historic interest, Jim busied himself with studying the great public works and manufactories taking an occasional ride on the omnibuses throughout a part of their lines. We met for dinner at some convenient place, and afterwards repaired, the first day, to Victoria Park, and the second to the Zoological Gardens. On the Saturday morning after our arrival, we concluded to take an excursion to Windsor. A ride of a few minutes carried us· to. the ancient town. As the queen was sojourning there, we could see only the portions separated from the apartments occupied by the royal family.

"The castle is about as big as the town," said Jim. "It is supported mainly by visitors who come here, they say. How old is the castle? old enough for you?"

"Yes, indeed; the Saxon kings resided here long before the Norman Conquest. But their palace was pulled down, and William the Conqueror began the erection of the present one."

"Well, I think it looks well for 'em to give their queen-bee a big establishment. She is the head of the whole, and such an institution makes her look greater to the world. More than that, she's a good woman,

married young the man she loved, was true to him, had
a heap of children by him, and when he died, behaved
like a sensible widow, and stayed single."

We entered through the gate next to the town, and
merely glancing at the chapel, ascended the royal stair-
case which led to the summit of John's Tower. The view
from this we enjoyed much. Below us, across the
Thames, was Eton College, where, since the days of
Henry VI, so many of the sons of the nobility and
gentry, afterwards become illustrious, received their
preparatory education. Lifting our eyes, we could
descry Stoke-Pogis, and to its right, Harrow, another of
the great schools of England. There, thinking of the
past history of the tower, my mind vividly recalled that
royal poet, James of Scotland, who, while listening to
the nightingale singing in a juniper tree in the garden
below, soothed his captivity by musing and writing thus
of his love, the beautiful Joana Beaufort. I repeated
the lines.

I.

"Now was there made fast by the Toures wall,
A garden faire, and in the corners set,
Ane herber green, with wandes long and small,
Railed about ; and so with trees set
Was all the place, and hawthorne hedges knit
That life was none walking there forby
That might within scarce any wight espy.

II.

So thick the bewes, and the leaves green
Beshaded all the alleys that there were,
And middes every herber might be seen
The sharpe, greene, sweete juniper,
Growing so fair with branches here and there,
That as it seemed to a life without
The bewes spread the herber all about.

III.

And on the smale greene twistes sate
The little sweete nightingale and sung
So loud and clear the hymnes consecrate
Of love's use, now soft and loud among,
That all the garden and the walles rung
Right of their song, and on the couple next
Of their sweet harmony, and lo, the text.

IV.

Worshippe ye that lovers been, this May,
For of your bliss the kalends are begun.
And sing with us, Away, Winter, away,
Come Summer, come, the sweet season and sun.
Awake for shame, that have your heavens won,
And amorously lift up your headdes all ;
Hark Love, that list you to his mercy, call."

"What little I could understand of that sounded moderate   But no more than about half of it was English, eh?"

"All of it was English: old English. That is very sweet, Jim. It has been greatly admired as well as very much more that he wrote of the same sort; for he was a captive here eighteen years."

"Did he get the girl at last?"

"Yes."

"Well, women, so you praise 'em, it makes not much difference what foolishness you talk."

We descended, and went through the royal mews.

"And horses and carriages according," said Jim. "The widow keeps a full team certain. So-so, Flora (patting gently the queen's favorite riding pony), carriage-horses, barouche-horses, phæton-horses, buggy-horses, saddle-horses, *and* ponies. Grey seems to be the favorite color here; mine, too, next to chestnut sorrel."

Emerging from the castle, we took a carriage, and
drove upon the Long Walk, in the shade of those
magnificent elms planted two hundred years ago by
Charles II, by Frogmore, the equestrian statue of George
IV, towards Windsor Forest."

"Hearn's oak!" exclaimed Jim, when we had reached
it. "Here those Windsor wives had their final settle-
ment with old Jack. Was'nt that Ford a fool? Still
that wife of his was, for a married woman, right sassy.
And Shakspeare wrote that just to oblige the queen,
who wanted to see old Jack in love? Fine, genteel set,
those ladies must have been, sitting up there laughing at
such talk and such carryings on generally."

Without going on to Virginia water, we took the first
turning and drove around by Datchett's, thus making a
semi-circle of the castle. Returning by the famous Datchett's Mead, Jim again apostrophized the knight.

"Poor, dear old Jack! they were too many for him,
were'nt they? But he was slow to take a hint certain,
and give up the chase. I should have thought that
after coming out of the river alive, and that buck basket
to boot, he would have concluded it was a lost ball.
But he had to be beat half to death afterwards, and
pinched all over before he could come to his senses.
And not to know that he was'nt the beau for that sort
of business. Haven't you noticed, Phil, that men who
are the quickest to take up the notion that women are dead
in love with 'em, have the least showing for such notion,
and are the easiest flattered and made fools of?"

"Often. That's the compensation which nature be-
stows, or which they make for themselves in the absence
of pleasing qualities. None but the abject like to feel
that they are objects of disgust or commiseration. Men

ignore their own infirmities, and by frequent endeavors to induce others to regard them as advantages, learn in time to do so themselves. Thus it is, I think, that such weaknesses become sometimes well compensated. Ignorance of their existence keeps down envy, which, after remorse, is probably the most painful emotion of the human heart. We seldom meet a person, who, whatever little he may have to brag about, does not believe that little better than what other people have of the same sort, and simply because it is his."

"No doubt about that. I know a case in point. There's Jim Hester; you remember him?"

"Very well."

"You know what a clever, good-natured, good-for-nothing fellow he was. Well, low down as old Jim went, after his father and mother died, who had kept him up, he had a notion that in spite of his laziness and poverty and general good-for-nothingness, he was still holding up tolerably well. His brother in-law, Dave Towns, let him live with him, you know. Dave fed him, but he told him he must get his clothes for himself. Jim got pretty seedy in time, and at last he wore out his last coat. This made him stay more about home than he used to; but it didn't *phase* his good humor. I never shall forget a remark he made to me one morning. It was before the war, and before I had quit fox-hunting. It was a mighty frosty morning. As my hounds were running near Dave Towns' house, old Jim came out on one of the plough-horses without any coat on, and joined in the race! 'Hello, Jim,' says I, 'good morning; pretty cold morning to be without your coat, aint it?' I wish you could have seen him smile, as he opened his shirt, and showed another underneath. 'Major Rawls,'

said he, 'haint you never found out that two shirts and
a westcot is the warmest dress a man can war?' And
then he looked as if he had me where it wasn't any use
to try to get away. What do you think of that?"

"A capital illustration. Jim believed what he said,
or, what was better, he thought *you* did: this compensated for the want of a coat, and served to subdue
his shame for not owning one. When conceit takes that
shape, it does no harm. Jim Hester was a philosopher
without knowing it."

"He was that, or something, certain; and so it was
with old Jack. He had carried that mountain of flesh
so long, that he at last, not only got reconciled to it, but
believed it becoming, and that it made him a woman-
killer, until at last the prince, now become king, threw
him overboard. That undeceived him, and killed his
heart. It was a mean thing in the king to do it. He
might have given the old fellow some little office or
other that would have kept him from breaking completely down. I don't believe in anybody getting too
good all of a sudden, and dropping old companions."

Hastening back to the city, we took a cab for Hampton
Court. Lingering for a short visit at Kensington
Museum, in about an hour's time we were at Kew, once
the favorite residence of George III. In a not preten-
tious palace on one side of the green, then resided a
prince and princess of the blood royal. The view from
the corner of the green next the gardens is very pleasing. The mansions seen through the trees overshadowing its borders, and the church standing diagonally
across, make an agreeable picture.

"There's the everlasting photographer," said Jim, as
we stopped near the gate. "We are getting too old to
keep up that foolishness, eh?"

But the man and the woman who worked with him were so solicitous, and we saw that in the fine sunlight they executed with such dispatch, that we concluded to stand.

"I see," said Jim, after he had finished with us, "that you have improved by travelling in good company, and putting on new clothes and a London hat."

We walked through these gardens, probably the most extensive and various in the world. Jim was especially interested in the Palm House, with its enormous collection of evergreens from all countries. In spite of the oppressive heat therein, we mounted the stair-case to the galleries in order to get a better view of the lofty trees as they towered on high with the same freedom and pride as if they were standing upon their native plains. After strolling through the conservatories and amidst the flower beds and plantations, and the winding walks, overshadowed with stately forest trees and extending down to the river, we sat down to rest awhile beneath a spreading fir.

"Nothing," said Jim, "that I have seen since I left home has made me wish to have Emily with me as these gardens. I do wish she could see them. *She* would enjoy them. The mischief with me is I never can remember how such things look so as to describe them afterwards. But, I'll tell you one thing, Phil, I have'nt seen any roses over here that are prettier than her's, nor any greater variety. That will be a consolation to her when I tell her so. Somehow, flowers, when I'm away from home, make me think of her more than anything else does, especially roses. Its always been so. Oh! Come, let's go on."

A few minutes drive, on leaving Kew, brought us to Richmond.   11*

"An aristocratic town I take this," he said, as, after
stopping at the Star and Garter and ordering dinner, we
strolled out for a short walk, and looked upon the
splendid villas in the outskirts. "You notice that, like
Hyde Park, no cabs can enter this. But for our walk
at Kew and the want of time, I should like to go down
into that deep shade yonder. Richmond? Richmond?
Why, old Queen Elizabeth died in Richmond, did'nt
she?"

"Yes, the town takes it's name from her grandfather,
Henry VII, who, you remember, was the Earl of Richmond. This has always been a favorite resort for the
aristocracy. See what a splendid view there is here."

"This is a great country for the rich, Phil. It does
look like it was made and laid off for rich people.
These magnificent views, and parks with shade-trees and
deer. As for poor people, they seem right well in the
country, such as I've seen; but those in the big towns
are of another sort. They are the poorest and the
worst-looking in London that ever I saw or ever imag-
ined to be in the world. Yesterday, I took a notion to
roam about among some of the poorest parts of the
town. I rode around old Whitechapel and places like
that; I forget the names of the streets. I was glad at
last to get away. They looked not only poorer than
I had ever dreamed of, but they looked savage, men
and women. They stared at me as if they had a notion
of dragging me out of the carriage and mobbing me
for having on good clothes. The driver laughed
when I told him I had had enough, and he said I
had'nt seen anything yet; but that to see the worst I
would have to take a policeman along with me. I
stopped once out there, near Whitechapel, at a court-

house. In a little room, not twenty-feet square, they were trying one woman for cutting another with a case-knife. There were the judge's seat, high up like an old-fashioned pulpit, the lawyers' benches and jury's, a prisoner's box, and room enough besides for about a dozen or fifteen others. I gave the officer at the door a little piece of money, and he let me in and set me right down by the prisoner's box. Of all the court-rooms that ever I saw, that was the smallest, and of all crowds, they were the hardest-looking, except the lawyers and the judge. With their wigs and gowns, a body could'nt say what sort of clothes they had underneath, nor whether they were poor or rich. The judge was a man of sense though, and seemed to understand the law and the sort of people he was dealing with. He as good as told the jury that he believed that what most of the witnesses, except one little boy, had testified to, was a pack of lies, especially as they (all except the boy being women) were drunk when the fight occurred. I don't know how they found. When the judge's charge was done, I left, and I told the driver to bring me back into the white settlements. That was about four miles the other side of the Langham, and nowhere near that end of the town. The truth is, if we were to count this London as we count towns in our country by keeping on counting until the stores and dwelling houses stop, there's no telling where the everlasting place does end. What are you laughing at?"

"I was amused at the discursive ways your mind and you" talk were taking. You have sadly mixed up the aristocracy and the poor, Richmond and London."

"*I* did'nt mix 'em; they mixed themselves. There's more mixing up of people and towns in this country

than anywhere else on top of the ground. London city
proper, you know, is rather a small concern. I did'nt
know that until I got here and found people talking
about Bishopgate without and Bishopgate within.
London city ends on the west at Temple Bar and on the
east at Ludgate Hill, and it has something of a distinct
government of its own. And there's even in that centre
a plenty of poverty along with all the riches. The two
extremes of uncountable money and un-something-ed—
I don't know what word to find for it—poverty have
come together here in this London town and go on side
by side. Now, not that there isn't a very large majority
of people in moderate circumstances, as, of course, there
is everywhere. Three-fourths of the tax paying people
here live on incomes of less than three hundred pounds.
Yes, sir, things are mixed over here. In our country,
when you get out of a town you *are* out. But with this
Babylon of a London, when you've been travelling along
for hours and see scarcely a particle of change, they tell
you you're eight or ten miles outside of it, and been
through half a dozen other towns besides. But you
make me do pretty nigh all the talking, while you are
everlastingly looking over your books and maps trying
to find some *new* old thing or another. What's that
you are spying out now?"

"Twickenham," said I; "that lies in our way to
Hampton Court, and, if possible, I should like to have
a peep into the grotto of Alexander Pope, who used to
live there."

"The *universal-prayer* man?"

"The same."

"Why, we must see that, of course."

"But it is private property, and they tell me that
strangers are not admitted there."

"Nothing like trying; only you let me manage that."

After a first-rate dinner, we set out. Crossing again the Thames, we ascended the hill on the opposite bank, and were soon in the old village. We drove by the elegant mansion and grounds of the exiled Bourbon, and looked over towards Strawberry Hill (now owned by Lady Waldegrave), once the residence of Horace Walpole. How much of gossip, but of the politest, most entertaining, most instructive sort, had been talked, and, fortunately for posterity, written down in that country place. By inquiring among those persons whom we met we ascertained the precise spot in the street beneath which was the grotto. On the grounds to which it extended, stood a handsome villa. After passing it a few rods, we halted, descended from the carriage, and approached the gate, Jim in the lead. A neatly-dressed woman was standing before the door in one of the walks. Jim advanced respectfully towards her, as she turned on seeing us, and, taking off his hat, gave her a bow and a good afternoon.

"I beg pardon, madam; but we called to beg the liberty of seeing, but for one moment, the—eh—the—"

He hesitated and looked at me.

" Grotto," I said.

" Certainly; the name escaped me for a moment,—the grotto of Mr. Pope."

"Very sorry, sir, but strangers are not allowed—my orders are to—"

"I beg your pardon, madam, we heard that was the case, but not until we had left our homes. We are Americans who have come over to see your beautiful country, and we have been delighted, madam, not only with the country itself, but with the people whom we

have seen thus far. As for myself, madam, and I am
sure I can say the same for my friend, a friendlier,
politer people we would both, seldom, in fact, never
wish to see. We did hope, indeed, just to look for one
minute into the grotto (intending, of course, to leave
immediately afterwards), just to say that we had seen
it, especially as both of us, which you can see for yourself, are somewhat advanced in life, and could hardly
expect to make such a trip again and—why, bless me,
what a beautiful place this is, and you notice, Philemon,
how well it is kept? in what taste? and everything of
the kind? Healthy, too, I don't doubt. However, you
English have such elegant complexions, especially you
English ladies, that, it's not worth while to inquire—
though some do have better than others—and, indeed—
the grotto, I understand, is just *there*, and runs under
the street—a very convenient place. Well, Mr. Perch,
we can tell our friends that they were very polite to us,
and if it had'nt been strictly against the rules—but,
upon my word, a better kept place I should, indeed—"

He was turning slowly around, looking persuasively,
alternately at the woman and the shrubbery which he
knew covered the entrance to the grotto. She smiled,
hesitated, and said:

"I suppose there is'nt any harm just in *looking* at it."
Then she led us through, taking pains to show us the
stump of the willow that the poet had planted. Jim
thanked her so cordially that she valued his words, I
believe, more than the present that he forced her to
take. She looked at him, as we left, as if she believed
him to be one of the best of men. If that was her
thought, she was not mistaken.

"You see, Phil," he said, when we were again in the
carriage, "nothing like being polite to people."

" You don't think that you pushed the figure any too far with the good woman ?"

' Not a bit of it. I suppose the owner is often worried by people, many of whom have no better manners than to almost demand admittance. They are genteel people, and while they wont show the place for money, I've no doubt they let in other genteel people sometimes when they apply in the right sort of way. My wife loves to hear her front yard praised, and I knew this woman, although nothing but a servant, would too, and I'd have said what I did, even if I had'nt wanted anything. And then, Phil, I did'nt know, you see, but that her husband, or brother, or sweet-heart might be the one that kept it in order."

" But what about the complexion ?"

"Oh, you get out. If it had been you, you would have been met at the gate and turned back, and probably had the dogs set on you. What did you think of the grotto, as you call it? I call it a hole in the ground."

" It is smaller than I expected ; yet, I am much gratified to have seen it."

"I'm glad I've seen it myself, that is, one time. I can't understand how any smart man would want to stay in such a place as that. But poets take up mighty strange notions. Then he was a little scrap of a fellow, and wanted to be seen seldom, I suppose. I expect he made it, to hide in sometimes when people called on him that he did'nt want to see."

"No, he was very fond of it, studied and wrote in it, and entertained his friends there."

"Many men of many minds, many birds of many kinds, as the copy-book says."

As we approached Hampton Court, it was easy to see that the great cardinal, who, in search of healthfulness

and fitness of situation, founded it, had been abundantly
successful."

"Another mean thing," said Jim, as we rode along the
road in Bushy Park, "in Henry VIII, in taking this
place, dry so, from old Wolsey. Well, sir, he was an
interesting fellow to me somehow. When he wanted
anything, he took it, without making any bones about
it, whether it was a new wife, or a palace, or land, or
money. He set out with the notion, or he got to believe
so at last, when they turned him out of the Church, that
every man and woman, and building, church or what
not, belonged to him, and if this doctrine did'nt suit
any particular person, he cut his head off, and shut his
mouth. But, I suppose the people had got so tired of
the everlasting wars, that they thought it as well to let
him cut off the heads of as many big men, and have as
many pretty women for wives as he wanted, instead of
resisting and breaking out into war again. He was
smart enough to see the situation, and he took it."

We entered the court, and ascending the King's grand
stair-case, passed through the several chambers. What
a flood of historic reminiscences here! I thought of
the marvelous rise of the butcher's son, the entertain-
ments, literary and festal, he had given here to lords and
ladies of his own and other lands, little foreseeing that
in that same grand hall, some of these same lords and
ladies would in time listen to the tragic recital of his
own downfall, while himself, in the Abbey of Leicester
would be warning his follower of the dangerous heights
of ambition. As little had the beautiful Anne Boleyn,
despising the faded beauty of her royal mistress, foreseen that dark room in the Tower, and that scene in the
court below. Indeed, could the powerful tyrant fore-

see that even there would be ever an end to his own life? It would seem that such disregard of God and man must have counted on living on always. But he would be king to the last, and even endeavor in his dying hour, to bid death wait, until he could hear that the head of Norfolk had fallen beneath the axe. Following along the track of history, I beheld Edward, and the imperious, godless Somerset, Elizabeth and Mary, the two sisters, so widely different in their characters and careers, and in the charitable speeches of the next ages; the Stuarts, Cromwell, dreaming, after allying with nobility, of founding another line of dynasty; William and Mary, husband and wife, yet not lovers, laying out this beautiful park in which he was destined to be thrown from his horse and killed; Queen Anne, reminded, at the consecutive deaths of all her numerous offspring, of the infelicities of kings, when they see the glory departing from their houses; and then the line of Brunswick, until, with the demise of the Second George, Hampton ceased to be the favorite residence of princes, and was consigned to the remnant of the decayed old nobility. "How many more among those who lived and ruled in this stately pile, the cups of disappointment than the cups of joy," I said, as after coming out of the gate, and entering the carriage, we were driving again through Bushy Park.

"Yes, sir," answered, Jim, "they paid high for what they got. The more I think of it, Phil, the more I'm thankful that I was'nt born, as Weller says, in that sitooation of life, or that I myself ain't a big man. That's a blessing, I know, that's very common. Still, every common man don't appreciate it like I do."

Returning to Kew, we dismissed our carriage, and

12

took the boat which we saw just then slowly descending the river above us. We walked down the bank towards the landing. As we were nearing it, Jim suddenly exclaimed:

"Where's your overcoat?"

I had left it in the carriage. The boat was now at the landing, where it would remain but a couple of minutes. I looked back, and to my surprise, there on the bridge, on which we had already crossed when we left him, stood the cabman, holding on high the missing garment, and motioning to us to proceed, rushed towards us with all his might. I rewarded the man, while Jim, who could not keep his hands out of his pockets, gave to him also, and shaking him by the hand, said:

"My dear fellow, *if* you ever come to Georgia—"

The laugh of the captain and passengers who had seen our strait, drowned the rest, and we were off.

"Honestest people I ever saw, cap'n," said Jim.

"Who, the cabbies?"

"Yes; but not them in particular: the whole English nation, by gracious."

"Oh, thanks; but he dared not keep the great coat. He's an honest lad, I daresay; but he dared not keep it."

"In our country, sir, many a one would have dared to keep it, and would have kept it. You see this aged person here, cap'n," he continued, laying his hand on my shoulder, "I have to keep my eye on him constantly. If I take it off him for a minute he's lost something. He'd lose everything he's got twas'nt for me. A little advanced, you know," whispering very loudly, "memory not good as it used to be."

"Even loses his thread sometimes, Jim, eh?" I said.

"You get out."

The weather was fine; the little steamer passed along down so leisurely, that the many row-boats that were out seemed to think it not worth their while to get out of its way until it had reached within a few feet of them.

"And here's Chelsea. At the hospital here, they take care, inside and out, of several thousand children of seamen. Here's where the great water-works of London begin."

"And here," I said, "also Queen Elizabeth once had a palace, and right yonder on that rising immediately on the bank was the house of Sir Thomas More, the loveliest character in British history."

By Putney, Battersea, Fulham, Lambeth. We debarked at Westminster bridge, and taking a cab, as the sun went down, drove to the hotel, both feeling and both saying that it was a most agreeable day's excursion.

That night Jim entertained me with an extended account of his travels in the city by omnibus and underground railway, his investigations concerning the Holborn Viaduct, the Thames Embankment, the Tunnel and other great works of London. "While you were poking about," he said, "to find out what the town *had* been, I was seeing what it is now." He had gathered up the statistics of many of these works, and the figures of their cost and the extent to which they were used were surprising and rather interesting to me.

"I did'nt," said he, winding up his account, "I did'nt have any idea of the bigness of this town and the tremendous business that is done here, before I saw it with my own eyes. I've ridden through and through it, lengthwise and crosswise. The people! the people that live and work here! How rich are the rich, and how poor the poor! These poor the rich *have* to take some care of, and so far as money is concerned, and hospitals, they spend and build, and build and spend. St. Thomas' Hospital alone, receives sixty thousand people a year! But to see the crowds of poor people that I have, one would'nt suppose there was a hospital in England. In some places they are as thick as worms in an old rotten log; and they almost are like 'em as they go crawling and dragging themselves about. But, you know, people have got to have the poor always. The Bible says that."

"So you see, Jim, that you have something else to be thankful for besides not being a king."

"Yes, indeed, and I don't know for which the most. I'm sorter like Agar, Phil. Neither poverty nor riches for me. I always would want enough to live on decently, and to keep from having to steal, or feel like stealing from other people. But I'll be blamed if I believe I could stand being as rich as some of these people over here."

CHAPTER XII.

HAVING determined, contrary to our first expectations, to make a flying visit to Scotland before passing to the Continent, early on Monday morning we were on the train for York. Shortly after taking our smoking-car, an Englishman, stout, fair, side-whiskered, hearty-looking, came in, and after placing his luggage carefully, took his seat without seeming to notice that any but himself were there. We had barely moved out of the station, when he took out a cigar, lit it, and read his newspaper. Jim and I, with maps extended, studied the region over which we were to journey, which like all the rest we had seen of this beautiful country was full of ever varying interest. The villas, the hayfields, and market-gardens of Middlesex and Herts, in the latter, the apple-orchards, as the city-like and suburban prospects subsided into the rural, and the fields became larger and the shade trees more abundant, made us glad to be in the fresh air once more. We flew into Bedford (where we again saw the Chiltern Hills), along the pleasant banks of the Ivel on its way to join the Ouse; then into Huntingdon, where I thought of the brave Iceni who had dwelt here, and Boadicea, their queen, and how, at last, at Caister, they went down before the Roman legions under Silanus; and then of the less ancient, yet far remote rule of the Forest Laws,

12*

and the great Earls of Huntingdon, descending to bold
Robin Hood.

Riding in the same carriage, seated silently by a
good-looking man, who seemed as if he might have some
good talk inside of him, was one of the things that Jim
Rawls was not used to. In speaking before this of some
of the acquaintances he had made, he said to me:

"These English people will travel with you a month,
and say not one blessed word to you unless you speak to
them first; and then, at the start, they'll just answer
your questions and no more. But if you don't put 'em
too fast, and then if you'll ask sensible questions—as I
generally try to make it a point to do—they will get
right sociable, if they ain't busy."

On this morning, after some talking among ourselves,
and while I sat ruminating over the past history of this
section, I noticed Jim open his cigar-case, and after he
had fixed the attention of our fellow traveller, with
apparently great care, select a cigar, and hand it to him
with this remark:

"I see you smoke, sir. We have some very good
American cigars; won't you try this one?"

Such cordiality few could have withstood. The gentleman, whom Jim found to be a Mr. Flynt from Yorkshire, accepted with thanks, and very soon the two were
on terms of reasonable good fellowship. Their interest
in each other gave me opportunities to meditate without
interruption. Jim was delighted to meet a person who
could answer all his questions about the present state of
the country, the character of the crops, and their condition, the lands and their prices, the manufacturing
interests, etc. As we went through Peterborough, I
observed, as well as I could, with the help of my opera-

glass, the old Cathedral, with its turrets and pinnacles and monastic edifices adjoining. Within was the dust of Catharine of Arragon. Neither her innocence nor her misfortunes had obtained for her a different resting place. Not so with the Queen of Scots, whose remains, first deposited there, were afterwards removed by her son, James I, to Westminster Abbey. Yet this had been no common place, but for centuries had been the favorite shrine of the pious, whether prince or noble, knight, or gentleman, or yeoman; and, from the gifts of the devout Edgar, had been called Guldenburgh, "the Golden City."

Our companion was no more able to refuse Jim's invitation to partake of our lunch than to decline his cigar. Having gotten on easy terms, both of us were entertained by his conversation. While not a man of liberal education, he was well acquainted with the resources and the business of his section. As we passed along through the great county of Lincoln, I listened as he talked of the undulating wolds of the northeastern portion of the county, the moors, extending north and south through the centre, and the fens in the southeast, fenced off by embankments from the German Ocean. I, but not Mr. Flynt, could occasionally detect on Jim's face an amused smile, as the former spoke, with some pride, of the four rivers of the county, the Trent, the Welland, the Witham, and the Ancholme, as if they were well known rivers of Damascus. Passing into Nottingham, our guest—for such Jim considered him now—spoke yet more knowingly of general interests and industries. While he was discoursing to Jim of the immense business done in the lace and hosiery lines, I could but recur to the Druids who once held here their solemn reign. Away

to our left were to be seen some remains of Sherwood
Forest, where the *gestes* of Robin Hood were enacted.
Along where we were travelling, doubtless he and Little
John, and Friar Tuck and the rest had passed; and not
far off was Kirksley Hall, where, having been betrayed
by his kinswoman, the bold outlaw ended his career.   I
said how I regretted not being able to visit that spot.
Mr. Flynt expressed some surprise, and Jim asked:
"What's Kirksley Hall?"
"Where Robin Hood died and was buried," and then
I repeated the ballad beginning thus:

> ' When Robin Hood and Little John
> Went o'er yon bank of broom,
> Said Robin Hood to Little John
> We have shot for many a pound."

"That's right good," said Jim, "I always liked that
Robin Hood.   He never hurt woman, nor man in
woman's company.   Still, he might have known that
following that sort of business he would be cut off suddenly somehow, by rope, or something else."
    Mr. Flynt smiled approvingly, and they returned to
the lace and hosiery business.   This turn shut me up
at once, and sent me back to my meditations.   For the
rest of the journey to York they sat opposite each other
at one side of the carriage, while I was by the window
at the other.   We were not far from the station, when
Jim turned to me and asked with an air of one who
was seeking honestly for useful information:
    "Phil, can you tell this gentleman about how far it
is from Boston to Buenos Ayres?   He asked me, but I
disremember, although I did know once, and am surprised that such a plain thing should have dropped out
of my mind,"

I was figuring in my mind preparatory to giving an answer, when Mr. Flynt arose, commenced getting down his luggage, and, looking out of the window, said:

"We are at York, gentlemen."

After we had parted, and were on the way to our hotel, Jim said:

"You want to know why I asked you that question? Don't you think that man believes that the war we had lately was between North America and South America? And he a man that owns land, and has plenty of sense besides. I wish you could have heard him asking about our negroes, and our feeding 'em on cotton seed, and working 'em in chain-gangs, and locking 'em up at night, and our having to stand guard and all such. But he's a clever fellow, and a sensible. He had heard such things, and he believed 'em. I've heard a good deal of just such as that since I've been over here. I don't know whether they believe me or not, but I poke all the information into 'em I can. I told him I thought it was about ten or fifteen thousand miles between Boston and Buenos Ayres, a right smart distance for two armies to pass over before they could get up a fight. But, bless me, here's another old wall. I'd have bet that you'd stop where there was one of *them*. The *Black Swan*, eh? Well, I'm ready for whatever good things she's got in her smoke-house and pantry."

Our expectations concerning this excellent hotel were fully realized under the care of Mr. and Miss Penrose. We supposed at first that the pretty bar-maids were their daughters, so fond of them they seemed; but we found that the host and hostess were brother and sister, and unmarried. Their uncle and aunt, then argued Jim. But no; it was only that the employed were so sweet and efficient, and the employers so orderly, considerate, and kind. The Yorkshire mutton chops and ham, and ale, the snug smoking-room, and clean, cosy bed-chamber, would have inclined us to rest here several days. Our host, we thought, might have provided us with a somewhat better horse than the old white jade that took us out to Bishopthorpe, the Archbishop's palace. But we did not complain; for the fields and farms on either side of the road were so fair to look upon, that we could have been content to travel at a yet slower pace. A sweeter spot (always excepting Guy's Cliffe) could not well have been chosen for retirement and religion. The Ouse, laving the palace walls and smoothly gliding amidst shades and flower-beds, the deep green grass, the magnificent roses (the finest we saw in England) engrafted upon lofty stems, all seemed to form a retreat where a scholar and devout prelate might dwell in quiet and felicity. A drive about the town on our return showed us its objects of special interest. Old Walmsgate, yet preserving its barbican, with the arms of the city and Henry V; Micklegate, that, although now without barbican, yet called to mind that here were wont to be hung in bloody times the heads of the executed; and Clifford's Tower, which though now occupied by those who manage the public business of the county, still could not fail to recall the days of feudal ascendency. The most beautiful of ruins seemed to those of St. Mary's Abbey, near Marygate, the multangular tower of which is now a musuem. But it was while wandering near Christ Church, and along by Goodram gate, the site of the ancient Roman palace, that I was most interested. Here Hadrian had fixed the British capital, after he had subdued the islanders and carried a wall

from Carlisle to Newcastle. Here Albinus commanded
with his legions, when, on the assassination of the good
Pertinax, Septimus Severus beguiled him away with the
argument of patriotic revenge upon Niger to rescue the
people from the base Julianus. Here the same Severus,
Niger and Albinus being overthrown, repaired on the
revolt of the Britons with his sons Caracalla and Gaeta,
whose ingratitude, crimes and dissensions rendered vain
his successes, and broke his heart. Here the accomplished Julia Domna reigned and dazzled, and did not
foresee the wounds she was to receive while lifting
her hands to rescue the beloved Gaeta from the
murderous knife of his brother. Yet more interesting
than these the reminiscences of Constantius and his
dynasty. Here died he, and on that day the legions
declared emperor the son, who was to erect the standard
of the Cross, and remove the centre of political empire to
New Rome on the Bosphorus, leaving the Eternal City
to become that of religious unity.

But vain were walls and towers against the moun-
taineers, unless the Roman legions were within and
around them. With the decline of the empire, another
power must come from beyond the German Ocean, and
after six hundred years of rule, while the last king, in this
same ancient city would be holding high festivity after
the battle of Stamford Bridge, the dread news be brought
that William the Norman was at Pevensey, and in another week the Saxon dynasty be laid low. The mind
saddened in retracing the bloody scenes enacted here,
both in war and in peace, Briton, Saxon, Norman, Lancaster and York, Stuart and Parliamentarian, Druid,
Christian, and Israelite.

"In the name of common sense," said Jim, winding

up another tirade against the preservation of those relics
of cruel times, "I can't see why they should want to
keep that old Micklegate that's in everybody's way, just
to look up to where the heads of their great, great
great grandfathers were hung up and left to feed the
buzzards."

"My dear Jim, it is to remind themselves and their
children and all the world from what oppressions the
courage of their nearer ancestry delivered their country."

"Humph! That's like the old nigger who, when he
was fishing in the creek, his under lip poked out about
two inches, and a white boy from the bridge above,
dropped on it a piece of mud, got up and started off,
saying: 'I don't 'tend to take it off. I don't 'tend to
take it off. I gwine kyar it right thraight and thow it
to your daddy.'"

The next morning while my friend and Mr. Penrose
were out inspecting the glass-works and the market, I
repaired alone to the cathedral. Fitly named, in this
central place of battle and blood, was that temple to
Bellona which was standing here on the day of Constantine's ascension to empire. On the very spot, after other
alternations, the Northumbrians erected a Christian
Church, when they had accepted the faith which Au-
gustine had introduced into Kent. Four centuries later
began the erection of the work which two centuries yet
later ended in the completion of the great Minster. Superior to what I had anticipated was the exterior view—
the lofty, square-topped towers in the west; the pointed
arches and the marigold windows in the south; the yet
more magnificent window of the east; the Five Sisters
of the north, and the great Lantern Tower lifted high
above all. But within! Not St. Paul's, not Westmin-

ster Abbey seemed to me so fitting for the worship of
the Creator, and so accustomed to His presence as this
whose nave, and aisles, and transepts, and choir, so varying in architectural excellence, yet so harmonious, told
of a long history, and seemed so typical of the varying
religious faith of this ever earnest people. To enter by
the west end, stand in the central door, and look down
that nave, one's vision extending beyond the organ into
the choir into which the mellowed light descends from
the great east window, and then slowly tread beneath
those solemn arches, and amid the aisles and transepts,
and look upon the tombs therein, and in Lady Chapel, of
archbishops and earls, divines and scholars, of Hatfield
and Wentworth, Medley and Saville, these are such as to
impress one's mind with as solemn awe, I believe, as
would be felt in any temple on earth. As I was about to
come forth by the door through which I had entered, the
great organ began to sound for a special morning service. Never before did that instrument seem to me so
fit for making the music of worship and thanksgiving.
But the hour for our departure was drawing nigh, and I
hastened back to the hotel.

Quite a friendly acquaintance had grown up between
Jim and Mr. Penrose, and on departing from the *Black
Swan* we had sensations akin to those with which we
had left the *Red Horse* at Stratford. After we were
fairly off for Edinburgh, he, as usual, began with the
dutiful task of speaking of our late entertainers with the
grateful praise which it was ever his delight to bestow
upon whomsoever had treated him with kindness.

"Phil," said he, "do you believe in lotteries, as they
call 'em, in people's marrying?"

"Why, what put so grave a question in your head this
fine m rning?" I returned.

13

"Because I just happened to be thinking about it. I have thought a great deal, and somehow I never have been able to make up my mind about it. It's a question that people may argue about all their lives and never settle. Now there's Mr. Penrose and his sister, neither one of 'em married. And yet I never saw two apparently better contented people in my life; and if they don't know how to keep a hotel it is'nt worth while for anybody else to try. What a good husband and wife they would have made—that is, to all appearances. But there's the point, you see. We can't tell about such things. Maybe it was'nt their lot to marry, and maybe they would'nt have done as well as they've done single. For many a man, there's no doubt about that, and woman, too, makes a poor out of it in marrying. Still, nine out of ten can't be satisfied until they do marry, and, as a general thing, that's what makes old bachelors and old maids so crusty. They go on the idea, or they think other people do, that they have lost something that other people have; and so they get to be at last what they suspect other people believe them to be. Now, this Mr. Penrose and his sister seem to me to be exceptions to this rule. I have an idea that they are always congrat- ulating themselves that they *ain't* married, and that they don't have the troubles of married people generally. But here's another thing that I've noticed, Phil. When this thing of not marrying runs in the family, it don't serve people as it does when only one stays single. It's especially the case when a brother and sister keep single and live together. Such a couple, generally, are quiet, good-natured, kind-hearted people. Marrying certainly makes some people better than they would have been without it; but then it makes others worse. Then again some couples get together in such strange ways; and then some fall in love at first sight, just like I did with Emily. And then you know the Almighty instituted marriage; and as for Adam, Eve was made expressly *for him*, and he *had* to take her because, my gracious, she was all there was. That was the first case, and after that, why not a lottery, or a special providence for the rest of us? But then, on the other hand—oh, pshaw! when I get on that subject my mind always gets confused. Oh, you may laugh, but you don't know any more about it than I do."

"I do not. But I suppose you mean, by what you say of Mr. and Miss Penrose, that if there was a lottery, they never went to the drawing, or they drew blanks."

"Blamed if I know exactly what I *did* mean, except that they are two mighty clever people, and know how to keep a hotel."

"You know somebody that drew a prize."

"That I do; and I never knew half the worth of her till I've come so far from her."

How lovely was that morning. Though we rushed along with the speed of the hurricane (for we made no stop until we reached Newcastle-upon-Tyne, eighty-six miles distant), yet the sweet prospects along the Ouse, and afterwards, the Cod-Beck and the Wistol, were so abundant, that we had no time to regret the instantaneous passing of any one among them. On and on, to Northallerton; we had scarce time to think of Standard Hill, where the battle of the Standard was fought, before we reached the Tees, and our thoughts wandered up its banks to Barnard Castle, and the days of Baliol.

"And now," said Jim, "I see from the map that we

are in Durham, and sure enough, here's the short-horned cattle. I've read that they come from Tees-water. This is one of the great coal counties in England, too. Did you know that?"

"No."

"So I supposed; I bet if there's any old cathedral anywhere about you know of that."

"I supposed everybody knew of the Cathedral of Durham. This is one of the richest sees in England."

"I hope those old Romans never got up this far."

"But they did. Here was some of their hardest fighting, first in subduing the Brigantines, and afterwards in keeping off the Scots and Picts. I wish we could stop for a little while at Durham town. The cathedral is one of the best specimens of Norman architecture. Besides, I should like to see the shrines of St. Cuthbert and Bede the historian."

"Bede! I never heard of a historian of that name."

"He wrote eight hundred years ago, and in Latin."

"Well, I never expect to read, the works of Mr. Bede, if you'll allow a rhyme."

We were soon at the Wear, and, flying along its lovely banks, noticed how it encircled the ancient town. We got only a brief look at the cathedral, and the castle on the lofty, immense rock, surrounded by gardens and plantations, when we were out of sight again, and in a few minutes, the speed slackened, and passing slowly through Gateshead and over the Tyne, halted at Newcastle.

"A live town, sure. I noticed some old walls still standing as we came in, but none to hurt."

"This place was the Pons Aelii of the Emperor Hadrian, and those walls were built by Severus. Long afterwards, it was noted for its monasteries, and was called Monkchester. Pilgrims in great crowds used to congregate at The Holy Well of Jesus. One of the sons of William the Conqueror built a castle here, and from that the town took its present name."

"No cathedral?"

"No; but the Church of St. Nicholas is next to one."

"Those old fellows never dreamed of the coal that was under the ground here, nor what it was to do for the world. Ah! Yonder's the German Ocean. Some distance from home, old fellow, let's brace up a little."

He took down the lunch-basket, and opened a bottle, and soliloquized thus, in audible tones, as he made things ready:

"I've found that when a fellow is travelling a long way from home, and with rather an oldish person, one of the best things to have against home-sickness is a good appetite, that is, provided, of course, a fellow can get something good to eat and to drink at the same time. Next to a good appetite and the et ceteras, of course, is young, pleasant company, if a fellow could get it; but, of course, it is the part of prudence to put up with what company a fellow does have, if it's the best he can get, and make the most of it. If a fellow could once get out of the region of old walls, and castles, and graveyards, some people might not appear to be quite so old. I am thankful to see, though, that they take kindly to beer, and that it seems—"

"Morpeth!"

"Morpeth? I've heard of that. That's it, is it? Was'nt there a Lord Morpeth?"

"Oh, yes. Morpeth gives the title to the Howard family, as the whole county Northumberland gives that to the Percies."

13*

Crossing the Lyne, the Cogent, and the Aln, the scenery grew rapidly more picturesque as we approached nearer and nearer the German Ocean, until we were upon its very shores. The ground to our left, though yet in faultless green, rose higher and higher until it culminated in the Cheviot mountains. As we neared Berwick-on-Tweed, I looked over the waters towards Lindisfarn, and my memory again called the saintly Cuthbert, and the sweet influences that the lives of him and his brethren of the Holy Island had wrought upon the fierce inhabitants of that mountain region. Crossing the Tweed, we were now in Scotland. Through Berwick and Haddington, getting only a glimpse of Dunbar House as we sped through Dunbar. The richest, loveliest plain we had seen was that which extended from the foot of the Lammermoor Hills in the south, and further on, from the Morefoots in East Lothian to the Firth of Forth. We had not ceased talking about the battle of Preston Pans, begun by our passing over that famous field, when, looking out to the left we saw Arthur's Seat looming up, and shortly afterwards were in Edinburgh.

CHAPTER XIII.

T eight o'clock P. M. we had enough daylight
left in that high latitude to make some observations in the afternoon. We sallied out, therefore, for a walk in the New Town, which this
street (Prince, on which, at *McGregor's Hotel,* we were
quartered), formerly a deep gulch, separates from the
old. We traversed alternately from end to end Prince's,
George's, and Queen streets, lingering severally at the
site of the Ambrose Tavern in Register street, St. An-
drew's Square, and the late residences of Brougham,
Scott, Hume, Jeffrey, Cockburn, and at Charlotte Square,
Moray Place and others. That night, while I' spent an
hour or two in reading up on the foretimes of Edinburgh, Jim, who had made acquaintance with the land-
lord, was engaged in getting an acquaintance with its
present conditions. I had taken a fresh interest in the
old Scottish kings—the pious David, founder of Melrose,
Kelso, Dryburgh, and Holyrood—the Holy Rood, so
eventful in its fortunes, all along from the time of
its importation by Queen Margaret; and Neville's Cross
and its enshrining in Durham Cathedral. I had wandered along to King James IV, and mingled with the
throng in that splendid pageant, when another Margaret,
daughter of the first of the Tudors, was led by the gallant Surrey and Archbishop of York to espouse the Scot-

(151)

tish king. The royal husband, in the fullness of con-
jugal happiness and princely power, could not foresee
that this same Surrey would afterwards lead an army to
Flodden Field, where Scotland's spear would be shat-
tered, and broken her shield. Then I thought of Magdalen of France, who came to preside in that same palace
(named from the abbey, Holyrood), and a month afterwards was laid in the abbey tomb, when Mary of Guise
was chosen to take her place. Lastly, I mused of the
daughter of this second marriage, Mary of Scots, so
beautiful, so imprudent, so unfortunate, with whom
passed away the glory of Holyrood.

In the midst of these musings Jim came up, and said
that he would bet "'arf a crown" that I did'nt know what
was the principal and most money-making business in
the present burg. I gave it up.

"Ale. A-l-e ale—beer. Yes, sir. They do a considerable business here in shawls, and in the book and type
foundry trades. But the big business is ale-brewing.
This is a great barley country, you know. Not that the
people drink the ale themselves, for *they* drink whiskey
instead; but the barley, what is not fed to horses and
poor folks, is made into ale and sold in England and
other countries."

This announcement served to divert my thoughts from
the pathway in which they had been traveling, and soon
afterwards my friend and I went in search of sleep
and found it. After early breakfast we took a carriage
and drove into old town, High street, Netherbow, and
Canongate, passing slowly along, through Morocco Land,
full of romantic traditions, St. Anne's Yards, the Debtors'
Sanctuary, made so widely known by the Chronicles of
the Canongate, Queen Mary's Garden, near where Rizzio

dwelt, then over the ruins of the ancient abbey to Holy-rood Palace.

The satisfaction on entering this renowned structure was subdued by the melancholy of contrasting its present humbled condition with the splendid adornments of old times. The ruins of the abbey, the disappearance of the gardens and parks, the poverty of whatever relics of art are yet preserved, the smallness of the chambers, that poor, ruined bed, with its faded, ragged coverings, all hindered us from wishing to linger among them.

"Where's the blood of that fellow Rizzio?" asked Jim of the guide, in a subdued, respectful whisper. Stooping down, he looked closely and thoughtfully at the stain upon the floor, and rising, whispered again to me:

"No business being so thick. It's always dangerous; though I always believed she was innocent of the worst they accused her of."

Emerging, we visited St. Giles' Cathedral, famous for John Knox and the Covenanters, paused for a moment at the figure of a heart made in the pavement where once stood the great prison—the Heart of Midlothian, thence to the Grass market, thence making a short visit to the hill and the castle, and after viewing these for a few moments, and looking over that almost inimitable prospect of the Salisbury Crags, Pentlands and Hills of Fife, descended and took the train for Stirling. Fertile in abundance are the level fields of Edinburgh and Linlithgow. As we emerged from the region of the Lothians and the Firth of Forth, the land rose in undulations, increasing in height and depth as we neared Stirling. Jim pretended to be not much interested in the talk I had of the ancient struggles of the Scots on one hand with their alternate enemies over the border—the Britons, and Romans, and Saxons, until the cession of the Lothians to the former in the time of Malcolm II; so about the wall of Antoninus at Falkirk. But he brightened up at the stories of Wallace, Edward I, and Charles Edward. What took him more than these, however, was what he had found out about the great Carron Iron Works, near the Trysts, and the cattle-fairs that are held here.

"Three hundred thousand head of cattle a year, sir; not *men* to be butchered, by gracious, but cattle. Old walls in this country moved away, spears turned into plow-shares, and swords into pruning-hooks. More good is done here in one year by these cattle shows than all the wars of all the times of all the Romans and all the Saxons and all the rest of 'em, by George."

"Still, Jim, it is interesting to know the places where these famous wars occurred; they are parts of the history of the world, and we must study that as we go."

"Oh, yes, certainly, certainly. I'm merely making remarks, and—comments, so to speak—on the history lessons, just to make 'em more interesting. Go ahead, you old schoolmaster: fetch out the big names. And, by gracious, they *are* getting bigger, I notice, and harder to call as we get higher up among these hills, these Linlithgows and such; and I see from the map that they are going to get longer as we go on. But go ahead, I like to hear you tell about it all. I want Emily to know that I've seen everything on the route that was worth seeing. That's what she cautioned me not to fail to do. She said I was to take in all I could of what you told of the history part of the trip. I shall tell her that I've seen all the old Roman walls, and where all the old battles were fought, and the heads cut off and hung up, and where all the old kings and queens were born, and lived, and kept in jail, and wrote poetry, and their lovers got stabbed and left their blood on the floor, and the whole conflutement of 'em. I want you, before we part, Phil, to give me a list of all of 'em, so I can study 'em up and get 'em at my tongue's end, and, when I get home, I can rattle 'em off and make Emily proud, and the other women in the neighborhood jealous. Go ahead; what old Roman was it that built the dirt wall along here? Old Antony?"

"Antoninus, you wretch, ANTONINUS."

"All the same, or nigh enough for my use. And so Queen Mary used to come out this way and spend some of her time at Linlithgow, crossing the Almond Vale, Queensferry and on by Barnbough Castle. Here's to all of 'em. I don't like this Scotch ale as well as the English. It's too frothy, and fussy, and fiery. Still here's to old An-tonicus, and may nobody else ever have to build another such wall along here nor any other decent and respectable country; and may the Scotch and English have plenty of cattle instead of men to butcher, and may they both treat old Ireland right, and all live in peace and harmony together."

"An extensive and varied toast. I join, however, with all my heart; *ab imo pectore*, Jim, you know."

"Certainly, that's what *I'm* after."

"And now, for Sir Walter's sake, especially, we must study well the ground from this to Glasgow, for it is all classic."

"All right."

After leaving Falkirk, the country, interesting from its varied scenery, became intensely so henceforth from

its historic and romantic associations. From our window
we looked out upon the Lennox Hills, from which the
Carron water descended and flowed across our path.
Not far off were Airth Castle and Dunmore Park, and
Tonwood Forest, at one time the hiding-place of Wallace, at another, the scene of the excommunication of
Donald Cargill, the fierce Covenanter. Soon we were
at Bannockburn, seeing to the right, on Abbey Craig,
the monument of the patriot, and, on the left, the Rare
Stone of Bruce and Gillie's Hill, where the camp-follow-
ers struck terror to the English army, and gave victory
to the Scots. Even from our windows we could see how
the gathering hills on either side of the Forth made
narrow the pass from the Lowlands to the Highlands,
showing how Stirling must have been, of old, a fortified
position.

Arrived at the station and taking a carriage, the toiling horse drew us up the long acclivity to the castle.
In singular contrast with the narrow streets and squalid
tenements of the old were the fine promenades and
groups of villas of the new town. Alighting from the
carriage, and passing over the esplanade and the draw-
bridge, we entered the castle beneath the gateway from
which the portcullis hung threateningly over our heads.
Most interesting to us both were those places which the
poet had specially celebrated; the chamber wherein
Ellen Douglass rested when she came to plead the cause
of her exiled father; that wherein Rhoderick Dhu
breathed out his life, while Allan Bane sang the battle
in which Clan Alpine's honored pine was laid low; the
great hall, now occupied by the Highland regiments in
barracks, wherein the blushing maid discovered in her
bold suitor the King of Scots. My dear old Jim

declared that he was enchanted—"is that how you call it"—by the sight of these places. He was even glad that these old walls had been preserved, as well to guard the places where such thrilling events had occurred, as for the prospect they gave below us of the winding Forth, the fair vale of Menteith stretching miles and miles northwest along the Teith, Cambus Kenneth Abbey and Bannockburn on which was yet marked the spot where the banner of the Bruce was triumphant. Above and beyond were Tinto (the Hill of Fire), Arthur's Seat, the Lennox, Ochil, and, yet further, the blue outlines of the Grampians. "I don't wonder," he said, "that they fought so long to determine which should have such a country, and that they had to compromise at last. Look down yonder at those wheatfields. They look so peaceful that a fellow could hardly believe so many battles have been fought upon 'em."

At this moment we heard the bag-pipes, and turning around saw a squad of Highlanders moving to their music.

"I tell you what," said Jim, "don't those tall fellows step it right with their gowns and bare legs? And that's the bag-pipe. Poorer music, I would *indeed* seldom. I could do as well with a split goose-quill, or a pumpkin-vine."

On the return, we drove about the town, taking hasty views of the Military Hospital (once Argyle House), Cowane's Hospital, and Grayfriar's Church, in which James VI was crowned. Taking another train at the station, after passing the Brig of Allan, we soon were at Dunblane, not valued by us for once having been an episcopal city, or for giving the title of viscount to the Osbornes, as for the little Jessie, it's famous "Flower."

14

While the main railway stem proceeded to Perth, we diverged, and coursing down the Teith, came to Donne Town, and even here we thought less of the baronial castle of the Earls of Menteith and the visits of Mary to the Earl of Moray, than the first of that long line which made its author the greatest of the romancers. We would have checked, if possible, the rushing train in order to view more leisurely this region. Thanks to the Buchanans, their love for Walter Scott, and his love for them. It was here, at Cambus More, he learned these mountains, and meads, and lochs, in the midst of which he dreamed that sweetest of poet's dreams. Across here fled the stag when, startled in Glenartney, rushing along Benvoirlich and Uamvar, and despairing to reach Lochard or Aberfoyle, he turned and made for

> " The copsewood grey
> That waved and wept on Loch Acray,
> And mingled with the pine trees blue
> On the bold cliffs of Benvenue."

Jim had had special admonitions from his wife and daughters about seeing all he could of this particular region, if we should pass over it. He had read over again, while in London, *The Lady of the Lake*, and now he studied the map and the poem carefully.

"It won't do, Phil, for me to be nonplussed about that when I get back. I'm going to get all that by heart, and make it my trump-card. But I should say that that was a slow way of coming at a deer. If I had been in that hunt, I should have *stood* for him. I don't believe in this way of breaking down horses as well as dogs just for one deer, and, by gracious, not get him at that."

"Ah, my old Jim, *you* would have been after the *meat*. That royal hunter and his gallant followers were for the sport, enhanced by the risk, the toil, and the adventure. Besides, in those days, game was allowed a chance for its life, instead, as in these degenerate times, of being waylaid and shot in ambush."

"Umph! That all sounds well enough in a love story. But in those days you talk about, they might give a chance to game, but they did'nt give much to *folks*. They did'nt stick at hiding behind a tree to shoot at *folks*. However, I'm going to see 'em through. It was a good long old race, I should say, judging from the map, and to let him get away at that. About the most sensible thing that Fitz James did, it seems to me, was when he acknowledged to his grey horse that he had paid too dear for his fun. But like many another acknowledgment in this world, it was too late to do any good."

I was on the point of remonstrating with him for holding and giving utterance to such commonplace views of this masterpiece of romantic poetry, when the cars suddenly slackened their speed, and we drove into Callander, where, in a few minutes, we were seated before the door of the *Dreadnought Hotel*, and looking upon the Teith that flowed rapidly by. After supper, while we were starting on a stroll, we heard lively songs, which seemed to proceed from the rear part of our hotel.

"That sounds like old Georgia, Phil. They are laborers from the country, who have come to town to spend their holiday to-morrow, and are drinking whiskey in the kitchen. It's the first whiskey music I've heard since I left home."

The boys were having a good time. We approached near the room where they were feasting, situated on the street crossing that on which the hotel fronted. Jim listened attentively. After some time, he turned and said:

"It *sounds* right, but I can't understand one blessed word they say. That isn't English. I never heard such a language."

"It is Gaelic," said I.

The party broke up after finishing their supper, and came out upon the street. As soon as Jim ascertained that they could speak English, he began to make acquaintance with them, and by a timely contribution for their next day's dinner induced them to talk about their work, and translate several expressions from one to the other language.

"Well, that's a language that I did'nt know was yet in the world. That language, Gaelic, as you call it, seems to be that of the poor people in their talk with one another. The learned folks, they tell me, don't speak it, and don't know it."

"With some exceptions, that is true. The Gaelic is the native language of the Highlanders, and they have not yet given it up. This seems to be the last liberty that the vanquished will part from. These people would feel that they were unfaithful to the memory of their forefathers if they were to do so. They learn the language of their conquerors; but in their domestic and social relations, they adhere to their hereditary tongue."

"I don't blame 'em; I like 'em the better for it. I believe in a people being true to their own folks. It's awfully outlandish, but it sounds pretty and affectionate like. That's right, boys," he said, turning again to the laborers, "hang on to the language that your mammies talked and sung to you when they were suckling and rocking you to sleep. And now let's all go in and take one more drink and then break up."

Hauling me along, he went into the kitchen, followed by a dozen or fifteen of the Highlanders, and ordered a bumper.

"Here's to your ancestors and forefathers, your fathers and mothers, your wives and children, uncles, aunts and cousins—Scotch, English, and Irish. Go ahead, boys, work hard, be honest, and hang on to your native tongue as long as you've got tongues to hang by, and let's all of us try to mind our own business and let other people's alone."

The very rafters shook with the applause which this sentiment evoked.

"Now, give me one more song, and then I shall have to leave you and put this old gentleman to bed. He's a good man, you see, and powerful high-learned and smart, but—feeble."

They applauded again, and at once broke out into a mountain song. When it was over, Jim said:

"Good, very good. I didn't know what it was about, but it sounded much like our Georgia corn-song:

> Ando, And-a-a-a
> Turn de wagon over-er-er,
> Ando, And-a-a-a
> Turn de wagon over.

Now good-bye, boys; may you always have plenty of work to do, and get well paid for doing it."

We shook hands with each one, and then leaving them retired to our chamber.

14*

The next morning, after breakfast, we were on one of
the great open-topped coaches for Loch Katrine. Just
before we would have reached St. Bride's we turned suddenly to the left and travelled up the vales of Venna-
choir and Loch Acray, having to our left Carchowzie
Woods and Bochastle Ridge.

"I see they've got a bridge over it now," Jim remarked,
pointing to Coilintogle Ford. Those two fellows, Fitz
James and Rhoderic Dhu, had pluck to go to fighting
there with nobody to part 'em."

On and on, by Lanric Mead, Duncraggon, the Brigg
of Turk, and the margin of Achray. Passing Glenfinlas,
Ben An rose in rivalry to Ben Ledi, the Trossachs
bristled before us, and Benvenue loomed to the left
across Loch Katrine.

"What!" said Jim to the coachman, who, in answer
to the question, what was the name of the Trossachs
hotel, as we halted to take in a passenger.

"Ardcheanachrochan."

"I give it up. Phil, you must put those names down
in my blank book, with some sort of pronunciation to
the right of 'em. For the present, give me another name
for this place."

"Well, what do you say to *The High End of the Rocks?*
for that is what it means."

"I thought it must mean something. But if their
idea was to give it a nick-name for short they missed it.
Now Ben, I can reconcile, and by the way, they name a
many a thing here Ben; but I know plenty of Bens in
Georgia. Right along here somewhere Fitz James lost
his horse, it seems. None but them that could afford to
lose horses would ever think of hunting with 'em in
such places as these. Read what Scott said when he got

on the top and took his view of the country around."
Here it is, said I:

"And now to issue from the glen,
No pathway meets the wanderer's ken,
Unless he climb, with footing nice,
A far projecting precipice.
The broom's tough roots his ladder made,
The hazel saplings lent their aid;
And thus an airy point he won,
Where, gleaming with the setting sun,
One burnished sheet of living gold
Loch Katrine lay beneath him rolled,
In all her length far winding lay,
With promontory, creek and bay,
And islands that empurpled bright,
Floated amid the livelier light,
And mountains, that like giants stand,
To sentinel enchanted land.
High on the south, huge Benvenue
Down on the lake in masses threw
Crags, knolls, and mounds confusedly hurled,
The fragments of an earlier world;
A wildering forest feathered o'er,
His ruined sides and summit hoar,
While on the north, through middle air,
Ben An heaved high his forehead bare."

Jim frankly admitted that he could not have expressed
it better, though he certainly would have used fewer
words.

Arriving at the shore where the little steamer had
been some time awaiting us, we hurried on board, and
in a few moments were slowly encircling the island.
With eager eyes we marked the "aged oak" from which

"A little skiff shot to the bay,"

and the Lady of the Lake peered across the pebbled

shore into the dense hazel shade, from which, instead
of Douglass or the Graeme, emerged the royal adven-
turer. Passing the island, we looked upon Benvenue
and the birch-covered Bealachnambo. The captain,
while drinking a cup of ale with Jim, pointed out to us
Coiran-Uriskin whither Ellen and Allan Bane retired
on the eve of the battle.

"English names, when they've got 'em, captain, if
you please. It is'nt worth while for me even to try to
remember the Scotch ones except these Bens."

The captain smiled, and anglicizing Bealachnambo
into Cattle Pass, and Coiran-Uriskin into Goblin's
Cave, did the like with others as we passed along.

"Yonder, you see, Phil, at that hole in the ground,
begins the aqueduct that carries the water from this
lake to. Glasgow. Well, I *envise* no man (as Gabe Nash
says) who has to drink town-water, but if I had it to do,
this is as clean and nice as I should ever expect to get."

Landing at Stronachlacker, and taking another coach
for Inversnaid, the four milk white horses rushed at
full speed along the declivities and levels of the way,
giving us little chance to notice the bracken on the
mountain side to our right, and the marsh-shrubbery
to our left on the tarn extending southward to Loch
Arklet. Beyond this we could see Ben Lomond the
loftiest of all beginning the long line of the Grampians.
Suddenly a shower came down white and soft like snow
upon us. The coachman did not even lift the leather
covering from the boot, and laughed at Jim and me as
we crouched under our umbrellas, which we could
scarcely hold as we dashed along.

"I don't see the fun," said Jim, "what is it?"

"Kiverrhing feerrom a mist," he answered, laughing
more and more.

"A mist? I call it a *rain.*"

"Na. Only a mist."

"But it'll make wet, for it's already got through my umbrella and shawl. Ain't you getting wet?"

"Na, na. The mist dinna wet the Scotch."

"I should say you had tolerable thick hides then. If you call this a mist, I should'nt like being out travelling in one of your rains."

At Inversnaid, besides a good dinner, Jim on the plea of having wet knees and shoulders tried the Scotch whiskey. But how anybody could like that smoky stuff except occasionally as punch of a cold rainy night, he could'nt see. He merely took it now as a brace against the mist.

The scenery on Lochlomond was even finer than that in Loch Katrine.

"Fact," said Jim, "I don't like to give it up, but it's so. Along here was Rob Roy's country. He was another rusher, like Rhoderick Dhu."

"Yes; just a little behind us up the lake was Craigroyston, Rob-Roy's Cove, and—"

"Look here, Phil, don't *you* be coming over me with them Scotch names. It's enough for these people to do that. They come natural to their throats. I say *throats;* for there's where they start from, and they get out of their mouths the best way they can. It's enough to give a fellow the asthma to try to pronounce 'em. I think a little spell of asthma would do good in this case. Rob-Roy's Cove, you say?"

"Yes; there is where he held councils with his followers; it was in the country of the Macfarlane clan."

"Clans, indeed! they were what ruined this country."

"No doubt their feuds contributed most to the

destruction of the separate existence of Scotland. We
are now in the midst of scenes where many of the most
murderous battles were had. It is sad to know that
such a lovely region as that around these lochs was ever
occupied by a bloody-minded people. Glen Finlas,
Glen Artney, Glen Fruin, Glen Luss: no tongue and no
pen can properly describe their matchless beauty, even
as they appear to the traveller while passing along their
borders, and noticing how they make their windings
among the mountains. One is always confounded to
know how those clans, the Stuarts, MacGregors, Calquo-
houns, Macfarlanes, so brave, so hardy, and (within
their limited spheres) so patriotic, should not have
striven, if they must have been rivals at all, to make
their own first among equals in a confederacy of States
that would have been unconquerable. What a sequel to
the history of Greece! But it is a fact, however unnatural, that the deadliest feuds always obtain among
those, whether clans or families, whose welfare and
happiness mostly depend upon peace and fraternity.
We ought to have taken at least one more day, Jim, for
this tour. Yonder is Rowardennan where tourists begin
the ascent of Ben Lomond. To say nothing of the mountains, we should have taken time at least to linger awhile
among these lovely islands."

" We would'nt remember the name of a single one of
'em ; at least I would'nt except the first syllable, though
there's a big family of 'em ; these Bens I know pretty
well, but I can't go the Inches, as they call their islands.
Let me hear you call a few of 'em."

" Easily enough. There's Inchlonaig, the Deer park
of Sir James Colquhoun."

" Go ahead."

" Inchconachan, Inchtaranach, Inchgalbraith, Inch-
cruin, Inchcalleoch, Inch——"

"That'll do. You need'nt go any further. You've
hawked your throat, and made mouths to no purpose.
You did'nt get one of 'em right; nowhere in the neighborhood of being right one single time. I looked and
listened both to one of those Scotch fellows a few minutes
ago when he was calling 'em over for me, and he looked
like another person altogether when he got his mouth
and face screwed up ready to start. You did'nt begin
right, Phil, and the longer you kept at it, the further
off you got. The spelling of 'em has nothing to do
with the pronouncing of 'em; not a blessed thing. Yes,
they are mighty pretty, the prettiest country *I* ever saw,
if they'd give names that a body could call and remember."

From right to left, from left to right, in constant
alternation, we walked in order to see as much as possible of noted places, Balmaha, Rossdhu, Buchanan
House, Glenfruin, Arden, Bilvetero, Cameron and others.
It was almost with pain we saw the boat come to land.
Taking the train at Balloch, a few minutes travel down
the banks of the Leven, brought us to Dunbarton, the
ancient Alcmyd, "Rock High on the Clyde."

"Dunbarton? Is'nt that the place they took Mary,
Queen of Scots, from when she was a child and carried
her to France?"

"The same. This old castle (how lofty and strong it
looks!) is full of historic recollections—Roman, Briton,
Pict, Saxon and Norman."

Not long afterwards we passed through Bowling and
Kilpatrick, where, in spite of himself, Jim had to notice
more of the remains of old Ant'ny's wall, as he called it,

and moving into Glasgow went to the *Queen's Hotel.*
Having only the rest of that afternoon at our disposal,
we took a drive through the Irongate, Queen and
Buchanan Streets to Kelvin Grove and the university.
In spite of the general unpicturesqueness of the town,
compared with Edinburgh, we were most agreeably
impressed by the many superb edifices, public and
private.

" The business, the business that's done in this town,"
said Jim that night, after reading an hour or two of its
operations and resources, " cotton, iron, ship-building,
medicines, etc., etc. There's one thing here, however,
which I expected to see, from the looks of the place : it's
very unhealthy, especially for children. We did'nt see
the cathedral, Phil. That's one more, if I had thought
about it sooner, I should have been willing to go to."

" I know why. To see the spot where Rob Roy was
once."

" Exactly. But we went through the Salt Market
where old Nicol Jarvie lived, any how."

" The thing in the cathedral I should specially have
liked to see is the crypt. That, they say, is the most
imposing in the kingdom."

" I don't care about seeing any more of such places
myself. I tell you, I believe in having graveyards out
of doors, under the trees, and where there's air."

Next morning, after a walk around George's Square,
we took the train for London. As we travelled southward, the lands in Lanark rose into hills, and in Ayr,
to the east and southeast, into mountains. Less fertile
obviously than the eastern shore, yet the crops showed a
thrifty population. Anything for a living, Jim pro-
pounded, as we passed along through the towns of Ayr,
in some of which, as Mauchline and Crumnoch, the

chief manufactures were snuff boxes. He had no fancy for the weed in that shape; but that was none of his business; and he did'nt care who had, especially when it gives a living to so many poor people. To get that out of this sort of land was an up-hill business. No wonder Bob Burns, after plowing all his life, looked out for a little office. "I've read a good deal about this county. It's better for farming now than it was in Burns' time, though no great things yet. That rich man—what's his name?—the Duke of Portland. He has done much for it by his extensive drainings. This county has a better system of artificial draining than any in the country. What mountains are those away over yonder on our right? It's a bigger country than I thought. Oh, I see now by the map, they are the Hills of Arran, on the other side of the Firth of Clyde."

As we passed along, I thought, and I made my companion interested in Border Minstrelsy. Of the ballads I recited, he said he liked best that of *Kirkconnell lee*, and wished, when we were rushing by Kirkconnell, that we had time to visit the churchyard where are the graves, side by side, of Fair Helen and her lover, who died on the banks of the Kirtle so long ago.

"Stop right there," he said, in the midst of my recitation of *Lord Lovel*. "Need'nt think I know nothing of those old fellows. Why, I can *sing* that one."

Then he lifted his voice high and sang the four remaining stanzas:

So he ordered the grave to be openéd wide,
    And the shroud be turnéd down,
And there he kisséd her clay-cold lips
    Till the tears came trickling down, down, down,
    Till the tears came trickling down.

15

Lady Nancy she died, it might be, to-day,
  Lord Lovel he died as to-morrow;
Lady Nancy she died out of pure, pure grief,
  Lord Lovel he died out of sorrow-orrow-orrow,
  Lord Lovel he died out of sorrow.

Lady Nancy was laid in St. Pancras's Church,
  Lord Lovel was laid in the choir;
And out of her bosom there grew a red rose,
  And out of Lord Lovel's a brier-ier-ier,
  And out of Lord Lovel's a brier.

They grew and they grew, to the church-steeple top,
  And then they could grow no higher;
And there they entwinéd in a true lover's knot,
  Eor all lovers true to admire-ire-ire,
  For all lovers true to admire.

In Dumfries pleasing was the contrast between the rugged country behind us with the gentle undulations along the Nith. At Langholm, we had a glimpse of Langholm Tower, once the castle of the Armstrongs, now of the Dukes of Buccleugh. At Dumfries town I alluded to the death of John Comyn by the hands of Robert Bruce.

"Such as that is all over with here now. You see little ships come up to this town to bring coal and slate, iron, tallow, hemp, bones, and carry off hats, stockings, leather, shoes, and even baskets."

"Well! if that is not a coming down from thoughts of claymore, and battle axe, and treading to the music of bag-pipes to—tallow, and stockings, and basket-making!"

"Coming down! thunder and lightning! they never commenced coming up in this country until they got to making baskets and such things, and having something to put in 'em. It was basket-making, as you call it, that kept from dying out what few of them had'nt got killed in the wars. As for those old bag-pipes, of all the music in this world, not even except bell-ringing, it is the poorest I noticed you, Phil, when they were blowing the everlasting things at Stirling; you looked as if you were trying your best to believe the music was good, but you could'nt make it out."

"Oh, I enjoyed it deeply, Jim. I was being carried back to the brave old days when—ah—"

"Yes, I think it *is*—ah! And as for stockings, these Highlanders never wore 'em because they could'nt afford to, and now, when they can, they don't, because their ancestors did'nt. But considering they don't wear breeches, I think stockings would come in now very well to hide some of their nakedness and a heap of their dirt."

Such and similar was the talk we had as we travelled along, through Ruthwell; and Cummurtrus, where we looked upon Kinmount House, the stately residence of the Marquis of Queensbury; and through the vale of Annan to Gretna Green. Jim expressed a curiosity to know the probable number of runaway matches joined here that had turned out well. I remarked that he was a great man for statistics. "Yes," he answered, "I always want to know *how many*. I never see a flock of geese that I don't try to count 'em, or, when I can't, guess at 'em. Somehow, this is a satisfaction to me. Well, here we part from old Scotland. Fare you well. Old lady: proud as you are of what you used to be with your claymores, and battle axes, and slogans, and coronachs, and what all, you are better off now with making snuff-boxes, and stockings, and baskets, and all such as

give your poor people a plenty to eat. Farewell, and
may you never go back on yourself, is the wish of yours
respectfully."

He waived an adieu backward as we passed the bridge.
More fertile and picturesque the country became as it
widened from the Solway. Passing through Carlisle,
while I dwelt upon King Arthur, the Round Table,
Adrian's Well, and the castle of William Rufus, my
companion talked of the dye, and prints, and leather,
and salmon trade of the new town. He calculated that
between us, we would get the most of what was worth
getting in this country, I the old and he the new.

"I'ts well you had me with you, Phil."

"No doubt about that, Jim. You've taught me
already more of the snuff-box and basket business than
I thought was possible to be in them."

"And you—if you would study more about such
things, you'd be a richer man, and—no, you are right,
and you suit me exactly, Phil. You are making me
notice the things which Emily and the girls told me I
had to see and tell 'em about. You better believe I'll
talk to 'em right about Ellen's Isle, and Dunbarton,
and the claymore, and all those old fellows. Still, I like
to find out, as I go along, what it is that makes the pot
boil."

More lovely yet the prospect from Carlisle to Penrith.
On the east and on the west, beyond the valleys and the
lower hills, were the Fells, and we could descry in the
west, towering high above all, Skiddaw. Penrith lies
snugly in the vale of the Edmont and the Lowther,
while on the neighboring heights are Brougham and
Eden Halls, and Dacre Castle. Crossing the Edmont
into Westmoreland, gliding along between the Lowther

and the tributary waters of the Eden, we looked out with continual delight upon the increasing fells and mountains.

"What a people these English are, Phil. It makes no difference what sort of region they live in, they are going to conquer it. See, on this map, what little ground is fit for cultivation. Not a tenth is plowed, and not a quarter fit for pasturage. Yet, see the large towns where money is made every year by the million, Appleby, Orton, Kendal, Kirkby, Ambleside, Tibay, Low Gill—what's his name? Still a fellow can call 'em. Out of these lakes they export fish, and from the mountains they get granite, slate, marble, copper, and lead; and what else would you suppose? Why, geese; geese by the hundred thousand. And now I see, we are leaving the valley of the Lowther, and getting into that of the Line, and at Kendal will enter that of the Ken, which widens into the Bay of Moncambe."

Again in Lancashire. Farming and cattle raising to Jim's content, and manufacturing, and everything else. None of your Lancasters and Gaunts now. John of Gaunt's castle, like that at York, holds business-offices. No more fighting for Roses, old friend, but working for victuals and good clothes, and houses and fat cattle, and living on till it is the good Lord's time to die, instead of falling down with daylight put through their bodies with sword or musket-ball. We don't stop at Lancaster; no, not until we get to Preston. Priest-town, eh? of old, because of the number of priests that used to live here. A solid town, he should say, from the looks, and much bigger than he thought. Three hundred thousand bales of cotton a year manufactured here. "I tell you what, Phil, we've been pretty well through this country, have'nt we?"

15*

"Rigodunum!" said I, closing my book.

"Rigger-what?"

"Rigodunum. That is the name of the old Roman town, on the ruins of which the present one arose."

"That's another bit of history that had entirely escaped my recollection. You would'nt have supposed, would you, that I'd have forgot as notorious a fact as that? Ah, a treacherous memory, as old Jack Pool told his brethren at Big Bethel when they reminded him of his promise not to get drunk any more before Christmas. Well, we'll let old Riggy depart in peace. I think a little chicken and beer and Scotch bread will do you good, Phil. A man that can think right along here of Rigodunum shows his stomach is empty."

He opened the basket and uncorked the bottles. We ate, and drank, and smoked at our leisure. The re mainder of our journey to London, as we had passed over most of the ground before, we spent in comparing our impressions from what we had seen in our rapid circuit. Jim said it made him a little homesick to turn his back on old Georgia again; but, oh! it was such a consolation to know how faithfully he was taking care of his feeble old friend.

"Just so."

"Adzactly."

CHAPTER XIV.

FTER much consideration as to a route for a brief journey to the Continent, we concluded to pass at once to Belgium, and after a visit to the Rhine and Switzerland, return by Paris. At the station in London, when we were about taking the train for Harwich, a trifling incident occurred that made known to us a system of travel of which, although considerably practiced hitherto, we were ignorant. We had already selected our carriage, stowed away our luggage, and were walking up and down the platform when we observed a short, brisk German, plainly dressed, wearing a small leathern valise at his side, which was strapped over his shoulders. He went about hurriedly among the crowd, speaking occasionally first to one then another, darting here and there as if in search of something of momentous importance. Those whom he addressed would follow him implicitly to the different carriages and be shoved in, while he would sing out, "Dish way, dish way, you, here," and "Dare, dish way!" to others to whom he was beckoning. Jim was amused by his actions, and remarked that, considering his size and looks, the little Dutchman seemed to have a surprising amount of business; and that in fact, by gracious, he believed he was actually shipping people. A moment afterwards, the man, returning near where we stood, and looking first upon a paper which he held in his hand, and, then around him, suddenly darted upon Jim, and seizing him by the coat-tails, asked:

"Arrah you a Cuke?"

Jim recoiled a step in blank amazement.

"Arrah you a Cuke?" persisted the German, with much earnestness.

" Well, now, my friend, you are a good deal smaller man than I am, and then I rather think you ain't in your senses. I don't care about raising a fuss with you, because I'm a long way from home, and you are too little a scrub for me to take the trouble to learn you some manners. But I recommend you to be off, and—"

"I pegs parten; I taught you was vone off te Cukes."

The rapidity with which all this transpired prevented me from explaining what, I had just ascertained from a bystander, was the man's business.

" What upon earth does the little idiot mean?" asked Jim.

Seeing me smiling, the ridiculousness of his own position occurred to him, and he laughed aloud. Yet he continued looking inquiringly at the retreating German:

" Is the fellow a fool?"

" Not he: far from it."

" My opinion is that he is, or, at least, out of his senses for once. I've travelled a good deal in my time. True, I'm further from home than I ever was before, and, maybe, am coming down in my looks more than I was thinking; but this is the first time that I was ever taken for a cook."

I could not bear to laugh at him further, and handed to him a circular of *Cook's Tourist Agency* that I had just gotten, in which it was to be seen that this person was one of that gentleman's agents, and on the eve of starting with a party of travellers on his tickets; and that he had mistaken Jim for one of those whom he was to conduct.

"Is that so?" said he, humbly. "Well, no; the little fellow ain't a fool. If there's any fool in the case —I always was too quick. I might have known—" he hesitated to pay himself the compliment.

"Certainly. And yet you know, Jim, that they have some cooks, or at least waiters, over here that are very fine-looking men."

"Oh, get out. I owe you one, and I owe that little fellow one more. Did you see how I jumped when he came at me? Blamed if I did'nt feel like I've felt sometimes when a little fice snapped at my legs. A little more, and I should have given him a kick, which I would'nt grudge a thousand dollars that I did'nt."

Jim was delighted with what it was easy to see, the agricultural advantages and industries of the county of Essex, which we crossed from southwest to northeast on the dividing line between the picturesque, rising, wooded country on the left, and the low-lying, well-drained arable land on the right.

"Just look at that wheat. I've heard of the Essex wheat and the Essex calves. They raise here thousands of calves and sheep for the London market. Great quantities of saffron, too, and hops, caraway and such. This county is the principal kitchen-garden for London. A big town, and a big garden. London keeps down all the towns in this part of the country. This is a right nice-looking little place, though; what do you call it? Chelmsford? Two more *rivers*, I see, the Chelmer and the Cann. They call every little spring branch over

here a river. I see they put down nine for this county.
All of 'em together would'nt make one as big as the
Savannah at Augusta."

The rush for berths at Harwich was great. But Jim,
with his usual good management, succeeded at once in
making terms with the steward, and, as usual, pleaded
the advanced age and infirmities of his old friend.

"Pretty good capital, Phil, for us both. You keep
quiet. You need'nt be afraid of being taken to be too
much older than I am. Besides, you don't expect to
marry in this country, no how."

"One would suppose you did from the manner in
which you vaunt your youth, and propose to fight young
men."

"That reminds me—" and he walked away. A few
moments afterwards, when the steamer was under weigh,
I saw him and the little German sitting down together
on one of the benches with a bottle of beer between
them, tipping their glasses, smoking cigars, and chatting
in a lively manner. Approaching where they were, Jim
rose and introduced me to—ah, Mr. Snapper?

"Schnauffer. Your fren was trought tat I call him
vone cuke, te cuke tat cuke te beeve and te sheeken. It
was ver funny."

"You have quite a number of Cooks with you," I
answered.

"Saxteen, Americ, Scost, Inglis, Wels. Te most
Americ. Tay spheak not te Ooropen langidge, and it is
more convenabble tat I go vit tem."

He showed us his route, and one of his books of
tickets and coupons. It is certainly a method of travelling convenient to those who speak no language but
English, and could be satisfied with the hotels to which

they are carried, the enforced companionship throughout of those with whom they start together, and the will of the guide as to the times of sojourning at the different places on the route.

We retired early and slept satisfactorily. When I awoke the next morning, Jim was already up and on deck. I rose, dressed myself, and joined him.

"Everything looks outlandish to me. The very ships, so black and flat, don't seem natural. We are already in the river you say Antwerp is on. What do you call it?"

"The Scheldt."

"You may call it that, or anything else you please for me. I don't expect to get anything right in pronouncing what little of that business I shall have to do over here. What a flat country; a dead level with the sea. But ain't there many a windmill? No wonder. Any quantity of wind always about to move 'em. Plenty of water, too, as to that, but it's got no fall. I feel like I was already a thousand miles further off than I was this time yesterday. I want to get through this part of the trip as soon as possible. You are the only man, Phil, on top of the ground that I would ever have come with this far from home."

The sight of the ancient city revived his spirits much. It does present a fine view to the approach with its immense basin; crowded with ships, and its numerous, lofty spires. Jim kept close to my side when the boat landed. Passing our luggage without difficulty before the custom-house officers, we went ashore and took a carriage for the hotel.

"Easier than I expected," said Jim; "what did that fellow ask you?"

. " Whether we had any tobacco or cigars."

" Tobacco and cigars! why that's what they asked us at Liverpool. They must be the main things they smuggle over here. But, now, do let me ask you: did you ever see such horses since you were born? I've heard of the Flemish horses; but these are a hickory over what I expected. Look at those two bays hitched to that wagon or cart, or whatever kind of a whimididdle it is. They'd weigh over two thousand pounds apiece. And what a load. A yoke of oxen could'nt draw as much, nor seem more awkward. They don't look as if they could *trot* at all. And those collars! They must have cheap leather to waste it that way in collars. I tell you everything over here looks outlandish to me."

Leaving our luggage at the hotel, we spent the couple of hours before lunch in driving around.

" Pretty solid buildings," said Jim, after we had seen the Exchange, the Hotel de Ville, the Maison Ansiatic, and the palace erected for the occasional sojourn of the royal family. " Better than I expected to see. As for this street, Place de—something—Meir, it's the prettiest we've seen anywhere. I should say, though, that this town isn't as big as it used to be. It looks, especially at the end behind us, as if its been worn out in that direction and then cut off."

" That's just the fact. Antwerp used to contain two hundred thousand. Now it has very many less. The towns on the coast have competed with it. It used to have a monopoly of the commerce on the waters of the North Sea."

"All right. I'm against monopolies of all kinds, for towns or folks. Let everybody have a fair chance."

I persuaded him to enter with me into the cathedral.

"I'll go with you," said he, "to a few of 'em; but I tell you, Phil, they're too tiresome and solemn for me to spend much of my time at."

He was, however, more interested than I expected him to be. Indeed, few persons could view without interest this great edifice, and especially those pictures that adorn its walls. He looked long at *The Descent from the Cross*, and remarked, after we went out, that it was the most natural looking picture of that kind that he had yet seen.

"Those faces look more like real people than any of them in the pictures of what you call the old masters."

"That is because Rubens painted from living persons. Some of the figures are portraits of his relatives and friends."

"I don't know so well about that," said he, with a somewhat troubled look.

"Nor I either."

We had dismissed the coachman on entering, and now but for Jim's clearness of head in the matter of locality we should have had some difficuly in finding the hotel. As it was, after winding here and there, often against my remonstrance that we were going precisely wrong, we made our way in good time.

"I can't speak their language, Phil; but I'm as hard to fool about places as a pig."

"A pig?"

"Yes, sir, a pig. There isn't an animal on the face of the earth, not even excepting a pigeon, that has as clear ideas about places as a pig."

Not having time for the discussion of this point, we hastily took our lunch and were on the train for Brussels. When we were fairly out of Antwerp, Jim began his remarks upon the country. 16

"A mighty difference between this and England—poplars instead of oaks, poplars, poplars—Lombardy poplars! and in straight rows. No hills either; no branches and creeks. Give me England and Scotland before a dead level like this. But this people know how to work it. By ditching and underdraining they've knocked the bottom out from the crawfish and tadpoles. There isn't anything like getting used to a thing."

As we traveled, the country became more picturesque; yet the long, double rows of poplars could not compensate for the clumps of wide-spreading oaks on English hill-sides, and the winding willow shades on the clear brooks. As we passed through Malines, Jim remarked that he had never heard of that place.

" But it is an important town," said I, "and bears to Belgium the same relation that Clapham sustains to England. One may take the cars here for any place in the country. That Cathedral is seven hundred years old. Rubens' picture of the *Last Supper* is in that; his *Adoration of the Magi* is in that of St. John's. In the Church of the Recollets is *The Crucifixion* of Vandyke.''

In Brussels, at the *Hotel de la Clos*.

Jim felt as if he was further and further from home as we sat, after dinner, in the court looking around at the quaint walls and windows, the flower-pots and shrubbery, and the small aquarium in the corner near the door of the dining-room, and listened to the strange mixture of French and Flemish of the busy domestics.

"So little like old Georgia. Such talking! Even if a body could pick up a few of their words, these people talk so fast they would all run into one. I always like to talk with people whenever I travel. I shall have to put up with you, Phil, until we cross this channel again."

I consoled him with the assurance that he would meet many Americans, and those among Europeans who could speak English.

The next morning he joined the Cook party, who had reached Brussels later, in a visit to Waterloo, while I went to St. Gudule, the Churches of Notre Dame, des Victoires, de la Chapelle, and the Hotel de Ville, wherein the abdication of Charles V took place in the year 1555. After his return we drove around, seeing, among others, the palace of Laeken, once the residence of Josephine, where Napoleon signed the declaration of war against Prussia.

Brussels is certainly beautiful—most beautiful, next to Edinburgh, and surpassing it in public walks. The Boulevards with their lime trees, the *Allée Verte* along the canal from the town to the Scheldt, the park, Royal palace, and the superb public offices, inspired us with admiration. Jim was running over with recollections of the sights at Waterloo. I tried to speak of the revolution of 1830, which resulted in Belgian independence and the elevation to the throne of Leopold of Saxe Coburg. But he came at me with Waterloo, whose great battle he had never fully understood until to day, when he went over the very ground. So we made short speeches apiece. As we passed a shop where the manufacture of laces was carried on, at his suggestion, we alighted and entered. Entertaining as this was, yet it was painful to look upon these poor women as they bent over their tasks, and with strained eyes brought almost in contact with the gossamer threads, they moved back and forth with marvellous rapidity, the numerous black, wooden handles that dangled upon the boards.

The next morning early we were off again. Jim was quite satisfied to diverge from the party of the Little Dutchman.

"Too much following like sheep. *He* did the thinking and the talking. It's convenient, but I like to think for myself, even if I can't tongue it out. Besides, he don't talk well enough for one man, let alone fifteen."

At Louvain we turned abruptly to the right, and sped along the fine country to the southeast. The approach to Liege through the fertile valleys of the Meuse and the Ourthe bringing us to the sudden summits of Sainte Walburg and Le Cornillon was enchanting. Jim said here was another Birmingham, but not half as healthy. Did anybody ever see such high houses and such narrow streets? The sun never gets into some of them. And what was I straining to see with my glasses—"

"St. Denis, St. Croix, St. Martin, and St. Bartolemy, and the cathedral. You have read Quentin Durward, have'nt you, Jim?"

"Certainly. I forgot that some of the scenes are laid here."

"The present Palais de Justice was the bishop's palace in the times of the Dukes of Burgundy."

"Those old fellows, according to Scott, made a mistake in taking up with the Wild Boar of—what was it?"

"Ardennes. This whole country used to be the football of the tyrants of Europe, and, you know, is yet the fighting ground for the neighboring great powers. But the people, who can't help that and who are naturally fond of peace, take the best care of themselves possible until the wars are over, go to work again, get richer and richer from all their resources, and now Belgium is the most populous country in Europe."

At Pepinster, we turned to the northeast, where another lovely valley appeared, that of the Vesdres, with its background of dark green hills. Shortly after passing Verviers, we entered the territory of Prussia, but without knowing this fact when we changed cars. Before starting off again, a stern-looking, full-bearded man, dressed in brown uniform, suddenly thrusting his head through the window, addressed to us some words in curt and apparently threatening tones. I guessed at his office, and, taking down my valise, started to open it. The man who brought him there, and who had acted as guard on the train we had left, showed his remembrance of Jim's civility in giving him a glass of beer not long before, by speaking to the officer in an assuring tone, and he immediately left us.

"What in this world did that fellow want, Phil?"

"He is, doubtless, a Prussian custom house officer."

"Upon my word, when he began—I was looking out of the window over there—I thought it was a dog growling at you; and when I turned and saw that hairy face, I was'nt much better off. He must have been cussing about something. If the balance of the people over here have no better manners than that, the sooner we get out of this country the better. Let's do the best we can with this lunch and Rhine wine. I've got my native appetite yet, if I have lost my speech."

A soothing influence upon us both, these, and cigars afterwards. Jim sat with his legs in the window as complacently as if he had been in his own piazza, and surveying his own cornfields. I told him after a while that he must stir about, as we were approaching classic ground.

"Explain yourself," said he, lazily shifting his cigar to the other corner of his mouth.

"This is Aix-la-Chapelle, the famous Aquae of the Romans. A little farther on, that little town, Duren

16*

on the Roer, which you see on the map, was the ancient
Marcodurum. The Emperor Charlemagne, destroyed
that town; this was his favorite residence.

"Right nice-looking old burg. Trace her back, Phil,
and tell me another time. That wine is first-rate, but it
has made me sleepy."

"What! sleep here in the very presence of the Roman
legions, of Charlemagne and his Paladins, of Tacitus
and his *Germania*, and within half an hour of the Rhine
and *Civitas Ubiorum?*"

"Never better; those very names make me go it
easier."

While he was taking his nap, I mused undisturbed on
the eventful history of the country. In half an hour,
this day's journey came to its end, and we were at the
Hotel Hollande in Cologne. Having at our disposal
only that afternoon, we made the most of our time.
Jim's observations of the old city seemed peculiar. I
shall let him speak for himself.

"Phil," he said that night, "my ideas of churches
have got turned upside down since we've been over here.
Now a church, I always thought, was a house—(big or
little, according to the size of the town or the member-
ship)—was a house where people could go to meeting of
a Sunday morning, hear a good, bad, or indifferent
sermon, and then shut up the house until meeting-day
comes around again. Over here they go to work building churches, like they were building towns. Now, the
idea of being six or seven hundred years at this old
cathedral, and, by gracious, not done with it yet. They
first put up one part. After a while, somebody comes
along, and runs another part across it, or alongside of
it. Two or three hundred years afterwards, somebody

else pieces on to it what he calls a chapel, and other people piece on more chapels, until it is perfectly astonishing how big and rambling it will get to be after a while. Why, a fellow might get lost—you would every time—in that building mixed up with those chapels and pillars. I counted a hundred of *them,* some of 'em ten feet thick. And then there don't seem to be any particular time for holding meetings, preaching or prayer meetings. People go in at all times, many of 'em one at a time, and everybody appears to have his prayers all to himself. But ain't they rich? But now, what good it does to keep so many jewels and so much silver and gold in a church I can't understand. We must have seen hundreds of thousands of dollars worth there to day. Who does it belong to? That's the question. And what good does it do locked up there? I know it isn't any of my business; but I would like to know what good it does, or what they expect it to do, this dead capital. But the having graveyards in 'em, that gets me the worst of all. I can't feel reconciled to people being buried in houses, and being walked over, and especially having their bones kept to show to people. They may be The Three Kings,* as they call 'em, but I've no fancy for looking at the head, even of a king, when it's off his shoulders. But as for that matter, don't that other old church, St. Ursula † take the lead in bones? Literally lined with 'em. Eleven thousand virgins! and that other one with the The-

---

* In the chapel of the *Three Kings* or *Magi* whose bones were brought there from Constantinople by the Empress Helena.

† In honor of St. Ursula, the English princess who, according to the legend, on her return from Rome, whither she had been on a pilgrimage, was murdered near Cologne with her 11,000 virgins, whose bones are preserved in cases placed around the church.

bans! ‡ I'm not going to follow you any more into
such places. I've got so confused already, that I'm
getting, it seems to me, to forget what churches were
meant for. Well, well, it's a curious old town, take it
by and large; and the dirtiest I should *never* wish to
see. I should think, with all the riches in their cathedral, they might raise money enough somewhere to have
some of the biggest of this dirt taken up and hauled
away. Did anybody ever run up against such smells?
They'll have to make more Cologne water than they do
to help that cause, and they say they make it here by
the thousand. Maybe they send it all away, and don't
use any themselves. No wonder it was invented here.
That old fellow, I expect, lived in one of the dirtiest
streets in the town, and learned how to make something
that would take the everlasting smell out of his nostrils.
It was a relief to get out of town this hot evening, and
take that boat up to the zoological gardens. They are
delightful. I've no doubt the people go there in such
crowds mostly to get rid of the smells in the town.
They work all day, and get their lungs and noses full
of 'em, and then go out there for a little fresh, clean
air before going to bed. That part of the trip here I
enjoyed in spite of that rascal of a guide   I knew he
was a scamp as soon as, without our asking him, he
took us to that cologne-water shop, and I noticed him
give a wink to the store-keeper. You'd have bought
there if I had'nt pinched you. I knew they did'nt have
the best article there, just from the looks of both of
'em. That guide won't forget us soon, I bet."

‡ st. Gereon! Dedicated to the Theban Legion with their captains,
Gereon and Gregory, who were martyred there in the time of Diocletian. Several hundreds of their skulls are arranged around the choir
under gilded arabesques.

The officers at the hotel were certainly not select in the matter of the guide whom they furnished to us. Jim had whispered to me at the cologne-water shop that he was not to be trusted. So we left without purchasing and went to another place. At the gardens we listened to the finest music that I ever have heard from a band of entirely wind instruments. They played several pieces of my selection. After which I sent, at Jim's suggestion, the guide to the musicians to join us in a glass of beer. In settling for it, I handed several pieces of money. Jim narrowly watched the guide as he made the change. The musicians having left us to return to the stand, I was about to put into my pocket the money returned to me, when Jim broke in thus:

"A few more of them *grochen*, or whatever you call 'em. You have'nt given back the right change. If my friend is willing to submit to the cheat, I ain't."

The man at first looked somewhat defiant, and then began to argue.

"Stuff and nonsense! I don't know what the Dutch for that is. But you understand me. Fork over the needful."

He put his hand to his head and frowned upon the money thoughtfully, and said:

"Yath, yath. I believe—"

"Yath! Yath! No doubt about it. There, that's it. Put it in your pocket, Phil. And now we've got sense enough surely to find our way back by ourselves, and may let this fellow go. See here, my honest friend," (turning to the man,) "you see this watch? We hired you by the hour. You've been with us for exactly three hours and twenty-five minutes to a second. Here's the money for four hours. Now, you can go. None of your grumbling. Off with you, or I will have you arrested for the money you kept when you bought us the cigars. You see that if I don't understand your language, I know some of your ways."

We found afterwards that there was a general complaint among tourists concerning these guides (*touters*) at Cologne.

Our chamber was within a stone's throw of the Rhine. For some time after Jim retired, I sat in the window looking out and listening to its waters.

"Suppose you talk me to sleep, Phil, about this town."

"Well, I was just thinking of the eventful destiny of her who was born here, and in honor of whom the town was named and a colony established."

"You don't mean that the town was named after somebody that was born in it? That looks like putting the cart before the horse."

"Yes, indeed. This was the old *Oppidum Ubiorum.*"

"You don't tell me so. That name needed a change, certain."

"While Germanicus was here stationed to keep down the fierce tribes that Agrippa had transported across the river, his daughter Agrippina, by his wife of the same name, grand-daughter of Augustus Cæsar, was born."

"Upon my word, I thought that woman was born at —somewhere else—a little farther up the river—or down it, I disremember which. Aggy, who, did you say?"

"Agrippina, daughter of Germanicus, grand-daughter of Vipsanius Agrippa, and great grand-daughter of Augustus."

"Gracious me! But I don't see how you get *Cologne* out of any of those names."

"I'll tell you. After the death of her husbands, Cneus

Domitius Ahenobarbus and Crispus Passienus, Agrippina married—"

"You don't mean to say she married again after bury ing all those men?"

"There were only two of them."

"I thought it was about five. Old Aggy seemed to like the married life. Go ahead; I have'nt heard better talking to put a man to sleep in some time. Who did the widow catch next?"

"The Emperor Claudius, her uncle."

"Her *uncle?* Get out! Was'nt there any law against that?"

"Yes; but in their case it was avoided by a decree of the Senate."

"That did'nt keep it from being a sin and a shame."

"And then she prevailed upon her husband to enlarge the town into a colony, and had it named Colonia Aggrippinensis."

"That was—very fine. How did they—get on after—"

"Badly. Claudius had already murdered his former wife, Messalina. After his marriage with Agrippina, she prevailed upon him to set aside from the succession his own son Britannicus, in favor of her son Nero. When Claudius intimated his purpose of restoring Britannicus she poisoned him with mushrooms. After Nero's accession, in her ambition to control him, she overreached herself, and he had her assassinated in her villa on the Lucrine Lake."

The measured breathing from Jim's bed announced that he was asleep. I sat some time musing upon the ancient and mediæval history of the place and went to sleep at last, thankful for having seen the great Dom, made, through centuries of pious endeavors, so fit for the worship of God.

CHAPTER XV.

N hour's ride next morning in the new part of Cologne and a stroll in the fine gardens without the walls, tended to subdue some of my companion's hostility. But, he urged, that of all the towns he had seen that which had "old walls" around them, this was the one from which it would be most sensible to have them removed, so as to give room for some of the worst of the noisome odors to get out of it. At ten o'clock we were on the boat for Mayence. At once I opened my map, a "Panorama of the Rhine," which I had purchased the day before.

"You look, from the length of that map, as if you had a good long geography lesson to get."

"Yes, sir; I'm going to learn all I can to-day about this river from Cologne to Mayence."

"Go ahead; tell me something occasionally which you think they'd be apt to ask me about at home, but not too much. My head's pretty well packed now, and not otherwise in very good order."

Among the Americans and English on board he soon made acquaintances. Occasionally, as he passed by me in his promenades on the deck, he would address some remark of playful encouragement of my studies or of praise of the scenery around us.

"Stick to it, my son; I know it's hard, for I've been all along there and got many a whipping. Still you can get it if you don't get discouraged and give it up, but will keep at it. And then you'll be so smart, you know, and feel so good that you had it to do. Pretty fair farming country this; and though there ain't as many windmills as in Belgium, still there's a plenty, I should say, for all reasonable neighborhood purposes. But, hello! here's a considerable of a town over yonder to the right. What is it? and tell me an item or two; I hope it ain't Roman. By the way, I went to sleep sure enough while you were talking about that widow. Those big old names were as good as a dose of laudanum."

"You don't need laudanum nor any other soporific when your head gets upon a pillow. That is Bonn. Read what the guide book says about it."

"No, sir; no time to be reading books now, and no great fancy for reading 'em very much any time, I'm ashamed to say—at least on such subjects as old towns. You were to do up the reading over here, you know."

"Bonn is not a large place, but a very old and important one. All I can say about it now is, that the Münster was started by the Roman Empress Helena, that a garrison is here, an observatory, a university, and botanical gardens."

"You may put off about the Roman empress until to-night, bed time."

"Here's a little bit of romance, Jim; you'll read that at least. We will come to the scene presently."

I gave him the guide-book and pointed out the account of the unhappy Roland, the remains of whose castle, Rolandseck, after passing the Seven Mountains, we reached.

17

"Poor fellow! But I should'nt have done any such thing as that. When I got back from the wars and found the girl, hearing I was dead, had gone into that convent—but look here, man, would'nt they have let her off when they knew that she had gone there under a mistake of the facts?"

"No, SIR; she was as dead to him there in Nunnenwerth as if she had been in her grave."

"Well, I should'nt have settled on that hill, just to be able to see all the time where she was, but I'd have gone off as far as I could get."

"And married some other woman, doubtless."

"Not improbable. However, that would have looked mean, and nothing good ever comes out of meanness. It was a hard case all around."

Surely there is no where else so enchanting scenery as that from Bonn to Coblentz. The country itself, aside from historic and romantic associations, seemed eminently suited as a theatre for stirring events. The variations of mountain and vale, the remains of fortresses apparently impregnable by all assaults except those of time, united with these the memory of Roman, German, and French prowess, of Paladin and Crusader, are so crowded upon the mind as one travels up the famous river that it is a hard day's work to note them all. At Oberwinter one has barely time to take that fine view backward to Rolandseck, Nunnenwerth, Drachenfels, and the rest of the Siebenberg before he must turn to the new beauties which lie in profusion on either side before him. To the right, in rapid sequence, Unkelbach, St. Apollinaris-Kirch, Remagen, the Valley of the Aar, Rheineck, Andernach; on the left, Unkel, Ochanfels, Linz, Neuweid, Bendorf, the Island of Neiderwerth, and many others.

"No wonder they call it strong, and are proud of it," Jim said, as we passed along by the base of Ehrenbreitstein, and looked up the long, steep, rocky ascent. "Cannon nor trick can take that, nor famine either, for they say the magazines and cisterns hold supplies enough to last a hundred thousand men three years."

"It is a great fortress; but yonder is a building at the confluence of the Rhine and the Moselle more interesting to me than that. It is the Church of St. Castor, founded in the ninth century. That old church has seen many a dynasty rise and fall from Charlemagne downwards. It was there, after his death, that his grandsons met in order to divide among themselves his vast dominions in Germany, Italy, and France—the great empire of the West"

' I think they might have taken some other place besides a church to settle up the estate. Coblentz! It's a curious name, but a sight easier to call than the most of them we've seen to-day."

"Coblentz is a corruption of the Roman *confluentia,* so called from the confluence of the two rivers."

"It sounds different now. Been through so many mouths, and German mouths at that, it's been smartly *chawed.* There's the dinner-bell. You won't go down? All right. I'll send you a beefsteak and half bottle of Moselle. Let me know when I get to Bingen. I promised Jake that I'd think of him when I got to 'Bingen on the Rhine,' God bless him."

"You will have plenty of time for that and get your dinner also. But would you, just for one dinner, Jim Rawls, would you miss seeing Stotzenfels, Oberlahnstein, Braubach, Rheinfels, the Lurlie, Schonberg, and especially the brothers Sternberg and Liebenstein?"

"Those two last were brothers, were they? What kin were the balance? No, sir, I give up my dinner for no places with names like that." And off he went. He came up just as we were nearing that curious structure in the middle of the river above Caub, called the Pfalz."

"In the name of common sense, what is that confounded thing?"

"It was built," this pamphlet says, "several hundred years ago for the purpose of having a convenient place for collecting tribute from passing vessels; but read that."

"In 1194, the Emperor Henry VI wished to marry the daughter of Count Palatine Conrad to one of his friends, but the young princess had already gained the affections of Henry of Brunswick. The father, dreading the emperor's wrath, would not consent to the alliance, but caused a tower to be built in the middle of the river below Bacharach, where he kept his prisoner. Her mother, however, secretly aided the Prince of Brunswick in gaining admittance to the tower, where his union with the princess was privately solemnized. When the princess was about to give birth to a child, her mother disclosed the affair to her husband, who, finding his opposition no longer availing, capriciously passed a law that all future Countesses Palatine should repair to the castle to await their accouchements. Such is the ancient and improbable tradition connected with the Pfalz, whence it also derives its name."

"No telling what young folks won't do, nor where they won't go when they take a notion to marry. Where did the old man live?"

"Just beyond the bend yonder, to the right, at Stahlek, the old castle."

"All come from meddling with young people's matches. My notion is, if you can't persuade 'em you need'nt try to drive 'em. We are getting into the great wine region, I heard at dinner."

"Yes. Just behind Stahleck yonder is Bacharach, celebrated for its wine."

Passing, in succession, Furstenberg, Heinberg, Falkenberg, Rheinstein and Ehrenfels, we reached Bingen.

"Is that another Piffals?" asked Jim, pointing at the *Meurth Thurm* in the middle of the river near the landing.

"Another what?"

"Piffals. Was'nt that what you called that concern back yonder where the young woman got married to that fellow unbeknownst?"

"Pfalz."

"I don't see much difference, and I bet you don't call it right. Is this another one?"

"No, that's the *Mouse Tower*, so called from a legend that, in former times, a very despotic archbishop was devoured there by mice. It was used, at one time, as the Pfalz, for collecting toll. Now it is a sort of lighthouse. You see how narrow the river is here? Rushing down those high mountains, it forms this, what is called the Bingerloch, over which it is dangerous for two boats to pass each other. The watchman who occupies it signals to any boats that may be meeting, so that they may avoid collision."

"That's sensible. A pretty town. It will do old Jake good to know I've seen it. Poor little fellow! There's another river coming in just above yonder."

"It is the Nahe; the old ruin is the Klopp, built by Drusus."

17*

"Of the same set that you put me to sleep with last night?"

"The same. He was the son of Livia, wife of Augustus and her first husband, Tiberius Nero. Augustus fell in love with her, and divorcing his own wife, Scribonia, took Livia away from her husband three months before her third son was born, and married her."

"What! Take a fellow's wife when she's borne him two children and pretty nearly three? No wonder that old empire broke down. Things can't last when God Almighty's laws are run over in that style."

Near Rudesheim, the river suddenly turned towards the north, and we were now at the beginning of the Rhinegau, the great wine region of the Rhine. Here I handed Jim another legend to read, that of Bromserberg, once the property of the old knights of Rudesheim. It ran thus:

"One of these knights who had distinguished himself by destroying a dragon in the Holy Land, and had escaped out of the hands of the Saracens, vowed that if he ever returned to Rudesheim he would dedicate his only daughter, Gisela, to the Church. The latter, during her father's absence, had formed an attachment to a young knight of a neighboring castle, and heard with dismay her father's fatal vow. The old Crusader was inexorable, and Gisela, in a fit of despair, threw herself from the tower into the Rhine. According to popular belief, her form still hovers about the ruined tower, and her lamentations are heard mingling with the roarings of the wind."

"It appears," was Jim's comment, "that the females in this region of country had bad luck in their love affairs; some of 'em getting to be nuns under a mistake, some made so against their wills, and some shut up in a box in the river to keep 'em from marrying according to their own choice. That last one had better married unbeknownst, like the other, rather than kill herself. But I suppose she could'nt get out. Meddling again. The old man thought he would do a great thing for the Church by devoting his daughter instead of himself. That is a business that ain't stopped yet. Plenty of people nowadays who think if they can make other people do right, they need'nt take any great pains with their own conduct. A great mistake, but a mighty common one."

The night closed in upon us after passing the Castle of Johannesberg, and soon we were landed at Mayence. Jim said that he intended to dine with me, because he felt so lonesome at the table on the boat without me that it took away his appetite. And now we must have a bottle of Johannesberger. We owed it to the satisfaction of having seen the vines that made it; we owed it to the country generally, and we owed it to ourselves. We had opened upon the great Rheingau with the Rudesheimer, we would now have a Johannesberger, and to-morrow we would wind up with a Steinberger.

"People that can afford to drink such wine as this," he continued, when we had opened the bottle and tasted, "ought to be a good people. Isn't it glorious all the way down? If I did'nt know myself, I should feel like making a speech."

After dinner we lighted our cigars and repaired to the smoking-room, and in spite of his pretended hostility to old things, we talked long upon the scenes through which we had passed during the day, and their history, ancient and modern. Next morning after a drive to the barracks, the cathedral, the confluence of the Rhine and Main, the fruit market, and Gutenburg monument, we took the road again.

"This is the cleanest-looking town I've seen yet in Germany," said Jim, as we were passing through Darmstadt.

"Yes. It was of small importance until the Archduke Ludwig gave it a start. The new part, built within the last twenty or thirty years, is larger than the old. That monument yonder was erected to his memory."

We had gone but a little way out of the town and turned squarely to the south, when, for the first time since we had left home, we saw a field of corn. The sight did us both good.

"Oh," said Jim, "if I could only get out and walk about in it, and feel of it, and hear the blades rustle, and catch a June-bug or two! How it does bring old Georgia to me! And, by the way, what splendid land it is for corn and wheat along this valley. What long mountain is that to the left?"

It was the Odenwald, and we were coursing down the Bergstrasse (mountain-road) between the Main and the Neckar. It was most pleasing to see the ripe wheatfields, the peasants reaping and harvesting the overflowing crops, and to lift our eyes anon above and beyond to the towering forest. After passing Weinheim, we diverged from the Odenwald, and, making a circuit by Ladensberg and Wiedrichsfeld, returned to it at Heidelberg. Here we stopped for three hours. Ordering lunch (to include, of course, trout from the Neckar), we hired a carriage for a brief inspection. We thought Heidelberg the prettiest of all towns of its size. At the head of the Valley of the Neckar, snugly ensconced between the surrounding eminences, the continuous green shades along its one prominent street impart a sweet coolness which the sun seems never to subdue. Passing by the university buildings in the Ludwig Platz, we first ascended to the Mulchencur, and returning, drove to the castle on the eminence opposite. Our time was too brief to allow us to view any but a comparatively small part of this, the hugest and grandest of all the ruins of Germany. In vain had many an army of besiegers attempted to destroy it. No wonder it was so long and so arduous to break down the power of the feudal lords, when they could hide themselves within walls that even gunpowder could only partially dislodge. As we drove by the university buildings again upon our return (which, as for age, Jim said showed for themselves), we saw several students walking along, some of whom were followed by dogs of a species such as we had never seen before.

"Did anybody ever see such dogs?" exclaimed Jim.

They seemed of the purest bull, but so extremely diminutive as not to weigh, I should say, over eight or ten pounds. Jim enquired about them of our host at the Schrieder, where we lunched.

"De shtoodens haf dem for combany in de valk, and dey make dem fight much. Yah? Day fight shtrong, dem leetle dog."

Our lunch was served in a veranda, in the rear of the hotel. Jim pronounced the trout delicious, but small, he should rather say, small but delicious. It would'nt do to bring out our bottle of Steinberger at the board of so polite a host. So we took one of his Hubberger.

"Well," said Jim, after we were on the move again, and we had fired up, "it's a beautiful little town. I notice, as we get down south, that they pay more attention to shade than we do. I'm glad we stopped here,

A beautiful little town. I say little, and it can't grow
much bigger, hemmed in, as it is, between the river and
these mountains. They jammed it in a snug little place,
and I don't wonder it's always been so hard to take.
That old castle is big enough though to make up for
the town. Some of those walls are twenty feet thick
and more, so that where they've been blown down by
powder they afford a defence still. That old wine hogs-
head took me; forty-nine thousand gallons. While they
were at it, they might have made it an even fifty. They
must have been good drinkers in those times before they
invented their lager beer. By the way, that was a capital wine we had—Humbugger, you call it? No humbug
about that, if you'll allow a bit of a pun. You might;
for I've heard you make worse often. But, by gracious,
what did you think of those little dogs? Don't they
beat the world? And is'nt it a nice business for college
boys to be at, instead of their books, and trying to get
back some of the money their fathers pay out for 'em?
Well, college boys will be college boys everywhere, I
suppose, like them at Athens and the other colleges in
Georgia. They learn how to dress fine, smoke, drink
whiskey, cuss, and be impudent to old people."

Richer and riper the crops, as, leaving the Neckar,
we travelled due South, having, on our right, the broad
plain of the Rhine, on our left, the low hills as, gradually growing higher and higher, they culminated in the
Black Forest. The villages on this dividing line between
the plain and the hills, embowered as they were in shade
and fruit trees, seemed perfect in their loveliness. At
Ettlingen, the Murgthal rose to view, the Black Forest
uplifted high, above all, the Mercuriesberg. At Oos,
our train turned suddenly to the left, and in ten minutes
we were at Baden-Baden.

CHAPTER XVI.

HIS is a place for richer folks than you and me, Phil."

We had strolled out after dinner (at the *Hotel Hollande*) across the Oos, and amid the rows of shops in the *Bazaar*.

"A small town, and few stores; but they look like they had a plenty of customers with a plenty of money. But money comes easy, and goes easy here. People that follow gambling spend freely when they are in luck, and I've no doubt these store-keepers know how and where to catch up the lucky ones. I've heard that these Dutch women are about as rapid gamblers as the men. When women take a start it's hard to head 'em off."

"Dutch? There are no Dutch here. We are in Germany, man, not Holland."

"I call 'em all Dutch; they are all Dutch to me."

"The gambling is almost nothing now, compared with what it used to be. The government has put an end to the excesses."

Many as there were in these grounds around the *Trinchhalle* and *Conversationshaus*, during the afternoon, they were few compared with the throng at night. A band of forty musicians played from a stand, and men, women, and children walked, and sat, and listened, and chatted. Jim's facility in making his way led us

into limited conversation with an intelligent-looking
German, whose table, as he sat smoking and sipping his
beer, was next to ours. To a direct question from Jim,
if he spoke English, he smiled and answered:

"A leedle beed."

It was amusing to me to observe the efforts the two
made to render themselves mutually intelligible. Jim
adroitly complimented the German military, and hinted
that perhaps the army might be getting ready to do
for some other nation what they had lately done for the
French. From the answer he received he gathered that
his remark had not been understood.

"Vot te Charmans vant mose now is bees."

"Bees!" exclaimed Jim, in astonishment.

"Yahs, bees," answered the gentleman, with an argu-
mentative look.

"Why—have'nt you got any *bees* in this country? I
should suppose that *bees*—"

I heard no more; but asking Jim to excuse me for a
few moments, retreated, so that I might laugh without
restraint. A few minutes afterwards he came where I
was promenading near the musicians.

"Why did'nt you come back?" he asked carelessly;
"that was a clever fellow."

I answered that the subjects of their conversation,
especially as he was talking about one thing and the
stranger another, confused me somewhat, and I concluded to take a little turn by myself.

"When he was talking of *peace* and you about *bees* I
could'nt see how you were going to make it."

The old fellow laughed heartily.

"Yes, sir, I thought the Dutch nation at large was
about going into the bee-raising and honey-making
business."

"How *did* you settle it, Jim?"

"I told him that I was surprised at what he said; that I thought, of course, that bees were a very good thing in their way; that I had a few hives myself, and most country people had a hive or two apiece."

"Hold on, Jim, and let me lean against this tree awhile. What did he say then?"

"Well, sir, he looked at me for a moment as hard as that custom-house officer yesterday; but he saw that I did'nt mean to be insulting, and that I was'nt scared. And then he laughed and said: 'Oh! you means te *peas*—te leedle peas.' I told him I did *not* mean *peas*— little peas, nor big peas. Fact, we raised *them*, too, in Georgia, where I came from in any quantity, but—"

"I'm going to fall, Jim," said I, "if you don't hold me."

"He took me up again, sir, and he said: 'I not mean *peas*, I means BEES—bees and VOR. Te Charmans not vont *vor*, te Charmans vont *bees*.' When he said *vor* he frowned and doubled up his fists, and when he said *bees* he looked as sweet as he could, spread out his hands and did like he was patting a baby on the head. And then I understood him. We laughed. I made him take a beer with me; but we both found talking together a rather heavy business, and I concluded to leave."

"Did'nt you ask him to call by if he should ever come to Georgia?"

"No. But if he should, I should treat him like a gentleman, and show him my bee-hives."

We were entertained by a little book which I purchased in the *Bazaar*, entitled "*Legendes de Baden.*" Jim was especially impressed by the legend of the miraculous intervention of the Blessed Virgin in deliver-

18

ing, many centuries ago, her convent of Lichtenstein,
situate a little more than a mile out of town, from the
soldiers of a fierce invading army when the abbess and
her nuns had fled from it and besought her protection.

The next morning we took the early train for Basle,
intending to deflect from our route at Appenweir and
make an hour's visit to the Cathedral of Strassburg. Jim
said he did not care so much about the old church, but
he wanted to see the clock.

"That steeple beats anything we've seen yet," said he,
as we slowly went up amid the throng of visitors.

"That at Cologne, when finished, will be higher. With
that exception, it is the loftiest in the world. Will you
go up it?"

"Not if I know myself. It's bound to fall some time,
and it might take a notion to-day just as I got at the top,
then good-bye Emily."

Grand as this structure is, it was less imposing than
that at Cologne. Jim thought that they must have run
mainly on their steeple, and that that broke them·
Nothing interested him so much as the clock. How he
did try to peer into it. We could not wait for the noon-
striking, and had to be satisfied with the slip-shod old
gentleman who came in at half-past eleven. As we
strolled along, remarking upon the different architect-
ures of eight hundred years, one of the servitors advanced
towards us, and raising his finger, intimated silence. A
moment afterwards we were at the opening of one of the
chapels where Mass was being said before a congregation
of about three hundred worshippers. We turned away,
and the sound of the service was again beyond our hearing long before we emerged into the street.

"I had no idea it was meeting-day," said Jim, when

we were out; "but they don't seem to have any regular stated meeting days over here. When we were at Cologne I got up early, you know, and walked out into the town. Blamed if I did'nt see at least a thousand people either going in or coming out of the churches. I doubt if they keep any almanacs in this town; because, you know, that old clock tells every blessed thing about the sun, moon, and stars, and I suppose these people go by her, and don't want any almanacs. I wonder how often they wind her up? Curious country. Going to meeting weeky days and before breakfast as well as other times. Let's move on."

Back to Appenweir. If our tickets had allowed, we would have preferred the direct route to Basle, in order to have a better view of the Vosges, and the mediæval remains on their slopes. As it was, we could only view them in the distance, while the Black Forest was better presented than in the direct line. The valleys are exquisitely beautiful. Busy were the laborers and their teams; most of the former were females. In a field where a dozen or fifteen might be harvesting, about three would be men—one with the team, and two with scythes, the rest women and girls. Behind each of the reapers a woman followed with a reap-hook to cut what stocks had been left.

"They make clean work of it, you see, Phil, and don't leave much pickings for the hogs. Now isn't it a shame for that sort of work to be done mostly by women? The men, what are not at trades, are in the army. They may talk what they please about *bees*, as they call it, but I tell you they mean *war* when the men are drilling and the women gathering the crops. Still, a woman will be a woman, in the wheat patch or ball-room. Look at those blue and pink jackets, and notice how stylish they set those straw hats on their heads."

Thus he rattled on during that sweet afternoon, often leaning his head out of the window, bowing and waving his hat, and halloing to the laborers, who sometimes gaily responded to his salutations.

We were at *Les Trois Rois*, in Basle, and were sitting at our chamber window looking down upon the rapidly rolling Rhine, from which, though after several divergences, we had not yet separated.

"*Consule Planco!*" said I.

"Certainly," said Jim.

> '*Non ego hoc ferrem, calidus juventa,*
> *Consule Planco.*'

"You and I read that together in Horace under old man Hodge, Jim."

"Did we? The old man tried to put Horace and Cæsar into me with a hickory, but they could'nt stick. Was he ever along here? not old Hodge, but—that other fellow?"

"Yes. Munatius Plancus founded this town. Rather it has supplanted another further up the river that was founded by him who was consul when Horace was a boy. When the Roman army mutinied under Germanicus, who had married Agrippina—"

"That same female you told about at Cologne?"

"No; but her mother, and a most excellent woman and devoted wife. Mother and daughter could not have been more widely different. The wife of Germanicus accompanied him in his wars, and when he was murdered by Piso, at the instance of Tiberius the Emperor, she charged the murderer with his crime openly at Rome, whereupon he stabbed himself."

"Good-bye for *him*. What became of the widow? Married again, I suppose. Marrying seemed to run in that family."

"No; being left with nine children, she—"

"Oh, dear! Not much chance to marry again with all that gang, without she could find a fellow like our same Bob Minton. But go on."

"No, sir; not another word."

"Go on, Phil; it's perfectly thrilling what you were saying, only I happened to think of Bob when you were talking about the nine children. Go ahead."

"Not I. You may substitute Bob Minton for the widow of Germanicus. What of Bob? You've put out the Cæsars for to-night, so bring in Bob."

"Bob tells it," he went on, after a hearty laugh, "that when he was a boy about fourteen years old he fell terribly in love, heels over head. He loved so hard that he began to get sickly, and his father got uneasy about him and gave him tansy bitters and vinegar-and-nails. But the old man found out somehow what was the matter with him, and that the one he was in love with was a widow that had nine children and weighed three hundred pounds. And then what do you think he did? Why, sir, he took Bob into the woods, and cutting an armful of hickories he gave him three hundred lashes, one lick for every pound of the widow."

"It cured him?"

"Yes, *sir*. Bob says that from loving he got to hate her, and he hated her as long as she lived. He always said that the best way to cure people who were foolishly in love was to give 'em the hickory. Now what about the widow Germanicus?"

"No more of her to-night. I refer you to the classical dictionary." 18*

After breakfast next day we left for Lucerne.

"Small but active for their size," Jim remarked, as we passed along by the rushing streams, on our way up the Bernese Oberland. In four hours we were at the *Schweizerhof* in Lucerne. In the afternoon we drove into the country overshadowed by Mt. Pilatus. Jim noticed with pleasure the luxuriant grass which takes its name from the town.

"I see," said he, "how it comes to have such a long root. The ground is so poor and hilly that it has to reach down deep in order to hold on in the first place, and then to get something to feed on besides this gravel. What in the world is that cross doing here?"

We alighted in order to inspect a small, wooden cross, the first we had seen of its kind, henceforth so numerous in this portion of Switzerland. In the wood a place had been hollowed in which, covered with glass, was a rude picture of the Blessed Virgin. Jim was touched most tenderly by this witness of the piety and faith of one who had erected this simple memorial for a credited deliverance, through her agency, from some calamity.

"It's a mighty comforting thing, I suppose, for them that can believe it," he said.

In the afternoon we went to see, on a rock by the brooklet's side, Thorwaldsen's *Lion of Lucerne*. A wonderful work of genius. The courage and grief exhibited in the fall of the noble beast, in whose side clings the broken spear, and the fidelity with which his huge paw covers the Lily of France were touching to contemplate. A brave people! Whether contesting for hereditary rights on their own soil, or in the cause of other peoples. No braver death was ever met by soldiers, not even the Lacedaemonians at Thermopylae, than when the Swiss Guards fell that fatal day on the threshold of the Tuilleries.

"It's about the only chance they have of showing their pluck," said Jim. "They can't get out to fight other people, and other people can't get in to fight them. These mountains and lakes, and these rivers that run like race-horses, stop such as that. Yet, they've got to make a living in some sort of fashion besides tending what little level land they've got, and so they hire themselves to fight other people's battles. It's a way of living that would'nt suit me."

It was delicious to sit, in the cool evening, in the piazza of this elegant hotel, look down the clear lake, and breathe the sweet air coming up from its bosom. Next morning we took an excursion upon it, leaving the boat at Vitznau for the ascent of the Rhigi. We took the least romantic but most comfortable and expeditious route—that by the railway. Jim was intensely interested in this enterprise, and, in what time we had, closely examined the locomotive, which, with its cog wheel underneath, revolving on the cross-teeth between the rails, drew, or rather *pushed*, the small car up the mountain. The morning was fair, and we could get all of this magnificent view. Once a little cloud gathered, and we could see the rain below, while the sun shone brightly above. As we stood upon the summit, mountains without number rose to the right, while in front, seeming white as silver, lay the cities and lakes of Zurich and Zug.

After another night in this delightful town, we took the steamer at the *Schweizerhof* quay. Passing down the Cruciform Lake, on reaching the west arm we turned into it, and disembarking at Alpnach, took our places in the diligence for Brienz. Slowly we ascended through

Sarnen and along its lake to Gisneyle, halting a little at
the relays of horses, to look into the small sideway booths,
and make our little purchases of woodware. More slowly
yet up the Kaiserstuhl to the town and Lake of Lungern.

And now for the ascent of the Brunig Pass. Out of
pity for the laboring horses, we alighted from the carriage and walked ahead the greater part of the way.
Jim said he had seen some hills and heard of some others,
but that this oversized all his experience and information. Such talk was between breaths, as we struggled
on, occasionally shying the rapidly descending vehicles.
The descent was delightful. The road, cut out of the
side of the mountain, winding along a precipice defended
from the abysses to our left only by a low stone fence,
added, from the spice of the danger, to Jim's enjoyment.
Our seats were on either side of the coachman. I could
but shudder sometimes as we trotted along the ever-
winding, rapidly descending way, when we would pass
a point where, over the narrow parapet a yard's distance
from the wheels, I looked down into the awful depths.
With my right hand I would grasp Jim's left arm whenever, on the slightest depression on my side, I almost
felt as if we must go over. He would smile, give the
coachman a wink, when the latter would flourish his
long whip and give it a crack that sounded like a pistol
over the horses.

"Oh, yes," said he, "got into trouble and you want
me. Care nothing about me when no danger. Danger
come, and it's Jim Rawls. Hold on, you need'nt blue up
my arm; but hold on. I've brought you safe so far, and
I'll try to put you through. Gracious! what a pretty
sight," he exclaimed, as the road brought us to a point
where we could look down upon the village of Meinrin-

gen and the long, narrow, fertile valley, with its crops of grain, which, though near the end of July, were just fading from green to yellow.

We could not linger at Brienz to inspect its wonderful wood-carving works; but, entering a little steamer, we sailed (passing with reluctance the Giesbach) the full length of the lake, and before sunset were at the *Hotel Belvedere* in Interlachen.

CHAPTER XVII.

 NOVEL sight it was—a small village, with five or six large first-class hotels, besides numerous boarding houses—*pensions*, as they are called. We sat in the veranda of the Belvedere, where a breeze from that direction would have brought to us the spray from the fountain in front that sent its thin jet high into the air, while vases of flowers and shrubbery were sitting in veranda, hall, and court, and even on the steps of the stairs. Before us, seeming only a few hundred paces through the mountain gorge, we could see the ever-white tops of Alpine peaks. Of all places for tired travellers, this must be the sweetest. Without, the scene shone as we had never seen. Within, the fresh, sharp air invigorated and exhilarated. Jim said it was a pity to have to go so far from home to find such sights and such enjoyments. Here, as elsewhere, he made friends with the English-speaking servants. It did his heart good, he said, after walking about the streets and hearing so much outlandish talk to get back and let himself loose in good old Georgia-talk with somebody else besides me ; because, as for us, he said, we had about talked out all we knew.

Of the many excursions to be taken from this central place, we had to be content with one. Early on the morrow we were in a double-horse barouche on the way to Lauterbrunnen.

"Don't she get over ground, and ain't she ashy?" said Jim, as we drove along the margin of the Leits- chein, almost continually crossing and recrossing it. "This river, Phil, and one on the other side, have made this town of Interlachen. You see, I've been studying up a little geography, too. This empties the dirt on this side, and the other, the Lombach, on the other, and the deposits have divided what was one lake into two—the one we came down yesterday, and that we are to go on to-morrow."

"*Tantum aevi longinqua valet mutare vetustas;* as Helenus said to Ameas about Scylla and Charybdis."

"Oh, hush! as the alligator said to the bull-frog."

"I'll do it."

Far above us we could see the goats as they felt their way cautiously along the steep acclivities, and cropped the thin verdure. Arriving at Lauterbrunnen, the horses were unhooked and saddled. Jim, avowing his recognition of the maxim, age before beauty and merit, selected the one he considered the best, made me mount him, mounted the other himself, and we began the ascent of the Wendernalp.

"Where's your horse, my friend?" asked he of the coachman, our guide, who could not speak a word of English. "There's nothing like trying 'em anyhow, Phil. I generally make 'em understand me before I get through."

The man smiled, pointed to his feet, and led the way.

On and on, up the weary ascent, sometimes wooded, then pasture land, then sudden acclivity. We halted occasionally at a little *chalet* to dismount and give rest

to ourselves and the toiling beasts; at other times paus-
ing to listen to the peasants, as, in expectation of a few
sous, they sang their country's airs or sounded the Alpine horn.   I can never forget the first impression made
upon me by this instrument.   The peasant had taken
his position beneath a lofty and rugged series of cliffs
projecting irregularly from the side of the mountain.
The echoes ascending, grew fainter and sadder, repeat-
ing from eminence to eminence until dying away in
whispers among the far heights.   I have never heard
sounds so solemn.   One could imagine them to be sigh-
ings of the ghosts of the giants of olden times.

When we had been about a couple of hours on the
ascent, I, who was ahead, heard Jim break out into a
laugh and say : " You've given out, old fellow, have you ?
Look behind you, Phil."   I turned and saw the coachman, as, having taken my horse by the tail, he suffered
himself to be pulled up the mountain.

" Look behind yourself," I answered, turning; and
there, similarly hanging to his horse, was a Swiss girl,
who on her left arm was carrying a basket of things she
had purchased at the village for the *Hotel de Jungfrau*
on the summit.

" Good gracious me alive ! " he exclaimed, and, immediately dismounting, said :

" My dear madam, or, most probably, miss, I can't
stand that.   This is a man's saddle, but I can fix it for
you.   Don't say a word," he continued, as she and the
guide looked wonderingly at his motions.   He drew the
right stirrup and leather over, and was proceeding to
shorten the left when the girl, with a merry laugh, darted
on ahead.   The guide roared, and then broke forth with
a mountain song.

"I saved my manners, anyhow," said Jim. "I was'nt brought up to ride horses when women had to get along by hanging to their tails."

About noon we reached the summit, when we dismounted for dinner and an hour's rest at the hotel. There, in full view, and apparently not further off than a rifle shot, though actually more than a mile, stood the Jungfrau—the *Young Bride*, seeming whiter in her nuptial array than all her maidens, and towering above them like Diana in the midst of her choir. It was unspeakably beautiful. The sun was terribly bright; so much so that we had to wear our blue-glass spectacles, with which we had been warned to provide ourselves. As we gazed, suddenly we saw what seemed a narrow drift of snow gliding rapidly down a narrow gorge. A few seconds afterwards, a roar, as of a hundred cannon, and we could scarcely believe the sound to come from what we saw, and that it was an avalanche of thousands of tons. Jim recognized in one of the waitresses the girl whom he had tried to serve. She had evidently told the landlady, for they both smiled graciously whenever their eyes rested on him as he ate. He called for another half bottle of wine and two extra glasses. The women looked curiously at him as he filled them. He passed one of them to the mistress, a very stout, fair woman, and the other he handed to the girl.

"You see, ladies, I never was raised, as I said to my old friend here, to ride a horse, especially on a bad road, and see women taking it afoot. You understand? I *nix* (*not*, you know) rides, when a woman,—got—no—*sheval*, (*horse*, you understand.) Here's to us four, and all the pretty Swiss women and girls."

There were half dozen other guests at the table, and

19

all shouted with laughter. The woman drank her glass readily; the girl took hers, blushed, and looked at her mistress, who signified her wish for her to join in the toast. She did so amidst much tittering and pretended reluctance. As we mounted our horses before the door, Jim, looking towards the Jungfrau, asked the hostess if she could'nt get up just one more avalanche for a couple of old fellows who could never expect to be back there any more. She shook her head laughingly.

"Nix?" said he. "Well, good-bye," and with adieu on both sides we commenced the descent.

"Did'nt you see they understood me? If you'll put the English to 'em slow and distinct as I do, you don't want but a few of their words to make 'em understand you. I have'nt got but two of 'em yet, *nix* and *sheval*, and you see what I made out of them. Give me about two dozen of 'em, and I can go through the whole country by myself. Of course, I should count on behaving myself like everybody, specially when they're away from home, ought to be expected to do. Well, she's a nice woman and keeps a good hotel away up here in the clouds."

As we descended, we encountered other peasants on the margin of the path who sang for our entertainment. Once, while we were walking along (for the way had now become so precipitous that this was less fatiguing then riding), we saw ahead of us two children, hatless and shoeless, a boy and a girl, neither of whom could have been more than six years old. They stood erect and still, side by side just out of the path, with their earnest little faces turned towards us as we neared them.

"Why what upon the creation of the earth," said Jim, "are those little chaps doing away up here by themselves? Hello little folks, where's your ma?"

Immediately they began to sing, the girl first, and the boy second soprano. A plaintive little song it was, and the sweetest my ears had ever listened to. My dear old Jim first stopped in amazement. He then walked on to where the singers were standing, and after look· ing at them for a few moments, sat down upon the green bank, took out his pocket handkerchief, and wept and sobbed. My eyes filled in sympathy. The guide, pleased with our appreciation, allowed us to wait for them to repeat their song. Jim rose, when it was over, and laid his hands softly on their bare heads.

"God Almighty bless you my children! I never heard such music before. If I had'nt seen you, I'd have thought it was angels. You don't know how much good you've done me. I know you are good children. You could'nt sing that way, and make me cry so if you were'nt. I bid you good-bye now. Keep on being good, and always mind what your ma tells you, and don't get bad as you grow big. Take this, and buy yourselves a hat and bonnet, and a pair of shoes apiece. I wish I could afford to give you more."

He filled their hands with coins, and for the first time since we had left home, made me add to what I had given at first.

"Give to 'em freely, Phil. You're never going to lose by what you give to such as them."

The children looked almost frightened by the dosses sion of so much money.

"Good-bye now, and remember what 1 told you, and especially mind what your ma tells you. I never felt in all my life-time, Phil, as I did then," he continued after we had parted from them "I did'nt want to try even, to keep from crying. I don't know what their

little song was about; but I tell you that it sounded
to me, away up here, as if it was two angels singing
the praise of God."

He would not even listen to either of the two other
bands of larger singers that we afterwards encountered,
but, throwing pieces of money to them, hastened his
gait, saying:

"No, my friends, I don't care about any more music
to-day. I don't want that I heard further up the hill
put out of my mind."

We reached the foot of the mountain at the village of
Grindenwald, where we found our barouche that a friend
of the guide had brought around the mountain. "The
idea of charging for ice here," said Jim, as, while the
horses were being put to the carriage, we were refresh-
ing ourselves at a hotel with a bottle of champagne.
"Why there's the ice *growing* in three hundred yards
of the house, and more plentiful than food for their
cattle.''

It did seem strange, for the glaciers extended almost
to within the village. As we drove rapidly out, we met
the goats coming in from the mountains, the udders of
many of them almost touching the ground. On the way
back, we halted a few moments at a bridge of the
Lutchen, and for a franc obtained a view of a couple of
chamois which were kept on exhibition to tourists in a
small covered pen.

"Ah, well," said Jim, looking at the doe. You've
got the finest pair of eyes *I* ever saw except one. Its
curious, Phil, that this little deer or goat—whatever it
is; should so forcibly remind me of Emily. But do
you know, sir? It was at old man Sereno Taylor's
examination, the first time I saw her, and immediately

fell head and ears in love with her. She came out and
sung that song. Somehow, it come down on me perpen-
dicular, like a gate-post, as Mose Grice used to say, and
then he broke forth with—

Oh, the wild chamois track at the breaking of day.

The frightened doe ran into a corner of the pen, and
her fawn crouched beneath her.

"They don't seem to be very fond of music," said
Jim.

"Maybe they object to the kind."

"Very probable, but its the best they can get from
this crowd. Don't be scared, you little beauty, I could'nt
hurt anything that had eyes like them. Good-bye to
you, and your baby."

"Were you ever much addicted to singing, Jim?"

"None to hurt. But Emily used to say I had a very
good voice. How did you like the stave I just now
tried?"

"You saw some of its effects."

We dashed along the smooth, ever-winding road, the
horses, whether stimulated by Jim's merriment or anxious to reach their stalls, pulling hard at their bits.
The night came on, and we began to see bright lights
high up among the mountains. It was the vigil of one
of the saints, and the peasants were paying honor to the
coming morrow.

"A more religious people, Phil, these than our people,
or the English. What they believe, they believe without any doubt, and try to practice it; and when they
don't, they blame nobody but themselves. I did'nt think
it was so, but it is."

An hour after dark we arrived in the village. As we

19*

dashed through the streets, the coachman warned, by the continued cracking of his whip, the foot passengers to get out of the way. After tea we strolled for a short time on the Cursaal, listened to the band, then went early to bed. Next morning Jim declared that he had never had a sweeter night's rest, not even in his own bed at home. Those little children, singing away up there on the mountain, kept him awake awhile, and afterwards he went to sleep, feeling as sure as if he had been there to see, that his wife and children were safe in the protection of the Almighty.

Leaving this sweet village, we took the short railroad with its double-decker car over the narrow peninsular, and embarked on the steamer *Beatus* at the southeastern extremity of Lake Thun.

"An outlandish name for a boat—*Beatus*."

"It is from the St. Beatus, who dwelt in the cave yonder on the side of the lake."

"What did he live there for? Why not in a house like other folks?"

"Because he desired to devote his life exclusively to religion."

"Could'nt he do that without going to live in a hole in the ground?"

"At least he thought he could not, except by removing himself entirely from mankind. Many hundreds in the annals of the Church have done the same."

"How did he manage to live there? It must have been a tolerably economical establishment?"

"His drink was the water of the lake, and his bread the fruits and the herbs that he could find near by, besides what the people around, who knew of his whereabouts and character, would bring to him."

"Tell me, Phil, why so many towns in this country are called by the names of saints?"

"The towns so named sprang from the various saints who, like Peatus, retired from the society of mankind and fixed their habitations in the forests or in the marshes. The reputation of their sanctity, their charities and the wonderful things they did drew multitudes from far, and these settling there, the towns which grew up they named after them."

"Their charities! I thought they were poor, and lived on water and blackberries. I don't see how they could do anything at charity, when they had no smoke-house and nothing to put in it if they had."

"A man need not have full barns and store-houses to be charitable. These monks managed very well. Among other ways, was this: the rich who were pious sent them the means to be dispensed to the poor. Then they taught the latter how to till the land and enrich it. The very richest tracts of country in France to-day, are those which lie near where the old monasteries stood, six and eight hundred years ago. You know, Jim, from your own observation, and your own experience, that when a man really wants to be charitable, somehow the means for his purpose come to him."

"Fact. The Bible says that whoever gives to the poor, lends to God, and He will pay at usurious interest, or words to that effect. But see yonder; would a fellow ever wish to find a sweeter place to live at than that?"

We were at the end of the little lake. The spot was most beautiful; on the narrow tongue of land, an exquisite chateau, surrounded by flowers and shrubbery, stood almost immediately on the banks, from whose veranda was a full view of the green waters and the mountains.

We at once took the train. Halting at Berne only for the purpose of dining at the station restaurant, we travelled along through Fribourg and Lausanne, reached Geneva at night-fall, and stopped at the *Hotel de L'Ecu.* Our chamber was on the third floor, immediately over the Rhone where it rushes out of Lake Leman. As we sat there at night, looking out of the window upon the rapid waters and the numerous laundry-houses in their midst, we had some talk on the subject of the classics.

"Jim," said I, "you did'nt seem very fresh about the *Munatius Plancus* of Horace; but you need not tell me that you've forgotten what Cæsar says about Geneva and the Rhone."

"Goodness! where I got one whipping about Horace, I got three about Cæsar. What was all that about old Orgetorix, and Dumnorix, and Diviticus?"

"Divitiacus, you mean?"

"Divy—something, and those old Allobroges, and Tulingians and Bellovaccians, and all those old fellows? We've come up with 'em at last, have we? Old man Hodge never could poke 'em into my head. I never could get 'em right and find out which was which. I knew some of 'em wanted to cross over somewhere, and that the rest of 'em were against it, and they were about a year disputing about it, and blamed if I ever found out whether they got over or not, or who wanted to go and who did'nt, or where they wanted to go away from and where to; only I remember there was a sight of rivers, and lakes, and mountains in the way, which it is very plain now to see was a fact. But I know that Cæsar astonished everybody by building a bridge in a mighty quick time over one of 'em; and if I was to live a hundred years I should'nt forget the whipping I got about that. Ah! that was a bridge, Phil, as *was* a bridge. None of your pontoons. But *I* could'nt cross it by myself. I should have stayed over on this side if old man Hodge had let me. But that old fellow killed himself, did'nt he? Old Orgetorix, I mean."

"So it was supposed. You remember, *Nec abest suspicio, ut Helvetii arbitrantur, quin ipse sibi mortem consciverit.*"

"Just about that, if I don't disremember. Considering how I was handled by old man Hodge all along in there, it seemed to me that I was to be made responsible for putting the fellow up to it, and would be made to follow him on—

Into the dark and silent grave,
Where there's nothing else to crave.

That's from the Ohoopie poet. And this is my same old Geneva, is it?"

"It is. That bridge yonder over which we drove this afternoon in the omnibus, stands about where the Helvetians tried first to cross over to the Allobroges. Over there is Jura, that *altissimus mons*, which you surely have not forgotten?"

"Forget *him!* Some things I might forget, Philemon, but *him*, never. I rather think I liked him better than the rest of 'em. He did'nt have to be crossed by any bridge, you know. You might sorter get around him. Oh, yes, he was a right clever old fellow, was old Jury. I—I remember him, Philip."

"Oh, Jim Rawls, Jim Rawls!"

Coming from anybody else but him, I might have been somewhat annoyed by such ignoring of the suggestions which the visitations to these classic grounds raised in my mind. Quotations from the *De Bello Gallico* of Cæsar were constantly rising to my lips, and I could but think it was most opportune to give them utterance. But my old friend insisted—to use his own phrase—that he could'nt stand it; and so I held them back, except the few that would break out of their own motion. Yet I must admit that for my disappointment in this behalf, he compensated many fold in all other respects.

CHAPTER XVIII.

'LL bet you a cigar," said Jim, next morning, as we started on a sail up the lake, "that you don't know why this steamer is named *Bonnivard?*"

"Bonnivard? Bonnivard? I ought to know, but I've forgotten."

"Oh, yes, you ought to know and don't. Well, sir, that's the *Prisoner of Chillon*. Know how I found out?"

"From your reading up, of course."

"I did'nt. That old gray-headed Englishman told me so just now. You see, my information costs less than yours. We can't go to the castle to-day; but we can see with our glasses about where it is, as we cross over from Evian to Lausanne."

A pleasant sail, with Ferney to our left not far off, and on the banks the Rothschild's palace, the chateaus of Sir Robert Peel and the Empress Josephine, and the towns of Nyon and Rosse, with the fair *Pays de Vaud*, and to our right Yvoire, Thonon, Evian, the rugged Savoy, and the Canton Chablais.

"See what a difference, Phil, a little body of water makes between the people who live on opposite sides. Over to the left, they are agricultural and easy-going in their motions. That is a rich country, with its wine and small grain. To the right, they live mostly by lumber business. See that barge of logs yonder; that has just come out of the mouth of the river Dranse, by which they were floated into the lake. They were cut last fall. They are a harder-working people over on this side. But don't they know something about making their towns comfortable? Just look at those women and children yonder sitting along the quay under the chestnut trees."

This last remark was made just as we were approaching the village of Evian. Women of all conditions were sitting upon benches beneath the trees, which, almost to the water's edge, lined the semicircular quay—some with their sewing and knitting, some reading, others chatting, while the children ran or were drawn by their nurses in carriages in the shade. As we passed across from this village to Ouchy, the port of Lausanne, we raised our glasses and looked towards the head of the lake and called to mind how Byron, in the little village before us, where he was detained by foul weather, had immortalized one of the prisoners in that gloomy castle. What anguish has been suffered behind those stones! Burgundians and Savoyards, not to mention the massacre, at one time, of those twelve hundred Israelites who had been so madly charged with the design to poison all the fountains of Europe. We lingered at Ouchy only long enough to meet the downward bound steamer, *Winkelried*. Of the individual objects seen in this excursion, Jim was most interested in the chateau of Josephine.

"A big man! A mighty big man. But that was where Napoleon made his grand mistake. He was so big that he thought he could get around God Almighty's laws and put away his wife. That's what HE don't allow. What HE has joined together man better not put asunder. What surprises me, is that anybody should ever want to try it."

" Every man has not an Emily Todd, you know, Jim."

" You are right there certain, old man; but my opinion is, that any man and woman can get along together if they'll both start right and keep on right."

"There was no special domestic unhappiness with Napoleon and Josephine."

"No; and that made it the meaner and less to God Almighty's liking. And you see right there was where He raised His finger. There ain't any telling where Nap would have gone but for that. But he never saw the finger, you know, and so the ground gave way before him on a sudden, and he went on down hill until he got to the bottom. She lived on and on until he *was* down, and then *she* died. She was a true lady, Josephine was. She never made any fuss about it. She let him have his way. She knew, though, who was on her side, and that it would win some time or another, and in some way or another."

In the evening we rode about the town, and later strolled along the gardens and the quay. Once, when we were on the bridge, we met a man who was intoxicated. It was the only instance of the kind we saw south of the Channel. Jim remarked how curious it was that we had not seen but this case in a country where people, rich and poor, never sit down to eat without drinking. I replied that there was a nut for the liquor-prohibitionists of our country to crack. It did certainly seem that where wine was used as food, there was little intoxication, and that better than legislation in non-wine-growing countries would be the abundant planting of the grape.

"I have come to believe it," replied Jim. "People *will* drink. They may join temperance societies and hold

20

off for a time, but they'll break over after a while, giving
as excuse that their president got drunk first, or their
treasurer stole their money and run away, or something
else, and then they'll make up for lost time. I've seen
often, Phil, that the very fact of taking a pledge made
people want whiskey worse than before. And then sometimes, all of a sudden, some of 'em go to getting sickly—
have a bad cold or a bronchial affection (that's the biggest
and longest-lasting disease), and then they have to take
a little for medicine, and so here they go. My notion is,
better leave such things with everybody himself. Let
him make a man of himself if it's in him, and if it ain't,
let him be a beast, and be treated as one, and not punish
the one that sold the liquor. The law in our country
seems to be always after the wrong fellow. It's after the
whiskey seller, when it ought to be after the whiskey
drinker."

After some discussion, we concluded to give three
days of the time we had set apart for Paris to an excursion to Chamouni.

Bright and early next day we were in the diligence,
Jim sitting between the coachman and one of the proprietors of the line, who, or one of whose partners, we
ascertained, accompanied every travel to and fro, for the
better security of all. I took the first front seat. Soon
we had crossed the Foron, and were trotting gayly along
in Savoy. Jim was interested in the manner of hooking
up the team of five horses (the three in front abreast),
and the dexterous use of the driver's whip. He noticed,
he said, that the dullest horse at every relay was placed
in the middle, and he called my attention to how the
driver gave this particular beast occasionally a gentle
caution, as he called it. With an execration, and with-

out a movement of any portion of his body, except his long, slender, wiry arm, he raised his whip, described with the long lash several curious rotary motions, and then, as he lifted suddenly the staff high in the air, the end of the lash flew with the rapidity of an arrow underneath but not touching the off-horse, and cut the flank of the dullard, sounding as if it had penetrated deeply into the flesh. It would be long before he would require another "caution."

Though there was much of the picturesque in the country through which we passed, along by Bonneville, Cluses, Sallance, and Ouches, we had become too familiar with such and finer views to be very much interested. We reached Chamouni (*Hotel des Alpes*) in time to take, before dark, a hurried excursion to the *Glacier Bossons*. As we toiled up the ascent, Jim was amused greatly when I would pause behind to recover my breath and mop my face with my handkerchief.

"Living in town on books and the other luxuries don't get a fellow up for this sort of exercise, eh, old gentleman?"

He had already gotten upon good terms with the guide, although the latter could not speak English, and Jim's own vocabulary of foreign words was yet quite on this side of his adequate two dozen. The guide smiled at the raillery upon myself, though he patiently waited until I could rest and renew the ascent. Jim would call to him, point back over his shoulder, and say:

"Sheval. Ee want sheval. Ee—not (nix) use—walk —much. Oui?"

"Oh, oui, monsieur," the good fellow would answer and lead slowly on.

"Slow and distinct, Phil, you see, with a few gestures

flung in to help.   They understand me about as well as
they do you with what French you've got."

Arrived at the point whence we were to make the passage, two boys presented themselves with what we·took
to be a couple of pairs of spurs.

"What in the name of thunder are you going to do
with them.spurs, my little chaps?"

The boys looked strangely at him and interrogatively
at the guide, who informed me for what they were
intended.

"They are creepers, Jim," said I.

"Creepers!   Well, I've heard of creepers; but these
here ain't the sort we have in Georgia.   What are they
for?"

"To walk with upon the ice; if we go to slipping
about here we may not be able to stop under half a mile."

"We live and learn.   Fetch along your creepers, my
little fellows."

They buckled them on, and we sallied forth.   Though,
compared with the *Mer de Glace*, this is an inconsiderable glacier, yet it was wonderful to us, as we walked
carefully along and looked upward and downward upon
the strange spectacle.   Soon we came to a point where
the glacier suddenly ascended somewhat, and the guide
stood before an open door cut in the ice, through which
we could see a passage lighted with lamps.   "*Le Grotto*,"
he said, and went in, we following.   The passage wound
around and around, and with the strangely colored lights
became more and more dismal and sepulchral.

"Look here, old fellow," said Jim to the guide, "how
long before we get out of this concern?"

The man smiled, continued to advance, and in three
or four minutes we emerged through another door.

On the following morning we were on the backs of mules to ascend the Montanvert.

"No choice of nags here, Phil. A mule's a mule. Do you call him a sheval, too? Take whichever you fancy. That's why they use mules, you see," he went on, when we found we were on a narrower, steeper path than that over the Wengernalp. "Look how steady and solid they come down with their feet."

By this time we had become quite used to foot travelling by holding on to the tails of the beasts. Jim said a Georgia mule would'nt stand that; however, these fellows, he supposed, had'nt any purchase to kick. Arrived at the point of crossing the *Mer de Glace*, besides the creepers, we had provided ourselves with a staff apiece about six feet long and armed with a sharp, iron point: for there are places on that wonderful road where one needs three legs and the utmost caution in their employment. The boys who had shod our heels advanced with hatchets and chopped, in especially narrow and dangerous places, notches in the ice for our feet to tread in greater security. We travelled very slowly, partly to avoid with extremest care the bottomless chasms, and partly to view the sublime scene. The rugged mountains far, far higher up above our heads, and this sea of eternal ice extending far away down and up the mountain gorge, hundreds of feet in thickness, the edges piled with huge masses of earth and rocks and stones that in the lapse of time had broken off from the mountains' sides and become fastened among the immovable glaciers, the huge chasms to our right and left, sometimes with a pass between of only a few inches; these were awful, but they were thrillingly interesting to see. I am quite sure I should have returned by the

20*

same route had I known of what sort was the celebrated *Mauvais pas* of which I had read, but of which I was afterwards surprised to hear tourists speaking as if it was not greatly to be dreaded. I have never thought of it since without some shuddering.

"You go ahead, Phil, next to the guide, I'll follow right on behind. All right, old fellow. Lively times, ain't they?"

I looked ahead. A mountain rising almost perpendicularly above me on the side of which I must walk on narrow steps cut into and running spirally for apparently six or eight hundred feet over a chasm down which I dare not look! How anyone could ever make this passage before the iron railing was fastened against the mountain, is beyond my understanding. Without it, I am confident I should have been lost. As it was, hanging with my left hand to the guide's right, I pulled myself slowly along with my right upon the railing. An occasional word from Jim, as if there was nothing especially remarkable in the situation, and the perfect coolness of the guide were of inexpressible value to me. When we reached the firm landing at last, on a small plain of the Flegere, where the little house called the *Chapeau* is situated, I sank down upon the ground exhausted. I had scarcely done so, when Jim brought to me a glass of brandy and soda.

"Speaking of groceries, and of their 'loose and lucid ways,' as Jack Moss used to say, it's a fine thing that there ain't any law against getting a drink here. If ever I saw a fellow who needed one it's you at this minute. You've seen her *one time*, Phil, have'nt you?"

"One time, Jim, *one time*."

He told me afterwards, that although he had felt a

little ticklish at first, he lost all personal apprehension in the sight of my condition, and that I should not be more pale when dead. After purchasing at the *Chapeau* a few trinkets which had been made ostensibly from the various minerals in the mountains, we mounted our mules that had been brought around, and descended the Flegere. On the way we met other tourists who were making the excursion in the reversed direction. As we approached the narrowest point of one of the ledges, where the path was not more than four feet wide, I had occasion to notice the sagacity of the mule. The foremost of our party met there the foremost of another, who was a lady. The mule that bore her stopped as he met the descending one, and leaned himself closely against the side of the mountain, and the others in his train followed his example until all of ours had passed, after which they straightened themselves and went on toiling upwards.

"That's what I call sense," said Jim.

The return to Geneva being a descent all the way, was shorter by several hours than the previous travel. It was an exalted enjoyment to sit on the lumbering diligence and travel down a spiral declivity of over forty miles, alternately on the sides of high mountains, and in ever descending fertile valleys. Early in the afternoon, we drove at a sweeping trot into Geneva, and had ample time to visit the jewelry stores, in one of which (Berguer et Fils) Jim had bargained for a watch for his wife and some trinkets for his children.

"How do you think Emily will like it, Phil?" said he, holding up a beautifully-enameled watch and chain.

"She'll be delighted, I am sure."

"She told me not to spend any money on her account."

"Why do you do it then?"

"Laws, Phil! Don't you understand women better than that? She just said that to keep me from spending too much. She knew that I should'nt think of going back without carrying some present to her, and she'd be disappointed if I did'nt. All women are like old Judge Dooly's wife, some more and some less. The old judge, who was a wild old fellow, you know, used to say that when he stayed away a long time on one of his frolics, and expected a scolding at home, he took pains to carry to his wife a new set of chainy. He always would call china, *chainy.*"

Our route northward took us along through the centre of the province of Ain, so variously picturesque, with its mountains in the east, its lakes and meadow lands in the west, passing into Saone-et-Loire near its capital city, Macon, and along the beautiful banks of the Saone river to Chalons, and thence into the Cote D'Or.

"This town looks as if it had been here for some time," said Jim, as we reached Chalons, while the train halted for some minutes as others, laden mostly with with wine-casks, were slowly moving up and down in the change of switches.

"This is the Caballinum of the Aedui. Your old friend Dumnorix used to cut a high figure all through this country. Just here, also, was one of Cæsar's granaries."

Travelling over the Cote D'Or, we had fine views of the rich vineyards, which the Burgundy wines, the *Yqem, Vougeot, Chambertin,* and others made famous. The afternoon at Dijon we spent in strolling about the ancient capital, the semicircular palace of the Dukes of Burgundy, now degenerated into a town-hall and museum, and the environs, which are very pleasing.

"More old walls," remarked Jim; "but then they leave room for the town to grow some, not like them at old Chester. Then these ramparts, with their nice shade trees, make walking here delightful. Another thing: a fellow can always tell where he is."

What we had done seldom hitherto, for lack of time, we dined at the *table d'hote*. We noticed that by each person's plate a quart bottle of Burgundy was set. Few of the guests called for more; yet scarcely one, even of the young men, failed to consume his bottle. We had both gotten to prefer the red wine to the white. That night we purchased for a trifling sum in one of the shops a bottle of *Chambertin* to help out our morrow's lunch. At about ten o'clock next morning, we were again *en route* for Paris.

"Ain't it a comfort, Phil, to have our faces turned towards home once more? I did'nt let you know it, but I felt mighty homesick as we started on that long journey to Chamouni. I begin to breathe freer with my face turned in this direction. I'm grudging every mile now between me and old Georgia."

We were in fine health and mood, with a plenty of what was good to eat, and drink, and smoke, on the express that flew along in the direction of home. On either side, as we looked from the windows of our *coupé*, the cornfields and vineyards smiled in the sunlight, and the laborers busily plied their hands or followed their teams. My old friend, now grown, if possible, more dear than ever, ran on in his alternations of serious and sportive conversation, now remarking on the culture and crops, and general productions of the country, and how they differed from our own, now with affectionate railing at me for some new evidence of absent-

mindedness or want of interest in present states of
things, and now with tender allusions to our best
beloved, from whom we had received at Geneva cheerful
tidings, winding up with words of gratitude to Providence who had taken care of all in the period of separation.   At Sens, in the province of Yonne, I had something to say about the Senones Gauls, from whom the
city derived its name, their achievements under Bren-
nus, and their final overthrow under Dolabella.

"That what makes you *look* so old, Phil. You are
always studying about old things, old people, old towns,
and old walls. Sometimes I think, from the way you
make 'em last you, that you rather have an old hat or
an old horse than new. It ain't because you're stingy—
because there ain't a stingy bone in you—but because
they *are* old. You've been so all your life. And,
speaking of old things," he continued, rising, and taking
down the basket, "let's try a little of this old wine.
Of all the old things in this country that's the one that
suits my fancy the most."

The westward bound travel, the choice lunch, the
Chambertin, the glorious day, the sweet valleys and
hillsides along the Yonne and the Seine, all gave to us
good appetites and spirits, and then we chatted and
smoked, and smoked and chatted in the full enjoyment
of all we saw.

"Oh, Jim!" I exclaimed once, when he had been
running over with the heartiest talk, "you are a glorious
old trump of a fellow. How could I ever have taken
this journey with anybody but you?"

"Hello! You breaking out in a fresh place all of a
sudden? Nonsense," and he went on to remarking
how, now that we were in Seine-et-Marne, the vineyards

were becoming less frequent, and pasture lands and cattle more abundant. When we had passed Fontainebleau, the train seemed to be endeavoring to rival the wind as it sped along the Seine. The splendid city rose to our view for many miles before reaching it, and our hearts beat quicker as we drew nearer and nearer.

CHAPTER XIX.

LTHOUGH it was late in the afternoon when we reached Paris, in spite of the long day's travel, we set out for a walk after tea. Taking up the Rue Rivoli, on which, opposite the Gardens of the Tuilleries, was our hotel (the *Meurice*), we soon reached the *Place de la Concorde*. The myriads of lights rendered this as well as the Champs Elysses almost as bright as the day. As we walked along, lingering occasionally at one of the Cafeés Chantants and mingled among the thousands of passengers on foot, on horse-back, in carriages with lanterns, returning from or advancing towards the Arc of Triomph, and heard the bands of music and the singing girls, we thought how inadequate had been any descriptions that we had ever seen or heard to give even an approximation to a just idea of this the most splendid avenue of the world. Jim had little to say at first. The theme seemed too vast for him, somehow.

"This is the place, Phil," said he at length, "where they had that cussed gulletin, this *Place de la Concorde*, as they call it."

"Guillotine, Jim, guillotine."

"I thought it was *gulletin*. I know it went through a fellow's gullet in a jiffey."

"You did'nt think any such thing. How gay, and how unlike the bloody scenes that have been enacted upon this spot, now so ineffably beautiful, during the hundred years from the frightful though unintentional slaughter of the crowds at the nuptials of Louis XVI to the battle with the Communists not long ago! How many of the illustrious of earth, men and women, cleric and lay, orators, poets, warriors, statesmen, Jacobin and Gironde, have poured out their blood here!"

"Everybody's got their time, you know, Phil. Yonder's something old enough for you, I take it—that Egyptian pillar. Fifteen hundred years before our Saviour. It's the handsomest *old* thing I've seen yet."

Next morning being Sunday, he said he would like the best in the world to be able to go to a regular old-fashioned Georgia meeting, and hear some good old-fashioned solid singing and preaching from a regular stated preacher. Sundays made him realize, more than any other days, that he was away from home.

"Not that I'm so very fond of going to church, for I ain't half as much so as I ought to be; but somehow I feel the necessity of such things over here more than I do at home."

He got his Bible, went to his room, and after remaining there for about an hour returned and was as cheerful as ever. Again we sallied out on the same route as the previous night, continuing our walk to the Arc de Triomph, and, returning on the southern side of the Champs Elysses, entered the Tuilleries Gardens. At every few paces wherever we went there were small booths, in which wine and confections were exposed for sale. Beneath the trees in the gardens boys and young men were playing at foot-ball and other sports.

21

"Ain't this a nice way of spending Sunday? Every
man, woman and child in the town, it seems to me, is on
the streets. Don't anybody here ever go to meeting of a
Sunday?"

"Yes, more than those of any town of its size in the
world. These people you see, the most of them, have
been to church already, some two, some three, and some
as many as five hours ago."

"You don't mean to tell me so?"

"Yes, indeed. Don't you remember what you saw in
Cologne? By this time four-fifths at least of the religious services are over for the day, except for Vespers in
some of the churches this afternoon, and the people are
out to spend the rest of the day in relaxation. The
churches have been opened ever since before five o'clock
this morning."

"Well, well. I don't think about such things as I
used to—that is, not exactly. Our people make some
mistakes, in my opinion, about keeping Sunday. But
over here they carry it too far 'tother way, it seems to
me. There's reason in everything. All this here, Phil,
looks to me just like a regular Fourth of July instead
of a Sunday. However, it's none of my business. I
did'nt suppose any of these out here had thought about
going to meeting to-day. Curious people. But they
go in strong for what they go in for at all—peace or
war, work or play. It's fight or play with them, whichever anybody chooses to have. Gracious! did'nt that
fellow make a good strike with that ball! Some of 'em
play like, as we say in Georgia, they *been* playing of
Sundays, sure enough."

Alternately sitting or standing or moving among the
gay throngs in these lovely gardens, our senses reeled

with the strange multifold sights. But for Jim's occasional homely remarks, I might have suspected myself to have been dreaming of the scenes of enchantment which I had been so fond of reading about in childhood. In the afternoon we walked down the Rue Castiglione to the Place Vendome. Turning into the Rue des Capuchins, we reached the Boulevard Madeleine that led us to the great temple. We sat on a bench beneath one of the trees in the Place and looked up towards this the finest specimen of Greek architecture now in the world.

"I give it up. It beats everything in that line I've seen yet."

"A proper memorial to the saint."

"What saint?"

"St. Mary Magdalen."

"Is that so?"

"Yes, indeed. She is the favorite of the female saints with the French. She died in France, you know."

"No, I did'nt know any such thing. I supposed she died about Bethany, where she used to live."

"No. After the crucifixion she removed with her brother Lazarus to France and spent the remainder of her life, which was over thirty years, in the neighborhood of Marseilles. Some of her relics are in this church."

"You don't mean that Mary Magdalen and Lazarus' sister Mary were the same person?"

"I do."

"That's news to me. What do they keep relics of her here for?"

"Why do you keep the lock of your mother's hair?"

He made no answer for a moment.

"Yes; I suppose it's sorter for the same reason; maybe a better."

At night, the *Champs Elysses* were, if possible, more brilliant, and certainly more thronged than the last.

"I never expected, Phil, to see such carryings on of a Sunday; but it won't hurt you and me, I suppose, to *look* at 'em. Their doings, as I said before, ain't any of my business; so let's see 'em through."

Having but a week to devote to Paris, we must work with system and rapidity. Taking a voiture early on Monday, we travelled slowly down the *Rue Rivoli*, halting to notice particularly the most notable places on the way, as the *Tuilleries*, *Louvre*, *Tour de St. Jacques*, the *Hotel de Ville* (rising, like the Vendôme Column, from its ruins), the *Place de la Bastille*, where the July Column now occupies the site of the old prison, and down the world-renowned Faubourg St. Antoine to the *Place de Trône*.

"The blood," said Jim, "the blood that has been poured out all along the way we have been coming. I've wanted often to see this—*forberg*, or whatever you call it, and the *Bastille*. I've read a good deal of the history of these people; and when I get back home, please God I'm spared to get back, I'm going to read it all over again now that I'm finding out how these places stand to one another. At the place where we are now, Robespierre and those other rascals had another of those cussed things to cut off the heads of the fellows in this end of the town. One was'nt enough to do all that sort of business. Ain't it curious, too, that like that *Concorde Place*, this one is where, on the great holidays, they have the fire-works and the big shows?"

Following the Boulevard Charonne into the *Menilmontant*, we alighted before the gate of *Pere Lachaise* and spent an hour within it. This cemetery was less impressive than I had anticipated. The difficulty, even with the help of maps, in finding the tombs of specially noted persons, and their wide separation from one another, diminished the interest. Jim remarked that as a matter of curiosity, graveyards were not his favorite, and he was glad to get out. Resuming our drive, we made for *Notre Dame* on that *Isle de la Cité*, *Lutetia Parisiorum*, *"Lutetia the Beloved"* of Julian the Apostate. Although I had been in so many cathedrals, I did not enjoy less the sight of this. Advancing to the spot where the great Napoleon had been crowned, we walked around the interior, musing upon its antiquity, its monuments, its marvellous windows, its vast organ, and, calling to mind the great events that had been enacted there mostly in the name, but some in the avowed dishonor of Christ. Jim never approached a shrine before which poor persons, especially poor females were kneeling, without exhibiting the utmost respect.

"This is all so new to me," he whispered, "and I tell you it looks becoming. These people pray like they *knew* there was something in prayer. Look at that poor old woman yonder. She has'nt taken her eyes off that picture of the Virgin since we've been in here. She has'nt noticed anybody, not even those that have been standing by where she is kneeling, and looking at and talking about the picture. Such faith as that is worth having." I turned and saw an aged crone in tattered garments kneeling, her withered hands clasped, and her lips silently moving, before a shrine. As we left the church, she was in the same attitude.

Crossing the south fork of the river, we lingered at the *Place de Termes*, where Julian was proclaimed emperor by the Gallic legions when the alternative was

presented of empire or death. A strange career for one
who, the greatest of his race, had been driven back into
paganism by the persecutions of the house of Constantine. His was the saddest career of all kings.

On by the quays *Montebello, de Tournelle,* and *Saint
Bernard,* through the *Jardin des Plantes,* returning
again and passing to the *Sorbonne,* the *Pantheon,* and
the *Luxembourg.* As we rode slowly along, we noticed
the people taking, some dinner, and some lunch, upon
tables on the pavement in front of the numberless
eating-houses on every street.

"These people literally live out of doors, Phil; at
least in the summer time. And the wine, the wine, the
wine they do drink here in one day. Yet we have'nt
seen but one man drunk yet, that fellow in Geneva.
Strange people, always drinking and not getting drunk.
There's a lesson in all this for our big men and good
men at home to study. I can't make it out myself, and
that don't run in my line. About joining temperance
societies, and signing temperance petitions, I'm about
like old Col. Blackford."

"How was that?"

"The old Colonel was a Methodist, you know, and
about the best man in his neighborhood. They had
started a temperance society there and tried to get him
to sign the pledge for the sake of the example, as they
put it. The old Colonel sometimes would take his
morning dram. He told the brethren that he was
seventy-five years old, and that liquor, what little he
had taken, had never done him any particular harm as
he knew of, and that sometimes he felt that he actually
needed a little stimulant. As for the example he said that
his ideas had changed on that subject many a year ago.

When he was a young man, he was very proud of himself, and thought that there was a tremendous amount of responsibility on him about other people, and that he ought to try to make everybody quit his foolishness and do right. But he was like the farmers who sometimes overcropped themselves and got in the grass, and he found at last that it was about as much as he could do, and *that* put him to his trumps many a time, to take care of himself. So you may go on, you French people. You can beat us, a hundred times over again, drinking, one thing and another, but we can whip you out all hollow in getting drunk. I don't understand it, and, by good luck, it ain't any of my business. And here's the place that of all in this town I wanted most to see."

We had reached the *Hotel des Invalides,* the *Temple of Humanity* (as it was first named), where France tenderly cares for her disabled soldiers. Many of these we noticed, some walking, others, without legs, rolling themselves leisurely along the spacious grounds in their wheeled chairs, all seeming contented with the care which their grateful country bestowed for their services and sufferings. We caught an occasional glimpse of the white bonnets of the Sisters of Charity, whose business it is to nurse the sick in the multitude of invalids there gathered.

"They know how to take care of their old soldiers sure," said Jim. "These without legs get more than those with 'em. That is, *they* are credited with what their shoes would cost. Everyone is allowed so much, and whatever one can save goes to his credit, and he can lay up a little something from year to year. What I want to see most is the place where the old fellow is lying."

It was touching to observe the respect with which he approached the centre of the noble building, and placing his hands upon the railing in the circular enclosure, leaned over, and looked down upon the sarcophagus which contained the dust of the great Captain. It is a tomb of exquisite fitness and taste, and it impresses the visitor even more than anything in Westminster Abbey. At that, one bows before the majesty of death and his power to bring into such small compass the mighty dead of many centuries, and the individual is merged in the multitude. But here, in the centre of this magnificent structure, in a circle defending by a railing all from approaching its centre, is the bier of that one hero, and him alone, and one imagines that he is required to feel that he stands by the tomb of the greatest of all times. After we had retired and were again in the voiture, Jim said:

" They had to bring him back there, but they waited until he had been dead twenty years."

As we passed along the *Champ de Mars*, we noticed several companies of infantry drilling.

" Go it, my fine fellows," said Jim. " Somehow, you did'nt have your hands in at your last fight. You'll have to try them Germans again some day. You'll have your hands full, too, but I think you can get even with 'em. It may not be in our day, Phil. But it will come. These are a freer people than the Germans, and love their country better. When they get a man who knows how to lead, they'll pay 'em back."

As we rode down the *Quai D'Orsay*, we were impressed by the large number of ill-looking washwomen about the laundry establishments on the river. Jim said that at the hotel an Englishman had told him that washing clothes was usually the last resort of the abandoned women of the town.

" When they begin to get old, and are still poor, they go to the wash-tub for a living, and many of them, when they can't make it at that, drown themselves in the river."

We crossed at the *Pont de la Concorde.*

" They seem to go for that name in this neighborhood. Do you know where the stones in this bridge came from mostly? Why, from that old *Bastille* prison. I read that last night. They've sounded to many a groan."

But a short time after dinner we had for a drive in the *Bois de Boulogne.* Besides that the season was past in Paris, it is not to be admired at any time as *Hyde Park.* We had now been going all day, and the wholesome fatigue invited repose. Yet, we lingered for an hour or two in the glass-covered court of the hotel, and talked over what we had seen during the day.

CHAPTER XX.

PROPOSED, next day, visits to the palaces, especially the Luxembourg and Louvre.

"Now, see here, Phil; one of the troubles on my mind before coming to this town was the fear that I might finish off what part of my neck has'nt been broke already looking up at old pictures; for I knew you'd want to see them here, and I thought I should be afraid to separate from you because I can't speak French. But I find I can get along with these people better than I expected. I don't understand a word they say; but by talking slow and distinct and with signs one way and another, I can make them understand in general what I want. Then I know they *can't* lose me. I'll travel around with you for awhile; but when it gets too bad, I'm going to quit and peruse on my own hook. But carry me first to some pictures that I can understand."

"All right. To the Luxembourg."

He was better pleased than he expected to be, and he admired, equally with myself, such pictures as Appert's *Pope Alexander III Disguised as a Mendicant*, Barrias' *Exiles of Tiberius*, Bertrand's *Death of Virginia*, Couder's *Levite of Ephraim*, Muller's *Prisoners of the Conciergerie*, and especially Delaroche's *Death of Queen Elizabeth*.

"My Lord!" he exclaimed, before the last, "I've

heard of pictures being called like life, but this is death itself."

A wonderful painting, indeed. The expression of those dying eyes will never be forgotten. They were the eyes of one who had been a queen to the last, and who, as she had not rendered mercy, had no expectation of it from her conqueror.

Jim lingered long enough in the Louvre to be able, as he said, to tell them that he had been there and taken in every blamed one of the old masters and left me to bring up the "drap-shot gang," then we parted with the understanding that we should meet for dinner at the *Palais Royale*. On repairing to this spot, I found him already there. He had become uneasy, he said, about me, and was afraid that, if I got there before him and did not find him at once, I might go to *boging* and prowling about looking for him and so get lost. And then again, he was hungry.

After dinner we promenaded for some time amidst the grounds and shops of this, so long styled, the capital of Paris. Nowhere in the world are to be found such magnificent shops. Sitting under the lime trees, we chatted long upon the events that in the several generations had transpired in that historic place, famous beyond all in the annals of mankind, for orgies, which cried out for punishment. In the matter of material pleasures, this area of a few acres has surpassed all others upon this earth. Epicures and debauchees, plots and conspiracies, what a long line since the death of the great cardinal! The princely libertines now resort to more secret haunts, plotters and conspirators allow other places to divide honors with this, yet luxury fully maintains its ancient sway.

It might have been amusing to hear Jim and me afterwards as each vainly tried to entertain the other with accounts of what he had seen in the interval of separation. While I would be enlarging upon some picture in the Louvre, or some great event enacted in one or another of its *salons*, he would be waiting to tell of the Ghobelin tapestry or the tumult of the Bourse. I had said, in speaking of the imperious tempers of some of the women of the house of Medici, that it really seemed as if they had been sent from hell.

"Hell, you say, Phil? I've been there or thereabout to-day. It was at the Bourse. I had heard of the fuss and confusion there, and wanted to see and hear for myself. I went first among the buyers and sellers. It was fun enough there, to see hundreds of fellows screaming and foaming at the mouth. One fellow would mount into a sort of cage, get on a platform, and bawl out what he had to sell, and the rest would bawl out what they were willing to give. At and around another cage another crowd would be doing the same thing, and everybody looked as if he wanted to cut everybody else's throat. I looked up and saw a gallery where whole crowds were coolly leaning over the balustrade and looking down. I went up there and stood awhile by a big Irish woman, who was gazing, evidently for the first time in her life, upon the scene. How she did enjoy it! From the way the concern is built, or something I don't know what, the noise that comes up is beyond anything that my ears ever heard. She laughed and laughed, and shook her big sides, as if everything that was sold belonged to her and was bringing the highest sort of a price. Once in a while she would grunt and say:

"'And shure it is, all the divils is turned loose.'

"She hit the nail on the head. I felt like, Phil, I tell you I felt like I was on the brink of the pit and was listening to the damned roaring with the pain of the fire and brimstone."

Next day, we took an excursion to Versailles by carriage, going by St. Cloud and returning by Sevres. It was a sweet day, and we drove leisurely along the fine roads. The great fortresses, notably *Valerien*, were within our view. It was sad to see the desolation in the wooded scenery that had been wrought all along the way by the Prussians and the government armies in the siege of the capital. The ancient Chateau of *St. Cloud* showed, even in its ruins, that it had been fit to be the residence of kings; and in spite of the dismantled state of Versailles, we could but wonder even then at the appalling sums that had been expended in order to make it what it was. Suites of rooms, a mile in extent, ornamented with pictures and statues of the best artists, grounds with terraces, parterres, and orangeries, basins, bosquets, fountains and quincunces, none but a grand monarch like Louis XIV, and none but a devoted people like the French could have created. I cannot say whether Jim was more entertained by the splendors he saw, or indignant at the enormity of their cost. He had gotten the figures and made calculations how much beyond the two hundred millions of dollars of original outlay these royal luxuries would have cost had no interruption been made to the design of converting the Eure from its channel and leading it through the palace grounds.

"Kings," said he, " are an expensive piece of property."

After a nice dinner at the *Hotel de Reservoir*, we set out again, and reached Sevres just as the porcelain works were being closed for the day.

22

"Missed 'em," said Jim, "and all for your hanging around them old pictures, and trying to study out the outlandish figures on the basins. It makes no difference though. I'm satisfied. I've seen the *place* where they make their chainy, as old Dooly called it."

For this excursion, Jim had secured the services of his coachman of the day before. His liberality, his heartiness of manner, and considerateness of others, enabled him, in spite of the want of understanding of their tongues, to hold considerable genial communication with whomsoever he met. He was always bound to have talk of some sort with his fellow-travellers. He had chosen our present companion because of his knowledge of a few English words. So, remembering, however, always to be "slow and distinct," he spoke without restraint to him whenever he wished, persisting until he had made some sort of understanding. Once, as we were driving along, noticing a dog in the way, he cried out:

"Coachee."

"Oui, monsieur."

"Dog there. Dog."

"Oh, oui, monsieur."

"Your Commune eat dog."

"Pardon, monsieur?"

Jim opened his mouth, and acted as if he was putting something into it, and chewing it.

"Eat, eat. Commune. Dog."

What a face he did make!

"Non, non monsieur; non chien? Non; trop mauvais—too hard—Nous mangeons—chat; chat bon—non chien; non dog. Non—non!"

"Shar? What's that?"

"Cat, Jim, cat."

"Oui, monsieur; cart."

"Not *cart*, my man. Cart's another thing altogether. *Cat*. *He'd* do, would he? but you could'nt come the dog?"

"Non, non, monsieur."

"But they did get to dogs at last, Phil, or at least a few. You know the reason why they did'nt eat 'em all?"

"Too bad, I suppose, as the coachman said."

"No, sir. *They could'nt catch 'em.* I've read in a paper somewhere, that when at last they got down to the dogs, the poor creatures actually held one or two meetings, and the first thing anybody knew, they were all gone. I suppose they passed resolutions not to be eat up if they could help it. When the siege was broke, and a plenty of good victuals got in, here came back the dogs as thin as snakes, creeping out of all sorts of out-of-the-way places, some even from holes in the ground. Just to think of two millions of people, as fond of good eating as these are, to be shut up in this town for months, and have to eat cats, and even dogs— and hard to get 'em at that."

The next three days were spent in visiting what was possible to see of the most noted things, travelling some- times together, sometimes apart. Jim had managed to gather a great amount of information concerning what he called the *live things* of the town, while I was searching among the dead. He studied the quays, the system of sewerage, and other generally controlling interests. Most of all, he admired the charitable insti- tutions.

"It's perfectly wonderful, Phil, the numbers and the different kinds of 'em. The poor are provided for here better than they are in London. I should'nt have believed it, but it's so. Some of these houses built for 'em they call *hospices* and some *hospitals*, and some a whole lot of outlandish names that I can't pronounce. There are some for old married people, and some for old widows, and some even for old widowers, and some for old bachelors, and some for old maids, and some for old preachers, and some for children. There are dozens of what we would call *nurseries*, where poor women who have to work out put their children in the day and take 'em home at night. There is'nt any kind or form of sickness or want that they have'nt places here where it can be taken care of. And as for these Sisters of Charity and the other names they've got, there don't seem to be any end of *them*. Then they have what I should call travelling hospitals. They have physicians who visit the sick poor at the public expense. They give the poor bath-tickets and such; and they hire nurses from the country who take sick children home with 'em and keep 'em till they get well. I did'nt expect this; I thought what they went for over here mostly was finery and pleasure. As it is, I find that they are or appear to be the most charitable people I've seen yet. The French are a great people, not only in big things, but in little. Travelling does away with a heap of prejudice, at least when a fellow keeps his eyes open and looks around. Don't it, Phil?"

" Indeed it does."

" Now, there's that *Foundling Hospital*, started by St. Vincent de Paul, they call him, two hundred years ago. It beats all. I declare it's enough to make a man cry, to see what care is taken of these poor children of sin. Then what I've noticed and found out about their going to meeting beginning at day-break, that struck me as much as anything else. I've seen 'em myself pouring out of a church when it was just daylight by hundreds, rich and poor, and another crowd pouring in right after 'em to another meeting. I had an idea that these priests were taken up mostly with good eating and such. The truth is, Phil, a man's a goose for condemning people and things that he knows nothing about."

The day came for us to leave, and we were both glad that we had chosen Paris the last place for visiting.

"It's a good rule, Phil, to save the best for the last— that is, if a fellow don't go and do like Bob Minton and eat so much meat and greens as to leave no room for pie and custard. If we'd seen Paris before the little places that we've been in, we should'nt have taken much interest in them. Take Brussels for instance. Brussels, it's plain to me, tries to be like Paris. I liked it mightily when I was there; but if I was to go there now I should be constantly thinking for awhile how much smaller it is than what it wants to look like. We've seen 'em all now, little and big, or as many as we had laid out to see, saving the best for the last, and now I'm ready for home."

We left after a too early breakfast; but then we knew we could make up with a good, quiet dinner on the boat which we were to take at Dieppe at one o'clock in the afternoon. We looked back towards the glorious city as long as we could see it. The last object of our sight was the great Arch.

"Far-you-well," said Jim, "all of you—Bonapartes and Bourbons, presidents and Frenchmen generally. I'm glad I've seen you one time. Far-you-well, I'm going now to see them that I think more of than all of

22*

you. They ain't—that is, in the special—they ain't but one good, in fact splendid woman and a parcel of—well, just good, common children; but I'd rather see them now than forty Parises and four hundred Arches of Triumph and forty thousand million of—let's try the weed."

We turned our faces onward. The country of the Oise et-Seine, though not naturally fertile, yet rejoiced with market gardens, and afterwards, in Seine Inferieur, with fields and pasture lands. The wheat in Normandy was now all cut and standing in yellow shocks.

"This is the Rotrimagus of the ancient Gauls, Jim," I said, as we passed through Rouen.

"Indeed? All I remember about this town is the burning of that poor Joan of Arc by the English, and a mean piece of business it was."

"That it was, and it was not long after the horrible outrage that the rule of that people passed away from this country."

When we went on the boat, Jim asked the captain how long it would be before dinner.

"I carn't say quite yet," answered he, looking out at the white-caps of the sea waves, and walking away.

"That sounds suspicious. What in the mischief are all these bowls doing here on deck, Phil? Why, here's at least a dozen under these benches, and see yonder, the stewardess is bringing up some more."

I had no idea for what purpose they were there. Fifty or sixty passengers were with us, mostly Americans and English. We were delighted to hear again from all tongues our native speech. All were so gay. Several gentlemen were standing near the bridge when the steamer moved off. We had not proceeded more than a knot, when suddenly a sea dashed from leeward,

and the spray drove us quickly aft. None seemed to
have had any expectation of sea-sickness. But it was
not fifteen minutes before the stewardesses were running
about with the bowls in their hands and setting them
down by ladies who had been taken so suddenly as not
to be able to repair to the cabin or even to reach the
railing.

"Well, don't this beat anything—eddy—eddy—
thig—" but Jim could'nt make it out. He managed to
get to the railing, but he was soon upon his knees, and
finally, holding on with one hand, lay on his side. The
chopping sea tossed the little boat, as a cork in a shal-
low running stream. All the suffering from sea-sickness
that we had witnessed on the Atlantic was less violent
than that endured in the few hours' passage from Dieppe
to New Haven. Ill as I was, I felt seriously concerned
for Jim, and especially for the women, who seemed to
have abandoned themselves to despair. Some lay on
the deck, others in the cabin, and rolled, and cried out,
and actually howled with the agony of nausea. In their
tossing, the clothes of some of them became sadly dis-
arranged; but there were none to criticise or to care.
The relief, when we reached New Haven, was as instantaneous as the attack. Having partaken hastily, but
heartily, of coffee and bread at the buffet, we were again
upon the cars.

"I never should have believed it," said Jim. "I
did'nt know that a fellow could have the cussed thing
twice. It gets worse the oftener it takes you. What
time it lasted, I do believe I was worse off than on the
Atlantic. I felt like I was going to turn inside out,
blamed if I did'nt. But some of those poor women
were worse off, if possible, than I was. One of 'em,

and she was a good-looking one at that, was lying just
behind me, and in rolling herself about, she kicked me
on the back of my head several times. I did'nt let on,
and I did'nt care. For my misery, as old Jim Williams
said, was all *innards*, and it would have taken harder
things than a sick woman's heels to hurt me on the outside. And did'nt they howl? I don't think I exactly
howled, but I done some tall barking. But that hot
coffee was good. I hid three cups of it, and ain't it
nice now?

> " Oh, de long time ago,
> I'm a rollin'!"

As the train dashed along, he broke forth into this
favorite old corn song.

I could not but almost envy that hearty, ingenuous
nature which, though with the tenderness of a child
ready to yield to suffering of whatever kind, was as
quick to mount into joyousness when it was past. How
he did rattle along in the sudden relief from seasickness,
being again among English-speaking people, and home-
ward bound. He said he was really *hongry* for old
Georgia talk, and declared that, if he had a chance, he
believed he could make a speech.

"All I want now, sir, is a subject and an audience."

" I'll be the audience, Jim."

"Ain't big enough, and ain't appreciative enough.
But will the audience, such as it is, start me off with a
little applause?"

" Certainly," and I clapped my hands loudly and
shouted huzzas.

" Give me a subject then. Be quick about it, while
the sperrit's on me."

"Oh, anything. Take Southdown sheep, for here we are now passing over the great Sussex downs."

"All right. These celebrated sheep—my client—gentlemen of the jury—how'll that do?"

"Won't do."

"Brethering and sisters—"

"Worse and worse."

"Respected audience."

"Right; proceed. Hear, hear."

"Make the rest of it yourself, confound you. If you had'nt put me out at the start I should have delivered a speech that would have made your hair stand and the goose bumps come out all over you."

"Oh, you Jim! You dear old Jim Rawls! You absurd, glorious, darling old scamp!"

> "Oh, de long time o' day
> I'm a rollin'."

"Mrs. Rawls is right about your voice, Jim. You have a—you have a plenty of *voice*."

"Ah, Philemon, my friend, nobody knows, the same as that judgmatical woman, what this world and society in general lost by me not being sent to a singing school when a boy."

"You always loved the corn-song. So did I. It is a strange music, but often very touching, not only in chorus, but in solo. Most of the airs, I doubt not, are national. That sort of music, you know, is peculiar to peoples who have had no foreign admixture. Thus, the Greeks had it, the Romans not; the Scotch and the Irish have it, the English not. Of course, Americans, white Americans, made from more elements than were in the image of Nebuchadnezzar, have it not. I have been told that since the war the negroes have given up much of theirs."

"Yes, sir, three-fourths of it, if not more. In old times one could seldom pass a field where they were at work without having a song of some sort from one or more of them."

"What, in your opinion, are the causes of the change?"

"Their minds have not now the leisure. Instead of having their thinking done by their owners, they now have to do it for themselves."

"How do you regard the prospects before them?"

"That's the toughest problem that the American people have yet had on their hands. The good Lord only knows how it is to be worked out; no *man* does. The negroes increase by births about as fast as the whites, but there are many more deaths among them. The difference will be greater as the country fills with population and the price of land gets higher. Land is so cheap now that they get an easy living; after a while things will be very different."

"Why, I have heard that a good many of them own lands."

"The tax books and the newspapers say so."

"But is it not true?"

"Quite a number in Middle Georgia (that's the only section I can speak about) have entered on lands for which they have bonds for titles. Many have made the first payment, some the second, a few, a very few, have gone further than that. The great majority never have, and never will. They have not the prudence, and their families have not the economy to lay up beyond a living on their yearly crops. If there is a people specially to be pitied, they are the negroes of the South. It is sad

to see a people, affectionate and grateful as they are, finding it more and more difficult to get what the most
reasonable and the least ambitious among them hoped
for immediately after their emancipation."

"You think they are a grateful people?"

"Remarkably so; that is, the old set, when not inter-
fered with and fooled by rascally politicians, black and
white. I wish that the education which we are giving
them in Georgia (for you know that public provision in
that respect is the same for them as for the whites), I
say I wish it would do them more good, instead of leading the most of them who get it to wish to be public
characters, as politicians, preachers and other church-
officials, school-teachers, etc. I tell you it is a tough
business, the negro problem is. I don't like to try to
argue it, and its because I don't know how. But in
that, Phil, I'm like Sam Spivey, when after being
whipped at school about twenty-five times for not getting the multiplication table, Pete Stricker asked him
if he knew how much seven times nine was, and what
was the difference between that and nine times seven,
he said, no he did'nt, and he did'nt believe there was
anybody in the world that did."

For some time the darkness had been hindering views
of this county and Surrey. We were in London in time
for a good dinner at *St. James', Piccadilly.*

CHAPTER XXI.

UR engagements were to return on the *Servia,*
which was to sail the coming week. We had
planned a three days' visit to the English
lakes and Ireland, arranging to meet the
steamer at Queenstown. So, lingering but a day in
London, and that mostly for making other purchases of
presents for our friends at home, we took the morning
train on the Great Northwestern Railway for Liverpool.

"Gardens, gardens; orchards, orchards," exclaimed
Jim, when we were out of Middlesex, and far on the
way in Hertfordshire. "It takes gardens upon gardens,
and orchards upon orchards to supply that same village
of London. The things, the things that go into its
great maw. But it's a rich little country around it, and
these people know what to do with it. Here we are
nearly through two counties, and everything that is
made in 'em goes to feed London, people or horses.
What a curious name this little town has: Tring."

"Tring? Tring? That's where Nell Gwynne lived."

"You mean that piece that one of those old kings
made so much of?"

"Yes; Tring-Park House was a fine mansion that
Charles II had built for her."

"But all he did could'nt keep her from the end that

such people are bound to come to. 'Don't let poor Nellie starve:' that showed that the old fellow had some heart, at least on his death-bed."

Into Buckinghamshire, the vale of Aylesbury now on our left, and the Chiltern Hills, extending into Bedfordshire, on our right. In Northamptonshire, the fields grew larger, and we admired those fertile pasturelands on which are raised sheep, short-horned cattle, and especially the famous immense black horses.

"Rich people live along here, Phil, I should say, from the looks of their mansions and parks. Weedon. Weedon. Another curious name."

"We are now, my friend, in what was the country of the Mercians, and Mulphere, their king, had his principal royal seat in this very town. There was another in Tamworth ahead of us."

"I'm thankful it was'nt the Romans. I've got right considerable tired of the Romans since I've been over here, Phil, and it's a relief to me to see you gradually coming down from their times."

"You have some rather unpleasant reminiscences, I think I've heard you say, connected with studying their language some years ago. Would it be too much for your feelings if I were to tell you that we had been travelling all day along by the side of a celebrated Roman road?"

"I would try to bear it for the sake—of your family. I've had to put up with a good deal from you since we left home. But make it short. Old Dumnorix never got up this far, did he?"

"Dumnorix was no Roman. He was an Aeduan, man."

"It makes no difference. I remember he had a heap

23

to do with Latin. I took him to be a tremendously
smart old fellow, for he said a many a thing that I
could'nt understand."

"Why, he could'nt speak Latin at all. Don't you
remember what Cæsar says in the conference about
"interpretibus remotis?"

"Excuse me, *if* you please. Well, sir, if Dumnorix
was'nt here, and if he did'nt travel along this road, I'll
be blamed if I know who did."

"Watling street again; the modern name of *Strata
Vitelliana,* in honor of the Emperor Vitellius."

"Why, that's as bad as the Weeklies of Hancock
county. Sixty years ago they came there, spelling
their name V-o-i-c-l-e. It got to be, first, Voicly, then
Woickly, then Wickly, then Weekly. But I don't want
to interrupt you. Go ahead, and follow old Watling as
far back as she'll take you."

"No, sir. Between Dumnorix the Aeduan, and the
Weeklies of Hancock, my mind is rendered incapable of
further pursuit in that direction."

"Rugby Station; five minutes," sang out the porters,
as they swung open the carriage doors.

Jim stepped out just to have it to say that he had
been where *Tom Brown* used to stay. When he returned,
and we were off again, he made some reflections.

"A great book, Phil, that *Tom Brown at Rugby,* and
a great teacher, Dr. Arnold. *He* had sense, that Arnold;
a thing that ain't so very common with school-masters
as far as I've known that tribe of folks. I'm not talking
about *books* now, mind you, but *sense.* Dr. Arnold had
sense. That was a curious old doctrine of school-masters of dealing with school-boys as if the whole kit was
one solid lump, and had to be handled *in* a lump. The

bother with school-masters often is that they don't seem to see any difference *in* boys. They can't, or they wont trust any one boy more than another. There seems to be something in school-keeping that confuses a man's senses, and makes him mix up things generally. Even if one starts right, it ain't long before he's in the groove, making his rules that take in everybody, and that nobody can follow. Now, Arnold had sense enough to see that there's a difference among boys as there is among men, and that they've got to be treated according as they are gentlemen or rascals. Tom Brown shows that. I took to Arnold as soon as I heard somebody say that he had made one boy give another who deserved it a thrashing. It made me read the book, blamed if it did'nt."

"You've always been a pugnacious fellow, Jim. If you are not in a fight yourself, you like to hear of one."

"Not at all. Fighting is a business that don't pay, and I've done monstrous little of it. Yet my opinion is that when it's necessary, you've got it to do, and when you get into it, you ought to do your level best to whip it. Sometimes a fellow *has* to fight, or show that he *will* fight, and that's often the best way to keep *from* fighting. Now, the old school-masters had a fool-rule about fighting, that whoever fought, no matter what it was about, or who began it, or who whipped, or who got whipped, had to be whipped by them afterwards. And they had many another no better. I'd like to know why it is that school-masters, as a general rule, have so little common sense?"

"*If* they have, it is because society thus requires or used to require of them. Society seems to believe, especially in the case of boys, that their sons need an ordeal of mean treatment and unreasonable management which they themselves are unwilling to take the trouble to inflict; and they are forced to devolve the business upon others, who, often unfit for any other, are willing to undertake that. Such an occupation separates them, to a degree, from the rest of the world, and they lose the important knowledge which comes from contact with mankind. Their associations are only, or mostly, with boys, and upon such terms as are naturally provocative of mutual hostility. The school is a little temporary absolute monarchy during a brief period, and that the most uninteresting in the life of a human being; known to be such by both teacher and pupil. The brief ruler's safety seems to him to consist in exacting every possible subservience, and the pupil's enjoyment is in rendering as little as possible consistently with his escape from punishment. Then, some parents desire a rigid rule, and some a mild. The schoolmaster, who seldom thinks he can afford to lose any of his pupils, tries to steer as well as he can between the two, assume to be rigid when he is mild, and mild when he is rigid. Then again the ceaseless routine of the same things, and generally small things, the habit of mind of moving everlastingly in circles, and small circles, at that, tend to belittle. In society the schoolmaster does not always seem to know what position he ought to take, because his own life knows of but two—the head and the foot. His deportment, therefore, is often a sort of compound of dictatorialness and subserviency. Arnold was a man who had strength enough to understand all such. He was a man of common sense, as you say, and governed his school as he governed his own family.

"You are right, sir. Now, my son, Buck, when he

came out of college, took a notion to keep a school awhile. I said nothing against it, though I had an idea that that business would'nt suit one of my tribe. The first time Buck came home to see us, when they had a holiday, I noticed that he was often bringing up Latin words in his talk. I happened to look in his hat one day and saw the lining all written over with little sentences from the Latin Reader. And then he would be frequently catching up his mother and the rest, except me, in their words. I told Buck if he did'nt mind he'd make a fool of himself. Old Buck quit the business and went to work on the land I had ready for him, and, though I say it, he's a fellow of sense and doing well. That business did'nt suit Buck, or Buck did'nt suit the business, I don't know which."

"It is a difficult business, certainly. The best way to govern boys, I think, is to leave much of their government to themselves. Constant watching, I think, is a great mistake. Boys are like men—the better you treat them the better they'll be. It is difficult for a man to be a detective and a gentleman at the same time, and none but a gentleman ought to be intrusted with the guidance of youth, especially sons of gentlemen. In late years changes are being made, some of them much for the better in the discipline of schools and in the relations of school-masters with other people."

That night, at the *Adelphi*, we saw several Americans, some of whom we had met before in our travels, who were there preparing to return by the *Bothnia*, which was to sail on the next day but one.

"Just to think of it," said Jim; "these fellows will all be nigh home at the time we start. By the way, Phil, about those lakes up there, are they such *great* things?"

23*

I replied that they were not large, and not so picturesque as those in Switzerland, but certainly were
jewels in their way and worth seeing. I rather expected
him to say more upon this subject, but he did not, until
we had gotten to bed.

"Phil, they say this out-going ship is one of the
stoutest of the line, and that McMickin is the cleverest
of all the captains. I wonder we did'nt find that out
before engaging return passage on the *Servia*."

"Is that so?" I replied quickly.

He laughed.

"What are you laughing at?"

"I'm laughing because I see, you old hypocrite, that
you are as anxious to go home as I am."

"Would you really like to go by this ship, Jim?"

"Would you?'

"What about the English lakes and Ireland?"

"Oh, *they*, especially the lakes, were your programme.
They're none of my business. However, it's no use talking: the ship's full."

"Don't you suppose—" I paused.

"Suppose what?"

"Nothing."

"Well, suppose I *do* suppose."

"Well, sir, suppose away; I'm willing."

He jumped out of bed, rang the bell, and ordered a
bottle of champagne.

"It's too good, Phil, to go to sleep on right away. I
was just a *waiting* to see what you wanted to do. It
would have *killed* me to see those fellows start home a
week before us, but I would'nt let on, and did'nt intend
to until I saw how you looked to-night when they were
talking about *home*. I saw you were as bad off as I was."

"And have you been homesick, Jim?"

"Nigh unto death."

He almost shouted with laughter, while his eyes shed tears.

"I did'nt know it, Jim."

"Of course you did'nt, and I should'nt have let you know it if I had'nt seen that you at last were in for it, too."

"But you say the ship's full."

"Never you mind about that; I'll fix that or die a trying."

The next day about eleven o'clock he returned from the Cunard office with our tickets exchanged, saying he had obtained for us the officers' quarters.

Captain McMickin was all that he had been represented. In the quiet but vigorous and efficient discharge of his duties, and his courteousness to passengers of every condition, there cannot be, I believe, his superior on any line of the Atlantic steamers. At Queenstown about one hundred and fifty steerage-passengers came on. Among them was a young man who played remarkably well on the accordeon. When we had been out three or four days and all were well over seasickness, they, on fine afternoons, commenced to have on deck dances and games, in which the sailors, when off duty, joined. Our eagerness, as we drew nearer home, was softened by the sight of the simple enjoyments of these poor emigrants. Even the aged among them, whose anguish we had noticed at Queenstown, when they had parted, knowing it to be forever, from their friends and native country, were led at last to look smilingly on as the young men and girls tripped it to the accordeon's notes, or won and lost at other sports and took and paid their forfeits.

As we neared the shore, we became more and more eager to reach it, and it was as if we had met a dear friend who had been long absent when the pilot came on board. Jim said that this officer looked so natural that he felt like asking him about Emily and the children, blamed if he did'nt. He eagerly seized the New York papers and devoured them.

"Oh, it's so homelike: it makes *home* come all over me in big spots to be reading one of our own papers. I want to make 'em last, you see, Phil. I'm going to read every line in 'em. I'm like old man Sentry about the *Southern Recorder*. It came always on a Wednesday, and he made it last till the next Tuesday night. It was the only paper he took. He'd always begin at the beginning, 'The *Southern Recorder* is published at Millidgeville, Georgia, etc.,' and then on to the rates of advertising. He read slow and loud, and when he got tired he'd make a cross mark where he left off and begin there the next time he took up the paper. He would'nt get to the news till about Saturday, and Monday and Tuesday he'd wind up with the advertisements. That's the way I'm doing with these old *Heralds*. I tell you that paper's a book. These advertisements get me. Here's women that want somebody to come and suckle their children, and women that want to suckle other people's children, and women that want to get acquainted with men, and men that want to get acquainted with women, with different *views*, as they call it, as matrimony, pleasant society, mutual improvement, and all such, but all of 'em views of devilment of some sort, I don't doubt. Oh, the diferent kinds of devilment that are in such a place as New York. However, there's a plenty of it everywhere, as to that," and he would turn again to the paper.

Next morning, I was roused from sleep by his shouting, "Hail, Columby!" He was fully dressed, and had come down from the deck where he had been to see the land, now in full view.

> " 'Come, arouse thee, arouse thee, my brave Swiss boy,
> Take thy pail and—'

"Come up and see your native country once more. I've been looking at her for an hour. I would'nt wake you, because I knew that when you're taking your morning nap, as you call it, you don't care a continental for your native country, your family, your friends, nor anybody, nor anything else in this wooden world. But it's breakfast time any how. So, fall to rising, fall to rising."

As we neared the landing, he again joined heartily in the waving of hats and handkerchiefs, and kissing of hands to those on shore.

"Blame it all, Phil, they're my countrymen, and I'm glad to see them whether they are so to see me or not."

While we were standing at Jersey City waiting for the south-bound train to start, I asked him if he did not intend to send a telegram to his family.

"No. It would have to go by mail from Augusta, and besides, would scare Emily half to death. We seldom use the telegraph in my neighborhood, except in case of death, or some other bad or urgent news, and a despatch always scares whoever gets it."

"Then there's something in operating an agreeable surprise."

"That there is, you bet. Phil, do you know, sir, I feel much like I did the day I started to my wedding, blamed if I don't; only I'm surer in my mind now than I was then that all's right."

The few hours that we were together before reaching the place of my residence, were spent now in retrospecting upon the various scenes over which we had travelled, and now in my listening to my companion's descantings upon Georgia. I found (what, indeed, I had all along believed) that the things which had impressed me mostly, had been much more interesting to him than he had before admitted, and that his apparent disregard of them had been assumed, partly from playfulness, and partly to subdue my too fond proneness for those that were antiquated. I am free to say that I found also that his observations had been more accurate and his reflections far more profound than my own both upon the past and present conditions of the peoples amongst whom we had been. Among many other things, he said :

"I'm glad we made this journey, Phil, and I try to be thankful to the good Lord that He let us make it in safety. Seeing foreigners in their own homes has done away with some big mistakes I've been making all of my life. I find that other people are as sensible as ours, as brave, as honest, as patriotic, and as religious. Travel is the thing to knock the bottom out of a fellow's pride and his prejudices. Yet all this don't keep me from being thankful, more so than before, if anything, for being born, and raised, and let live where I was."

Then he talked at length upon Georgia, its climate, its comparative freedom from exclusive knots in its social existence, its adaptability to generous production, not only of the grains and cotton, but of many of the fruits of the tropics, as well as those of more northern latitudes. He spoke heartily of the persistent industry with which the people had striven to repair the losses

caused by the war, and how in spite of some miscalcula-
tions and disappointments, general improvement was
always existing, and lately becoming more and more
clearly apparent.

"What we want down there, Phil, more than anything
else, is for some of these Northern people to come among
us, buy the land we no longer need in such quantities
as before the war, and settle on it, and, by gracious, be
of us. Many of them, I know, think we don't like
them, but they are mistaken. We would be glad to
have them, not only as citizens, but as neighbors, that
is, of course, such as are fit to be either. There are
thousands of plantations (I have several myself) with
good dwellings and out-houses on them, that can be
bought at from four to ten dollars per acre. Three
thousand dollars will buy a good plantation of five hundred acres, which a man who is sensible and industrious,
with the crops made on it, can pay for in two or three
years, besides supporting his family, and live in a house
that costs more than that money. Or, with five or six
hundred dollars paid down, he can get as long payments
as he wants for the balance of the purchase-money."

Other things he said on this line, and about the
negroes and their relations with the whites that were
deeply interesting to me. He regards the condition of
the negro, compared with those of the other races, as
one of childhood, childhood ungrowing, and incapable
to become adult. He is dependent upon the white man,
like a child is dependent upon a father, capable to be
led to good, liable to be led to evil, according as his
guide is sensitive or not to the behests of his relation.
Observations of results of emancipation have served to
make stronger this opinion. While these, after recover-

ing from the first prostration wrought by sudden revolution, have been beneficial to the white man, they have
saddened the negro by the evidences they have given of
his incompetency for the most important exigences of
his being. In this depression, his chief support is the
conviction that his white neighbors in the main, so far
from wishing his return to the condition of servitude,
would never consent to it; that they compassionate his
unalterable dependence, and are willing to do whatever
they can, while minding their own, to help in all the
development that is within reach of his powers. To
cheat at all is a vice; but in Georgia to cheat a negro is
regarded as about the meanest of which white men are
capable.

   Such and similar conversations that, during several
weeks, we had had, led me to remark how experience in
a long, energetic, honorable career had ripened his judg-
ment and made ever nobler his spirit. Our very last
talks I could not, if I would, rehearse. It was in vain
I tried to induce his tarrying with me even for a night.
My life-long friend, always loved and trusted, showed, I
thought, that he felt as I, that after a journey, long to
men at our age, we were knitted together, if possible,
more closely than before. When the time of separation
came, we took hands, and with trembling voices and
moist eyes, said good-bye. And I could not but yearn
as I looked after him journeying on alone.

[THE END.]